THE NOVA AFFAIR

A Novel by

Thomas Bloom

A RavenHaus Publishing Book

THE NOVA AFFAIR

Copyright © 1999 by Thomas Bloom

All rights reserved. No part of this book may be reproduced in any form without consent from the publisher.

Edited by Dolores Dowd
Cover designed by Lori Vogel

RavenHaus Publishing
227 Willow Grove Rd.
Stewartsville, NJ 08886

RavenHaus Books on the World Wide Web:
http://www.ravenhauspublishing.com

ISBN: 0-9659845-2-4
Library of Congress Catalog Number: 99-093050
First edition: March 1999
Printed in the United States of America
0 9 8 7 6 5 4 3 2 1

This book is dedicated to my family who both tolerated my absences and encouraged me to continue.

Acknowledgment

It is difficult to remember and thank all those who gave a little encouragement and support along the way. To all the various family and friends who gave me a little input or some positive reinforcement. I appreciate it more than you suspect.

Special thanks to my daughter Lisa, Robin McAlear and Bruce Link for wading through the manuscript and offering many suggestions and improvements.

1

Roger Courtney awoke with a splitting headache and a foul taste in his mouth. He knew from experience that the throbbing in his temples would increase as soon as he stood. Then he remembered what day it was and he felt even worse. He glanced at the clock on the night stand 8:00 AM. In an hour his attorney would pick him up to keep an appointment with the Cook County Prosecutor's office. It was Roger's day to cop a plea. He rolled over and was almost surprised to find a woman's naked body next to him. The previous night slowly came back to him. He had stopped at a bar on Rush Street to calm his nerves following an afternoon session with John Lipton, his attorney. He had not been looking for any action. The girl had found him. He realized that he could not remember her name Maria, Marie, something like that. He debated whether to try and take advantage of her presence and decided that, as bad as he felt, he would not enjoy it anyway. With a painful effort, he arose and entered the bathroom. He felt slightly better when he emerged, a half-hour later, wrapped in a towel--showered, shaved, after-shaved and eye-dropped.

The girl was already dressed and sitting in a chair in his living room, smoking one of his cigarettes and looking out the window at the morning traffic on Michigan Avenue.

"You're a hell of a lot of fun," she said in a monotone, not turning her head.

"How's that, uh, Marie," he answered, taking a chance. He could not remember much of the night before.

"Marcia, you asshole," she said, finally looking at him. She was very young and dark-complected with long, brown hair. She would have been cute except for an overly large, hawk nose.

"You promised me wine, a steak dinner and candlelight. What do I get? A glass of scotch, no ice, and a quick screw. Then you pass out on me. I mean on top of me! I've had more fun at funerals. It's too late to take the bus home and still get to work on time. Give me twenty bucks for cab fare and I'll get out of here."

Well, at least she was honest, he thought. A lot of women would have helped themselves and left long ago. He pulled two twenties from his wallet and laid them on the coffee table in front of her.

"Here, buy yourself a nice dinner tonight," he said.

"Christ, you're precious. First you screw me like I'm your wife and then you treat me like a hooker. What business did you say you were in insurance? I should have known better." She took one of the twenties, grabbed her coat and left.

A great day off to a great start, he thought. He watched from the window as she left the building and maneuvered her way through the piles of slush and snow along the curb to hail a cab. He looked up to examine the Lake Michigan shoreline that paralleled Michigan Avenue at a few blocks distance. The lake was covered with ice a mile or more out from shore. The sky was a low, fast moving mixture of gray and black. A strong wind whipped a few flakes of snow south, toward the Loop. Chicago in March could be a forbidding place.

Roger brushed his hand through his full head of wavy, black hair. He had an olive complexion and wide-set, brown eyes. His large, aquiline nose was set over small, straight lips that often broke into an easy, attractive grin. He had a heavy build and a massive upper torso covered with thick, black hair. Years of overeating and lack of exercise had expanded his paunch to an impressive, if not obese circumference. He was a good-looking man in a rough, raw sort of way. He stood just over six feet tall and weighed two hundred and twenty pounds. Other men found him intimidating. Most women found him attractive, although his size and aggressiveness repelled some.

He had just time to dress and mix a cup of instant coffee before Lipton would pick him up. Since his wife had left, a few weeks before, his diet had deteriorated considerably.

He waited in the building's foyer for Lipton's distinctive white Mercedes to pull to the curb. As always, the man was

The Nova Affair

exactly on time. Lipton was dressed in an immaculate, blue, pinstriped suit and a camel's hair overcoat. He wore a pair of leather driving gloves. He had sandy hair and a perfectly groomed mustache. He was a trim man, in his fifties, articulate, precise and intelligent. He took great care with his appearance. Roger had amused himself with the thought that the man must double as a model.

Lipton took one look at Roger as he entered the car and said, "You look like shit. Eat anything?"

"Cup of coffee."

"Christ, money in the bank, a Gold Coast apartment and the man can't feed himself. What did you do for dinner last night?"

"Nothing a piece of ass."

"And a bottle of scotch from the look of your eyes. Have you got the program straight? If you screw it up this morning we're going to trial and you're in a world of trouble, my friend. Read the deal back to me, so I know you remember it."

Lipton drove the heavy Mercedes with easy assurance, swinging the car from lane to lane on Lake Shore Drive as they made good time into the Loop.

Roger summarized the deal as Lipton had explained it to him the previous afternoon. "I plead guilty to one count of felonious conversion. I agree to turn all my records over to the Prosecutor and the Illinois Insurance Department and cooperate with them in any other way they ask. I declare corporate bankruptcy and pledge all my personal assets to the creditors. In return, I get a three year sentence, all but thirty days suspended, which I get to serve in a minimum security institution."

"You've got it," Lipton said. "It's a hell of a deal. The only reason you're getting it is because you have no priors, you're a decorated vet and because I convinced them that you're more dumb than dishonest."

"Thanks. That'll do wonders for my reputation," Roger replied.

"Your reputation is long gone, my friend. It's your ass we're trying to save."

Thomas Bloom

The Assistant District Attorney, William Grover, kept them waiting for an hour. This was unexpected. Grover was an old hand gruff, crude and unsympathetic. During his thirty years in the District Attorney's Office, he'd seen everything. He was also efficient. The hour's wait was not his style.

Lipton was obviously worried. Someone could have changed his mind and the deal might be falling apart. Roger sat in one of the overstuffed, leather chairs in the waiting room and gratefully nursed the cup of coffee offered by Grover's secretary. He decided to let Lipton worry about the deal. He already felt bad enough.

When they were finally ushered into Grover's office, they found him waiting with two other men. Both were in their forties and dressed in that particular style of suit, shirt and tie that labeled them government. For the first time, Roger was worried.

Grover looked highly displeased himself. He motioned Lipton and Roger to be seated across a small conference table from the two men. He made the introductions.

"This is Mister Smith, Treasury Department, Washington, and Mister Jones, Securities and Exchange Commission, Washington. They know who you guys are. They've got a deal for you, Courtney. I'm not for it but they've convinced me that I should let you decide." He sat down at the head of the table with a resigned, disgusted look on his face.

Roger looked at the two men. Smith and Jones, like hell, he thought. He must be in worse trouble than he had imagined. He lit a cigarette and blew smoke across the table at the two men. Neither one had any papers in front of him, nor were there any briefcases in evidence. They were not attorneys he decided. Attorneys never did anything without a file and a legal pad in front of them. Both men looked too hard and tense to be bureaucrats. Jones had a suspicious bulge under his left armpit.

"So?" Roger opened the conversation.

"We've got a peculiar problem, Mister Courtney," the man labeled as Smith began. "We need an individual with a

The Nova Affair

particular set of attributes. As best as we can determine, you're the only man in the United States that fits the bill."

"What attributes would those be?" Roger asked. He was a good enough businessman to know when to shut up and listen.

"Let me review your biography as we understand it," Smith said, extracting a single sheet of paper from the breast pocket of his coat. "Please correct any error. You were born forty-one years ago in Mexico City. You're an only child. Your father was an American diplomat. He was subsequently posted to Paris for seven years and then to Bonn for eight. You grew up in Europe and speak French and German fluently. You took a Bachelor's Degree in Romance Languages from Dartmouth in nineteen seventy-eight. You volunteered for the Marine Corps, passed through Officer's Candidate School and Flight School and flew ground support fighters for four years, including some covert operations for Special Forces, one Bronze Star and one D.S.C.

"After the service you entered the insurance business, where you have held a number of positions and, five years ago opened your own business dealing as an intermediary in the placement of reinsurance. You are presently under indictment for the conversion of funds from that business.

"We also show your hobbies to be Bridge, tournament or duplicate Bridge more specifically, at which you are an expert player and a Life Master. You also dabble in the theater and have played a number of parts in local amateur companies. We understand you're a better Bridge player than you are an actor."

Roger winced slightly. He regarded himself as an excellent actor. His last role had been an eight-week run as one of the only two actors in the play *Sleuth*, admittedly to mixed reviews. Smith continued.

"You're married, no children. Your wife left you a few weeks ago when she couldn't take the publicity surrounding your indictment. She's back in Seattle with her family and filing for divorce, which we understand you have not contested. Is that all correct?"

Roger still had no idea where the conversation was headed. It was best to let them play their hand. He nodded slightly in assent.

"So?" he repeated.

"We need a man with the following skills: fluent in French and German, an expert in insurance, in particular the specialized field of reinsurance, an expert Bridge player and a man capable of some acting. We also need someone with a certain incentive to accept our offer. You meet the criteria.

"We have Mister Grover's permission to make you the following offer. In return for your agreement to accept a two-to-four month assignment on behalf of the United States Government, the State of Illinois will drop all charges against you in the pending matter. The rest of your deal with Mister Grover still stands. You still give all assets, personal and corporate, over to the creditors of your business and agree to cooperate with the authorities.

"We can't tell you anything about the assignment except that you will be reactivated into the Marines Corps at your old rank and that you will be serving on foreign soil. I can tell you that it involves a small degree of risk. You will be under the control and protection of an arm of the United States Government at all times."

Roger looked at Lipton in dismay. The attorney raised his eyebrows and shrugged his shoulders.

"How long have I got to decide?" Roger asked.

"We need your answer immediately this morning," Smith answered.

Lipton turned to Grover.

"Do you confirm all this Bill?" he asked.

"I'm satisfied that these gentlemen represent the United States Government. I've been convinced that it's in the country's best interest to let your client accept the deal. My office won't be happy about letting Mister Courtney avoid all prosecution. Neither will I. It'll look lousy in the press. The decision's yours."

"Can we confer?" Lipton asked Grover.

The Nova Affair

"Sure, there's an empty office across the hall," Grover responded.

"It's ten fifty-five," Smith interjected. "Be back by noon or the deal's off."

Lipton led Roger across the hall to an empty office, which was bare except for a desk and several chairs. Roger took the chair behind the desk and turned to his attorney.

"Well, what do you think?" he asked.

"You've got a good deal now," Lipton answered. "Thirty days in a country club institution and you're free. This thing smells to high heaven. Whoever these guys are, their names aren't Smith and Jones and I doubt that they have a lot to do with the Treasury or the SEC. If they tell you there's a little danger, then there could be a lot. Once you're reactivated they've got you by the balls. Disobey an order and you could end up making small rocks for twenty years. I think they're looking for a sacrificial lamb and you're prime for the slaughter. Either way, you end up broke. Take the bird in the hand, Roger."

"Maybe you're right," Roger answered. "But I like the idea of having no record. Besides, I'm intrigued with the offer. Why those peculiar combinations of skills, particularly Bridge? Let me chew on it awhile."

Roger lit another cigarette, leaned back in the chair and put his feet up on the empty desk. He stared out the window at the Chicago skyline. The day was developing as miserably as its promise. A bitter wind was blowing small cyclones of snow down the corridors formed by the buildings of the Loop. Pedestrians walked at an angle, leaning into the wind, fighting to keep their balance on the icy sidewalks. The higher buildings disappeared into the low ceiling of clouds. The Sears Tower was cut off at mid section, a full fifty floors lost in the mist.

Roger reviewed the sequence of events that had led him to this impasse. He had left the service after his second tour because he was tired of the regimen and the constant danger. He had never been injured but had come close to death many times. His last two years of service had been spent in the gray area of covert operations. Using small, twin-engine civilian planes, he had flown U.S. drug agents into small airfields in South and Central America where they joined colleagues on missions never explained to Roger. He would often return days or weeks later to pick them up. The drug cartels that were the target of these operations had not the slightest qualm against shooting down a civilian plane suspected of being involved in the operations against them. In the jets in which he had been trained, he would have had no problem in defending himself. In the light, unarmed planes he was asked to fly on these missions, he was helpless. His only defense was to fly a few feet above the jungle foliage that covered that part of the world. Winding his way through mountain passes and down river valleys, he would rely solely on his skill and reflexes to avoid both the terrain and the larger, more powerful planes of the cartel which were constantly searching for flights like his. Once, when he was discovered, Roger was forced to fly even lower and faster while avoiding the volleys of automatic pistol fire directed at him from the windows of his pursuers. Fortunately, the Cartels never obtained access to true military aircraft or Roger would not have survived.

After one flight, he had returned to base with a plane so badly shot up that it had been scrapped. Another time, he had been even luckier. After a tough mission into Columbia, where he had taken several hits, his plane had lost power halfway back to his base. He had chosen to ditch in a small marsh, sliding the plane in on its belly, rather than risk bailing out at low altitude. He had stepped out of the aircraft directly into the arms of a government unit patrolling the area. They had trucked him to the nearest city with a U.S. consulate. He had hardly gotten his feet wet. The experiences had earned him two decorations and a lasting distaste for combat.

After leaving the service, he had been forced to face the fact that he had no plans for the future. He had no family in the States. His parents had retired to the Virgin Islands. Except for his four years at Dartmouth and his military training, he had never lived in the country of his citizenship. A bachelor's

The Nova Affair

degree in Romance Languages was not particularly conducive to any field of specific labor.

Roger had known a fellow pilot in the service who planned to join his father in an insurance brokerage firm in Chicago. He had taken the man up on a casual offer made during a drinking bout between missions and applied for a job with his friend's firm. To his surprise, he had been hired.

Roger discovered that he was a natural salesman. The technical aspects of the business fascinated him and he became quite competent in dealing with the multitude of forms and coverages involved in the industry. He served his clients well and was rewarded, for the most part, with their loyalty. He had been successful enough, after a few years, to be hired away from his friend's firm by the local office of one of the large, national brokerage firms.

Over the years, single and successful in a highly competitive business, he had developed a taste for the good life. He acquired a large apartment in one of the exclusive high rises on the "magnificent mile," that stretch of Michigan Avenue north of the Loop. He had used a liberal expense account to maintain a lavish lifestyle with friends and clients. He had still had time to indulge his two passions, Bridge and the theater. It was an easy life, too easy in fact, for it led to the unconscious presumption that it would always continue.

He had finally married, during the mid-nineties, to a woman who began as his customer and ended as his lover. It was a comfortable marriage, but based more on their shared lifestyle than on any deep feelings for one another.

Earlier, in the nineties, bored with direct sales, he had used one of his connections to get a job with a large reinsurance company. That had been the turning point in his career. He moved from there to opening his own firm, himself and a few assistants. He had only several clients but they were enough to support him in a comfortable style.

A peculiarity of Roger's business was that a huge amount of funds passed through his office. His share of that money was only a few percent, the rest he was obligated to pass on to various insurance companies. That money entrusted to him for a limited period of time was known as the "float." Roger had allowed himself to fall into the classic trap of the brokerage business. When he had lost a large client, rather than cut his staff and his lifestyle, he had "borrowed" from the float, fully intending to pay it back when things got better. But things did not get better and over time he took even more of the money that belonged to others.

He had never meant to steal a dime. He was only guilty of sloppy management and a lifestyle beyond his means, crimes serious enough of themselves. The result would have been the same if he had walked out to rob a bank. He had taken, by the end, several hundred thousand dollars that belonged to others and spent it to maintain a business that could not pay its own way.

Finally, the inevitable happened. A large payment came due which he could not meet. His comptroller, the only other person in the firm who knew the whole story, had sensed disaster and had reported Roger to their customers and to the Illinois Insurance Department in order to save his own skin. Auditors had descended on the firm in droves. In a few days he was out of business and under indictment, his corporate assets under the control of a court appointed Receiver.

Regardless of what happened, Roger knew he was through in the insurance business. As to affairs conducted in good faith between gentlemen, he could no longer present the necessary credentials. Such privileges are granted only once in a lifetime.

His money was gone, or shortly would be. His business was in the hands of others. His wife had left him. None of his former friends or associates would even speak to him. The weather stunk and he had no future.

The deal Smith had offered him would give him a chance to avoid a guilty plea and a prison sentence. It would take him out of the country and away from Chicago. More importantly, although he would never have admitted this to anyone, it might give him a chance to wipe the slate clean to balance his crime and the damage he had done to others with a service to his country. It probably would not make any difference to anyone else but it would help him live with himself for the rest of his life.

Other than the instance in question, Roger had never stolen anything in his life. His parents had taught him solid values and instilled him with a respect for fair play. He had always bent over backwards to give his clients the benefit of any doubt in a misunderstanding or difference of opinion. His military record was spotless. He had never cheated in school, in business, at cards or in life. It was just beginning to sink in to him that his one careless and selfish action had wiped out the record of an otherwise clean and honest life.

If he were reactivated into the military, they would have to pay him, a more than academic consideration for a man with no assets, no income and no immediate prospects. The possibility of danger did not concern him. It appeared that he had nothing to lose, a fact of which Mr. Smith and Mr. Jones were obviously aware.

He glanced at his watch. It was 11:45.

"I think I'm going to take it, John. Your advice to the contrary is noted for the record. Let's go give my new employers the word."

Lipton shrugged and rose from his chair.

"It's your life my friend. But I have the feeling that someday I'll get to say 'I told you so.'"

2

Roger was given the rest of the day to clear up his personal affairs. He packed two large suitcases, paid the building super to store a few other personal things in the basement and gave Lipton his power of attorney over all the rest of his assets. The furniture and furnishings would be sold at auction. Lipton's fee would be paid out of the proceeds of his estate. The legal system always took care of its own.

He spent the last two hours of the afternoon with Grover and a representative of the Illinois Insurance Department reviewing his files and books. Despite the circumstances, Roger took some mild satisfaction when everything was found to be in order. His files were complete. The books accurately reflected the condition of his accounts. There was only one problem. His liabilities exceeded his assets by some $412,362.18. His bookkeeper, the only continuing employee, was present. Roger even wished him well and forgave the man for reporting him. Roger's failure had not been the bookkeeper's fault and the man had covered for him for years.

He and Lipton had a goodbye dinner at a favorite steak house in the Loop. Lipton bought. Then, as Smith had ordered, the attorney delivered him to the Drake Hotel at 9:00 PM

Grover had allowed him to keep $500 in personal funds. He did not know when he would see any more so he carried his own bags through the lobby, past the bellhop, and up to the suite number given him by Smith.

Jones met him at the door and spoke his first words in Roger's presence.

"Welcome home, honey," the man said with a dispassionate smile. "Coffee's on."

Besides Smith and Jones, there was a third man in the room, a uniformed Marine Major. Obviously not understanding what was happening, the Major walked Roger through a maze of reenlistment forms and then gave him the oath. Roger was a First Lieutenant again. No one said anything about a uniform or when he might expect a paycheck.

The Major gave him a set of written orders. He was to report by the fastest possible means to the American Embassy in Paris, there to be assigned to special duty. As soon as Roger

The Nova Affair

had received his orders, Smith thanked the Major and escorted him from the suite.

Jones poured three mugs of coffee and they went into the suite's ornate sitting room.

"Now we can give you the whole story," Smith said. "Unfortunately, we have very little time.

"As you've probably guessed, we've somewhat misrepresented ourselves. My name's Craigwell, call me Jim. This is Howard Kronovich, Hal for short. We're both with the CIA. The reference to the Treasury and the SEC wasn't a lie. We liaison with those departments on certain matters, this operation being one of them."

Craigwell was in his mid-forties, tall, lean and weathered looking. He had a full head of blondish hair. If he had been a little better looking he could have played the lead in a western. He struck Roger as a man who had more than a few miles on him. Kronovich was younger, shorter and heavier. He seemed to defer to Craigwell. Both men had taken off their suit coats and seemed not at all awkward about the nine-millimeter pistols that each carried in a holster nestled under his left arm.

"Now that we've straightened that out, let's get to the matter at hand. Have you ever heard of a company called Mayberry Reinsurance Ltd.?"

"Heard of, yes. Done business with, no," Roger responded. "They're a Bermuda company, popped up several months ago and started doing some very aggressive things in the American market. I lost several pieces of business to them at prices I couldn't get near. I seem to remember that they've got European money behind them."

"That's right, as far as it goes," Craigwell said. "They're backed by a French holding company which we think is controlled be a man named Heinrich Goestler."

"Goestler's one bad egg," Kronovich continued. "He's a West German national, in his late forties. He was a counter-espionage agent for Bonn until about five years ago. He was dismissed under a cloud. The Germans were sure he'd been turned but they couldn't prove enough to prosecute him.

"Since then, he's been connected with several major business scandals in Europe. Each time, millions of dollars have disappeared but he's always been able to insulate himself from the actual wrongdoing. He's very clever. We also think that he's gotten some behind-the-scenes protection from a middle-eastern government."

"So you've found a crook running an insurance company," Roger said. "Unfortunately, it's happened before. Present company not excepted. There are agencies to deal with this kind of thing. Why should it involve me?"

"Because," Craigwell said, "we think it goes far beyond mere fraud. There's a pattern that we've been able to identify in each of the previous cases. A front, frequently an unwitting pawn, suddenly appears from nowhere and buys controlling interest in a healthy, well-established company. The company is then run into the ground in a very perverse, systematic way. It becomes highly competitive, stealing business at any price. This allows it to expand its activity. Many new employees are hired. Plans are made for even larger expansions. The company gets a reputation as a rising star. It arranges for large bank loans based on doctored books and records. Then poof! the star turns into a nova, blows up and disappears."

"That's the code word for the operation 'Nova'!" Kronovich said. "When the dust settles the damage is enormous. Not only is the company itself gone and all its employees on the street, but suppliers who have shipped huge orders go unpaid, the banks have to eat the loans, customers are left with unfilled orders and the economy in general is disrupted."

"What happens to the money?" Roger asked.

"That's where the story really starts to get interesting," Craigwell answered. "Most of it just disappears. But we've traced some of it as far as Berlin, which brings the Goestler connection full circle. In every case, he's been on the scene, but always in some unofficial capacity. He's masqueraded as a friend, a relative, a consultant, a technical specialist anything to

The Nova Affair

get him on the inside. Then, when he's milked the situation for all it's worth, he destroys the records and disappears."

"What about his people, his fronts?" Roger asked. "They must be able to give you some clue as to his methods where the money went."

"They would be able to," Kronovich answered, "except for one thing. None of them has lived to talk about it. That's one of the reasons that this goes far beyond fraud. Each exercise ends in a mass murder. And, because each job gets bigger than the last, each time it ends in more deaths. His last operation was a chemical factory in Marseilles. At the end, eight people were killed. It was made to appear as an accidental explosion at the plant. The French government figures just the total direct loss at several hundred million dollars. The indirect costs are probably just as large, not to mention the mental anguish and the loss of life."

"How can he possibly handle all that himself?" Roger asked. "Not just the murders, I mean the whole thing. It sounds like a far larger job than one man could manage."

"You're right," Craigwell said. "We know he's got backing, substantial backing, but we can't identify it. We suspect the Iranians but we can't prove anything. Remember, in each case the authorities only got involved after the job was done. The records were gone or destroyed and the principal witnesses were dead. There's been just enough evidence to point the finger at Goestler but never enough to warrant his apprehension, let alone to convict him."

"You mean he's still living in the open?" Roger asked, surprised.

"He'll probably be having his morning expresso in his favorite Paris cafe in just a few hours," Craigwell said.

"How did you get involved? The United States Government, I mean," Roger asked.

"Okay," Craigwell said. "This gets us down to the short strokes." The man rubbed his palms together and leaned forward in his chair.

"Every job has gotten bigger and more sophisticated, but up until now he's confined his activities to Germany and France. This Bermuda reinsurance thing is a whole new direction for him. It took us a while to psyche it out.

"First, he knows that he's under suspicion and being watched in Europe. He doesn't have the advantage of total surprise over there any longer. Second, he figured out that by working with a financial services company that he can get his hands on a lot more money a lot faster than by dealing in a tangible goods industry and being forced to convert everything to cash. Third, someone's tipped him off as to how much money flows back and forth in your business and how loose some of the procedures are. Your personal experience would attest to that, Mr. Courtney."

Roger blushed slightly, acknowledging the accusation. Kronovich picked up the thread.

"When his latest holding company took over the Bermuda reinsurance operation the French and Germans were stymied, so they shared their files with the British. When Mayberry started doing business in the U.S., the British took us in. It's the first chance anyone's had to catch Goestler with his hands in the cookie jar. We don't want to just scare him off. He'll only resurface somewhere else. We want to get enough on him to convict him and we want to find out who's backing him."

"Okay, that makes sense so far," Roger said. "I still don't see where I fit in. I've no experience in investigative work."

"Goestler has two problems," Craigwell said. "We've been coached enough in your business to understand what they are. First, the people who are running the Bermuda operation are legitimate. They just think that an overly aggressive parent has purchased them. They were only following orders from Paris when they started to underprice U.S. businesses. Goestler needs his own people on the scene before he starts playing any real games with the books."

"In other words, he needs a patsy who knows something about reinsurance," Roger said, the light beginning to dawn.

The Nova Affair

"Exactly," Craigwell said. "His second problem is that he can't penetrate the U.S. market significantly without having someone who knows the business in this country. There's only so much you can do long distance. What Goestler needs is someone who knows the U.S. market and who can run the business for him, but run it his way."

"Just a minute," Roger interrupted, "we've got some loose ends here. I understand the problem and where I might fit in but I see some things you haven't considered. After all my bad publicity, I'm too well-known in insurance circles to operate in the States, or Bermuda for that matter. Even under an assumed name someone's sure to recognize me."

"That's where the acting comes in," Kronovich said. "Remember those peculiar attributes? You'll not only be operating under an assumed name but also in an assumed identity. You'll have to play a role, maybe several."

"Okay, that makes sense. I can handle the acting," Roger said. "But where does the ability to play Bridge come in?"

"That's the key to getting to Goestler," Craigwell replied. "It's his only weakness. He likes to play Bridge for money big stakes."

"And he cheats, or so we're led to believe by our people in Paris," Kronovich added.

"I still don't see it," Roger said. "I'm sure he doesn't just allow strangers to challenge him to a game. And what if I do get to play him? That doesn't guarantee that he'll offer me a job, let alone the one you want me to get."

"Let us handle that part of it," Craigwell said. "That's the part we're best at devious manipulation."

"What about a partner? It is a partnership game you know?"

"Give us some credit," Kronovich said. "You're covered there too. We've got a partner lined up for you, a French operative who's an excellent player and who speaks English and German."

"I'll need time with him," Roger said. "It takes a while to work out a bidding system with a new partner and to learn their style of play."

"It's a her, not a him," Craigwell responded. "We'll give you as much time as we can, which won't be much. But you'll have an advantage, you're going to cheat too!"

Roger must have looked shocked. Despite his business problems, it had never even occurred to him to cheat at cards.

Kronovich laughed, "You'll get used to things, Courtney. You're in the big time now murder, criminals, deceit, international intrigue and all that shit. There's no honor in this business."

"Now, if that answers your questions," Craigwell said. "You can answer some of ours. For starters, tell us something about the reinsurance business."

Roger spent the next hour outlining the basic structure of the American insurance market and his particular specialty, the reinsurance business.

He explained that various regulatory agencies in the country acted to protect the insurance buyer. However, insurance companies themselves were allowed to buy insurance from whatever source they chose. The theory being, that the companies, as sophisticated buyers, did not need the same protection by the regulatory agencies as is required by the public in general. When an insurance company bought insurance to lay off part of the risk it assumed from the public, it was known as reinsurance. Mayberry was one of the companies that dealt in such transactions.

Roger also explained the origin of the Bermuda connection. Many large American corporations, recognizing that they were of sufficient size to assume most of their own insurance risks, had set up captive insurance companies, that is, wholly owned subsidiaries, in the period following the Second World War. In order to avoid the restrictive regulatory requirements of the various states, these captive companies were set up and operated "off shore," in a country offering a more liberal legal climate in which to conduct business. The inducement to the

The Nova Affair

host country to establish such laws was the large infusion of jobs and capital that followed. Bermuda was such a country. Not only was Bermuda geographically convenient to the United States, but it had the advantage of being an English speaking country with a stable government and a relatively sophisticated and well-educated population. In addition, as a member of the British Commonwealth, it offered an easy interface to the British insurance market, including Lloyds of London, a major source of reinsurance, and through England, access to the European insurance market as well.

It had proved to be an ideal relationship for all concerned. As a consequence, a large insurance industry had been built up in Bermuda by those dealing with and, in some cases, managing the captive insurance subsidiaries of major U.S. corporations. Over a period of time, various reinsurance companies had sprung up to service the needs of the Bermuda captives. This device served to provide an easy access to the American market for European capital seeking to expand into the United States.

Roger went on to explain how someone in Goestler's position, in control of a legitimate insurer and operating in a relatively unregulated climate, could cause immeasurable damage in the marketplace and yet, do business with near impunity over a long period of time. The majority of insurance premiums are collected to protect against claims which, if they occur at all, are relatively quickly known to all concerned. Either the building burns or it does not. The ship or plane reaches its destination or is reported lost or damaged. The life insurance carrier generally knows within a few weeks when one of its insureds has passed away.

A substantial minority of all premium dollars, however, is written on exposures in which the development of claims follows a considerably different pattern. These are exposures involving third party liability claims, claims for injury or damage due to negligence, which take many years to manifest themselves, be reported and then work their way through the court systems to some final adjudication. In exposures involving medical malpractice, for example, it is not unusual for an insurer to face a claim arising from an incident that occurred a decade or more before. These types of exposures are referred to in the industry as having "long tails," a reference to the extraordinary amount of time which passes between the collecting of the premium and the payment of the claim.

It is this type of coverage that lends itself to abuse by the consciously fraudulent, or the simply naive, practitioner. It is possible to write this coverage for many years at premiums that are sure to prove ultimately inadequate because it is so long before the bills become due.

The picture becomes further clouded if the insurer is enjoying a rising premium income. Then, premiums collected today can be used to cover deficiencies in accounts written many years before. The operation of the insurance company becomes, in effect, a giant Ponzi, or Pyramid scheme. These effects do not eliminate the day of reckoning for the fraudulent or the incompetent but they can delay the ultimate collapse for some time and make it all the more spectacular when it does occur.

"Okay then," Roger concluded, "given that background here's Goestler's likely game plan. He will go out and actively seeks this 'long tail' business at whatever price he has to offer to get the order. Remember, he doesn't have to worry about pricing the product because he doesn't intend to pay any but the small and routine claims."

Roger continued, "Once he gets a premium flow going, he will start to accumulate huge funds in Mayberry. Mayberry, in turn, passes the cash upstream to the French holding company. The Bermuda company will get some kind of note to balance its books, but it will be worthless for anything but wallpaper. When claim payments start to mount to the point that cash flow becomes negative, they just walk away from it and leave the shell. In the meantime, he can get away with tens of millions of dollars, maybe even hundreds of millions. The beauty of it is that it's almost impossible to prove any fraudulent intent until the shit finally hits the fan and, sometimes, not even then."

The Nova Affair

"Wow," Craigwell said. "If it's that easy, why isn't it done all the time?"

"It's been done," Roger said. "But never on the scale that Goestler could accomplish." He briefly told them of several of the classic frauds that had been perpetuated in the American insurance industry, frauds that had been conducted along the same lines as he had described.

"His next step then," Kronovich said, "will be to find someone he can control to manage the Bermuda operation and to increase his writings in the States. That's why we can't waste any time. It's imperative that we get you in that position before he finds someone else."

"It's 1:00 AM," Craigwell interjected, "Wednesday morning. Goestler has a standing Bridge date at a private club in Paris every Friday night. He always plays with the same partner and he always plays against the opponent who is willing to risk the highest stakes. We're going to get you into that game. That gives us less than three days to get you to Paris and introduce you to your partner. In the meantime, you've got to acquire your new identity and learn to apply enough makeup to at least superficially disguise yourself."

"I'm beat," Roger said. "Can we call it a night. This hasn't been one of my best days."

"Sure," Craigwell answered. "But don't get too comfortable. We've got a 6:00 AM flight to Dulles and tickets for the Concorde leaving for Paris at ten."

Roger groaned. "James Bond never had to catch planes at 6:00 AM."

Craigwell laughed. "Welcome to the real Army, Lieutenant Courtney."

3

Craigwell shook Roger awake at 3:30 AM.

"Drop your cock and grab your socks, Lieutenant. There's work to do. You've got ten minutes to shower and shave then report for duty."

A few minutes later, still bleary with sleep, Roger faced Craigwell and Kronovich across the small table in the sitting room. Both men were dressed as Roger had left them. It did not appear that they had slept at all. Craigwell pushed a mug of coffee across the table to Roger.

"While you slept, sweetheart, others were working. Here are your new papers. Take the cash out of your wallet and give anything else on your person to us."

Roger emptied his pockets and pushed everything across the table to Craigwell, who promptly sealed it all inside a large Manila envelope. Roger put the ten fifty-dollar bills that belonged to him on the small stack of material that Craigwell pushed back in exchange. His new belongings consisted of a passport, a wallet and a checkbook. He flipped open the passport. The name inside was Roger Forgeron. Cute, he thought, "Smith" in French. The passport held no photo. The wallet had an Illinois driver's license, also missing the photo, and several credit cards, all in the same fictitious name. The checkbook indicated an account in his new name at a local bank with which he had never traded. The address on all the items was one Roger did not recognize. He suspected that it did not exist.

"Is this stuff any good?" he asked.

"As phony as a three-dollar bill," Craigwell said. "Please don't try and use any of it. The banks have no sense of humor about this kind of thing."

"What am I supposed to do if I have to buy something?"

"Don't worry about it. Your government will provide."

"What about the photographs?" Roger asked.

The Nova Affair

"That brings us to item two," Kronovich replied. The man pushed a small makeup kit across the table. Roger recognized a bottle of water-soluble, gray hair dye, a false mustache and some makeup glue. There was also a pair of lightly tinted glasses.

"Gee, disguises and everything," Roger said. "Are you guys sure I'm ready for this on my first day?" He smiled in spite of himself. It all seemed overly theatrical. Kronovich ignored the sarcasm.

"You've used this stuff before, in the theater. Lighten your hair and put on the mustache and glasses. We need a picture of the new you."

Using the mirror above the dresser, Roger rubbed enough of the dye in his hair to streak it with gray and pasted on the mustache, which was a suitable salt and pepper shade.

"Okay," Kronovich said, producing a 35-millimeter camera. "Stand up against the wall and smile for the birdie." The man expertly adjusted the camera and flash.

"You look like you had two hours sleep, or something. Can't you smile a little? Jim, show the man the birdie."

Craigwell, sitting at the table with an amused smile on his face, gave Roger the finger with both hands. Despite himself, Roger grinned. The flash went off three times in quick succession.

"Great," Kronovich said. "Now for item three. Take off what you're wearing and pack everything away. I mean everything clothes, shaving gear, cigarettes, whatever you brought in here. You're in the Army now kid. Remember how it works? Everything is Government Issue. You'll get a receipt for all this stuff. It'll be waiting when you get back."

Roger remembered the uneasy feeling he had experienced during basic training as an endless succession of supply clerks had piled his arms high with clothes and personal gear. It had seemed that his identity was being changed in front of his eyes.

Kronovich went to the phone, dialed a number and spoke a few mumbled words into the receiver. Before Roger was done packing his things there was a knock at the door. Kronovich handed out a roll of film to a person Roger could not see and took a suitcase and a valet bag in exchange.

"Here's your new spring outfit, kid. Put on what's in the bag and check over the suitcase. We leave for the airport in twenty minutes."

The valet bag contained a conservative sport coat, slacks and a dress shirt with matching tie. Roger opened the suitcase. It held several changes of underwear and socks, a fully equipped shaving kit, a light topcoat and several more conservative outfits. All the labels were from Chicago area clothing stores. He dressed rapidly. Everything fit perfectly.

"I don't want to tell you guys your business," Roger said, "but if I'm assuming a new identity aren't we going to a lot of trouble to make it very similar to the old one? Why not a Denver address make me a cattleman, or something?"

"All things will become obvious in due course," Craigwell replied. "Let your Uncle Sam worry about the logistics. You just play your part."

Roger was getting a little tired of the patronizing attitude of both Craigwell and Kronovich. He was also uneasy about the fact that there were obviously facets to the plan involving him about which he knew nothing. Well, he was in and there was no choice but to see it through, he thought.

A cab was waiting at the front door for them. An hour later they were at O'Hare, waiting for the flight to Dulles. They even had time for a quick breakfast.

Someone Roger never saw delivered the two photographs necessary to complete his identification. When Craigwell returned with his papers, the driver's license was laminated and the passport was complete with his current photo.

Except for the fact that either Craigwell or Kronovich kept Roger in sight at all times, the rest of the trip was uneventful. They landed at Orley Airport, south of Paris, at 7:58 PM, exactly as scheduled.

After they had cleared French Customs, Kronovich guided them through the airport to the departure area where an unmarked limousine was waiting for them. The automobile was

The Nova Affair

driven by a small, dark complected, middle-aged man with a Charlie Chaplin mustache. A younger, good-looking man, dressed in a suit cut with a continental flair sat in the back seat. As they entered the car the young man held out his hand and introduced himself.

"Welcome to Paris, Mr. Courtney. I'm Paul Sullivan, Embassy Political Affairs Officer and your contact while in Paris." Sullivan had movie-star good looks, a nice tan and a very assured air. Roger guessed him to be about thirty-five. Roger decided that he did not like the man. He was reminded of some the brokers he had dealt with over the years too smooth.

Sullivan motioned Roger into the seat beside him. Kronovich and Craigwell sat in the jump seats that opened in the limousine's cavernous interior. A glass partition separated them from the driver. Despite the fact that Sullivan was at least ten years their junior, both Craigwell and Kronovich treated him with obvious deference. Roger quickly concluded that Sullivan was in charge. That led to the additional assumption that the young man must be very good at what he did to have risen so soon over others much older than himself. Very good and probably very tough, Roger thought.

"We don't have much time, Mr. Courtney, so I'll start your orientation while we're in transit," Sullivan said.

"Please speak French," Roger said. "I can use the practice."

Sullivan slipped easily into slightly accented, but otherwise perfect French. Roger had no trouble understanding the language but found speech more difficult than he had anticipated. He knew he would go through a transition period while he mentally translated everything from English. After a while, he would start to think in French and then the effort would become much easier. He was many years out-of-date on the slang. That would take several months to pick up.

Sullivan began by giving him a more detailed review of Goestler's history. He summarized each job as he proceeded through the dossier spread on the seat between them. Goestler had started with an auto parts manufacturer in West Germany, then a chemical supply firm. Switching to France, he had brought down a large furniture manufacturer in Leon and, finally, had ended his continental escapades with the chemical factory in Marseilles. At the end of each section was a group of pictures Goestler's victims. Roger stared at them in morbid fascination. They were mostly older men, but the photographs included some women and two small children.

"Why the kids?" Roger asked.

"They were just unlucky," Sullivan answered. "Their mother happened to come home from an outing at the wrong time and saw her husband's killers leaving the house. They shot both her and the children. That's her the brunette with the glasses."

As Sullivan pointed to the woman's picture Roger noticed that the nails on his hand were about half-size and strangely malformed. It seemed an odd imperfection for a man otherwise quite handsome.

"Why are you showing me these pictures?" Roger asked.

"I want to be sure you understand what this man and his backers, whoever they are, are like," Sullivan said. "We don't intend to put you in any undue danger, but your continuous concentration is essential. One slip and they will not hesitate to kill you on suspicion."

"In my business we just lose the order," Roger replied.

"Your ex-business," Kronovich interjected.

"Right on," Roger replied, in English.

Paul Sullivan was sizing up Roger as they spoke. He did not like what he saw. The man was untrained, undisciplined and soft. He had resisted his superior's decision to bring a civilian into the operation. Such things never went well. While he saw the logic in using a plant to break into Goestler's operation, the downside was significant. It was only because no one in the Agency knew anything about reinsurance the key to getting to Goestler that he had agreed. Now it was his problem

The Nova Affair

to guide this untrained agent through a dangerous and complicated plan.

Sullivan was a pro. He had risen rapidly within the Agency because he was smart and willing to accept dangerous assignments that others shunned. He had spent much of his career in the Mid-east, gathering intelligence on the many regimes in the area that considered the West in general and the United States in particular to be an enemy. He was single because the lifestyle made marriage impossible. He also had a side to him of which his superiors were only vaguely aware. When in danger he could be ruthless, not hesitating to take the first action against a potential enemy or to sacrifice one of his own assets to protect himself. There were few rules in the game that he played. Operatives were generally judged on their ability to complete their missions and survive. Their methods were not subject to scrutiny as long as secrecy was maintained and the involvement of the sponsoring government not made public. Sullivan liked being in charge and actually enjoyed the danger involved in his career. He also liked living in expensive and exotic places largely at the expense of his government, which was one of the trade-offs for his willingness to accept risk. He did not ever want to go back to Washington to push paper and live on his relatively meager salary. When the Agency judged him to have become too well-known in the Middle-East they had transferred him to Paris where he became the senior Agency officer, reporting directly to the Ambassador on French matters and directly to Washington on everything else.

They arrived at a small villa in what Roger guessed must be the southwestern suburbs of the city. The chauffeur unloaded Roger's bag and escorted him to a large, second-story bedroom overlooking an interior courtyard.

"I'll serve dinner in ten minutes, sir," the chauffeur announced as he exited the room. A multifaceted talent, Roger thought. He wondered how many other jobs the man performed.

Dinner was a collection of cold cuts, several excellent cheeses, freshly baked bread with butter and jam and iced tea. As soon as they were served the chauffeur-cook, called Abdul, left them alone in the dining room.

"We may as well get on with this," Sullivan said. "Jim, why don't you fill him in on your half first."

"We have a small confession to make to you," Craigwell began. "Your exit from Chicago wasn't as clean as we led you to believe. Here's the wording of a news release the Cook County Prosecutor's Office will be giving to the press in a few hours. Craigwell handed Roger a single, typed sheet of paper.

> *Mr. William Grover, Assistant District Attorney for Cook County, today announced that his office had discovered the illegal flight of Mr. Roger Courtney. Courtney is a local insurance executive presently under indictment for the illegal conversion of funds from his brokerage firm.*
>
> *Courtney had been released by the court on his own recognizance pending a trial on the matter. Until this date, Courtney had been cooperating with the authorities in their investigation.*
>
> *Grover indicated that his office had evidence that Courtney had fled the country under an assumed name in the company of an unidentified female. No other particulars are available pending a full investigation.*
>
> *Courtney's attorney, John Lipton, has denied any knowledge of his client's whereabouts. Grover stated that Courtney does not have any of the allegedly converted funds in his possession at this time.*

The Nova Affair

"What the hell," Roger cried in surprise. "This was never part of the deal. I was supposed to leave clean."

"We're sorry," Sullivan said calmly, a placating smile on his face. "This was necessary for two reasons. No one in Chicago would have believed that the case was just dropped for no reason not after all the publicity. More importantly, this is all a part of your plant over here. It's essential that Goestler think you're right for his operation. A man with your background, running from the authorities, with a need to stay undercover is a perfect setup for him. If he thinks you're also broke, it helps."

"But how will Goestler know who I am? I've already changed identities."

"A shallow disguise on purpose," Sullivan answered. "We'll give Goestler a hint or two and hope he can figure out the rest for himself."

"Very clever," Roger answered. "When does my name get cleared?"

"If you pull off your part of this deal we'll release the whole story, even give you a medal," Sullivan said.

"Shit, I've already got a medal," Roger said. "I wanted a clean start. Are there any more surprises?"

"Nothing that will affect your good name," Sullivan said. "But we can only plan this scenario so far. I'm sure that we'll have some improvisation as we go along."

"Okay, no more bullshit," Roger said. "I'm a volunteer, remember?"

Kronovich let out a snort. "Sure, the same as the Jews volunteered for Buchenwald."

Sullivan gave the man an icy stare and Kronovich immediately returned his attention to his plate.

"Now that we're over that," Sullivan said, "let me get on with my part. Here's a two-page summary of your new identity. Nothing fancy, just a rough outline. Remember, we want you to be found out. Note that you're supposedly traveling with your wife, who Goestler will think is the fictitious woman who accompanied you from Chicago. She will be played by one of our operatives and she will also be your Bridge partner. You'll meet her tomorrow. Memorize all this before you go to bed. Now for item three. Here's some equipment you'll need."

Sullivan put a matching ball-point pen and mechanical pencil on the table, along with a cigarette lighter and a heavy pen-knife.

"Don't touch anything yet," Sullivan said.

Roger stared at the items. They all looked ordinary. The lighter and pen were engraved with the initials "R.C." Roger was starting to see the plan. He was also becoming more impressed with the logistical ability of the CIA. Sullivan had not admitted to any identity other than that of Political Affairs Officer. However, even Roger knew that very few Embassy personnel in politically sensitive posts actually had anything to do with the running of the embassy. It was obvious that Sullivan was a CIA operative.

"Pick up the pencil," Sullivan ordered.

Roger did as he was told.

"Now, twist the pocket clip one hundred and eighty degrees upward," Sullivan said.

Roger turned the piece of metal so that it extended above the pencil.

"It's now an operating radio," Sullivan said. "When you twist the clip it turns on the transmitter. The clip doubles as an antenna. In case we're separated unexpectedly, just turn it on. The device has a range of two miles. We can hone in on you in a few minutes. The battery lasts for three hours. Now, turn it off and pick up the pen gently."

Again, Roger did as instructed.

"I have a dummy copy here," Sullivan said. "Watch me closely." Sullivan took a duplicate of the pen Roger held out of his own breast pocket. He slowly pulled the free end of the pocket clip away from the pen. When the clip reached a ninety-degree angle to the pen a hiss of air escaped from a small hole in the base of the pen.

The Nova Affair

"This is just an inert gas," Sullivan said. "Your copy's loaded with a strong anesthetic. It won't kill, but at close range it will put someone out for up to an hour."

"Great," Roger said. "James Bond lives."

"I saved the best for last," Sullivan said. "Try the lighter."

The lighter was an expensive, gold-plated model. When pressed on one half of the top of the mechanism, it would flip up the other half and produce a flame in the process. Roger tried the lighter. It worked normally.

"Okay," Sullivan said. "Blow out the flame, keep the top raised and pull the raised part all the way back."

As Roger did so, the top at first resisted and then gave about a half inch and emitted a small click.

"That was a firing pin striking an empty chamber," Sullivan said. "When it's loaded it fires one twenty-two caliber round. The bullet exits through a small hole on the bottom of the lighter that's disguised as a screw head. The screw is a fake. You can't really aim it, just point it. It has no accuracy but at close range you can surprise someone."

"I'll bet," Roger said. "Probably cure them of smoking. What about the knife?"

"It's what it appears to be," Sullivan said. "Except it's very well-made and razor sharp. You can do quite a bit of damage with it, even with such a small blade."

"Or just whittle?"

"If one wished. Do you have any questions?"

"Just one," Roger said. "If this job involves only a 'small degree of danger,' why do I need all this hardware?"

"That's why it's only moderately dangerous," Sullivan answered. "We take all the precautions."

"Sophistry," Roger remarked, "Government Issue sophistry."

"Time for bed," Sullivan said. "You've got a long day tomorrow. Your Bridge partner will be here at eleven in the morning. You can spend the afternoon practicing. You will play together at Goestler's club tomorrow night."

"Tomorrow's Thursday. I thought Goestler only played on Fridays," Roger said.

"That's true. Tomorrow night is to set the scene. We've got to bait the trap so that Goestler asks you to play on Friday. We'll explain the rest tomorrow. Be sure and memorize that biography before you go to bed. Once you're into it, stay with it. Don't expect to be able to turn on an assumed identity at a moment's notice. It's too easy to slip."

Roger spent a half-hour with the biography, long enough to memorize both sheets. By then it was after midnight. He put out the light and lay in bed, smoking a last cigarette. Smoking in bed was one of his several bad habits.

He tried to decide if he had made a mistake or not. Things had moved so fast in the last forty-eight hours that he had hardly had time to reflect on their significance. For better or worse, the government definitely had him on a short leash. He was very unhappy about the press release labeling him a fugitive. Not only did it obliterate the last vestige of his good name, but it also was an indication of the level of morality of his new employers. What had Kronovich said? "There's no honor in this business." It might also explain Grover's extreme displeasure. The man had apparently been forced to participate in the charade.

He was in too far to get out. Once he had taken that oath they had him by the short hairs. He would have to see the game through. But it was time to start looking for a way to cover his own ass. It was obvious that these people would not do it for him.

Strangely, he felt no fear at the prospect of facing the danger that involvement with Goestler and his schemes would presumably create. He recognized that this was more a matter of resignation than courage. Like a soldier about to enter battle, he had consigned his destiny to fate. Whether or not he would emerge unscathed was now a matter largely out of his own hands.

The Nova Affair

4

Roger slept until ten the next morning. Abdul served him a breakfast of fresh fruit, coffee and croissants. He also supplied several of the Paris morning papers. Roger had read one paper from front to back and was working on the second when his new partner arrived.

She was remarkably small, not more than five-foot two. She had a perfect figure and short auburn hair. She appeared to be in her early thirties. It was her face that surprised Roger. She had green eyes and regular features, but her expression was hard, not at all the smiling, pixie countenance one expected with a woman of her general appearance.

She was dressed casually jeans, sneakers and a white blouse with a green scarf that set off her eyes. She carried a small suitcase in one hand and large purse hung over the opposite shoulder. She sat the suitcase down and held out her hand.

"Delonge, Suzanne. I'm your Bridge partner and your alleged girl friend from Chicago. Shall we go to work." She spoke in French. Roger noticed that she emphasized the word "alleged."

Without waiting for a reply, she took several decks of cards from her purse, along with two pads of paper and some freshly sharpened pencils.

"How do you feel about opening four card majors?" she asked.

With no further introduction, she and Roger began a several hour conversation on their respective techniques and philosophies of the game of Bridge.

The bidding procedure used by expert Bridge players bears as much resemblance to the amateur's methodology as sandlot baseball does to the major leagues. Expert players use a number of conventions, bids that signify something other than their apparent meaning. The rationale behind such conventions is that it allows players to use bids that rarely occur in normal bidding sequences to convey some special information. Some players even use "artificial" systems, in which all bids have meanings different from any standard system. In the hands of an experienced partnership such systems can be used to arrive at makeable contracts, or to avoid hopeless contracts, that less sophisticated systems could not manage. On the other hand, because so many bids have meanings other than their traditional significance, the chance for error in the bidding process is multiplied. The Bridge world has seen many instances in which world-class players arrived at impossible contracts because some complicated bidding sequence was misunderstood.

There is nothing devious about the use of such bids. They are not meant to hide meaning from the opponents. In tournament play a team must indicate in writing every convention it intends to use. The use of a convention not previously declared brings penalties. Also, in tournament play it is accepted procedure for a member of an opposing team to ask one member of a partnership to explain a bid of the other partner. (A player is never allowed to explain his or her own bid. To do so might give that player's partner the chance to correct his or her own misunderstanding.)

It was this procedure on which Roger and Suzanne worked all afternoon. After agreeing on a basic system, they dealt dozens of hands and bid them as practice. Then they would lay the hands down and decide if they had reached the optimum contract. There were also a number of other techniques on which they had to agree how to pass information to a partner by "sluffing" or leading cards in a certain order, how to handle

The Nova Affair

intervening bids by the opponents, and how to respond to unusual bids or playing techniques by the other team.

At 6:00 PM, when Abdul reentered the room to serve them dinner, they were still far from done. They had a good idea of each other's philosophy and technique, but there were still many situations they had not discussed. The conversation had been all business. They had each satisfied themselves that the other was a competent player.

Roger had formed little other opinion of his companion. She was obviously intelligent and organized. Beyond that, she seemed curiously reserved and unemotional.

By unspoken consent they laid aside their playing cards and notes and turned to their meal.

"Are you with the Embassy?" Roger asked, making conversation.

She hesitated momentarily, choosing her words carefully.

"I'm a French citizen. I work for the Americans occasionally, when they need special skills."

"You too," Roger said. "What are your special skills? Besides Bridge, obviously that can't come up too often. Don't tell me you're in the insurance business."

"No, hardly." She smiled for the first time. "I am very good with cards. I speak a number of languages. I can sometimes go places where others might arouse suspicion. I owe Paul a debt. When he asks, I am available."

Roger decided not to ask about the debt not yet anyway.

"What's Paul's history? He seems very young to be in such a responsible position."

"Paul is very good. The best. He is good because he thinks. He plans for every contingency. He is always two or three steps ahead of the opposition."

She spoke with obvious admiration. Her voice had warmed for the first time. Roger suspected that Suzanne's relationship with Paul might involve more than business.

"What happened to his hands his fingernails, I mean? I couldn't help noticing that they were unusual deformed."

She hesitated again, obviously debating if he needed to know. Finally, she shrugged.

"It is a well known story now," she said. "Paul was serving in the Middle-East several years ago. He was undercover, working with one of the anti-government factions in the country. He was betrayed by one of his own people and captured by some government troops. They were in the desert, miles from anywhere. They tortured Paul for several days, trying to get information from him. During that time they removed, one by one, all his fingernails. Finally, when they decided that he would not talk, they left him tied to a tree in the bush and covered him with honey and rotten meat. The ants and the animals would have finished him in a day.

"Abdul was one of the government advisors. He had planned to defect for some time. After they left Paul, he doubled back and released him. Together, they made it out of the desert and back to safety. Paul has kept Abdul with him ever since. They have a special bond."

"And the man that betrayed him?" Roger asked.

"His skeleton was found later, tied to a tree," Suzanne said.

"Interesting," Roger said. "Is Abdul an embassy employee then?"

"No," she answered. "These things are taken care of separately."

Roger decided that he had run that line of questioning as far as it would go. He tried another tack.

"What are your other card skills?" he asked. "I still don't believe that the demand for Bridge or Pinochle is that high in this business."

"It is not the number of games I play, it is how I play them. I am a manipulator."

"What is that? Polite for cheating?"

"If you wish. But I cheat only for legitimate purposes."

"Show me," Roger said.

She picked up one of the decks of cards on the table and handed it to him.

"Look at the top card and then cut the deck toward me."

The Nova Affair

Roger looked at the top card. It was the six of diamonds. He then divided the deck roughly in half and placed the top half next to the remainder of the deck and nearest Suzanne. It was an automatic gesture, performed before every Bridge hand in casual play as a matter of universal custom.

Suzanne, using only her left hand, picked up the bottom half of the deck, furthest from her, and placed it on top of the other stack of cards. It was a perfectly normal movement. The half of the deck topped by the six of diamonds had never left the table. If he had not been warned, Roger would have bet anything that that card was in the middle of the deck.

"Turn over the top card," she said.

Knowing what was going to happen, yet still not believing it, Roger turned over the top card. It was the six of diamonds! He quickly leafed through the whole pack, to be sure that it was the only such card in the deck. The deck was normal.

"Now hand me the deck," Suzanne said. "Leave the same card on top."

She began dealing him the cards, one at a time. Even watching her and knowing what was happening, Roger could not tell that every card was not coming off the top of the deck.

"Tell me when you would like the six of diamonds," she said.

Roger watched until she was two-thirds of the way through the deck. Finally, he signaled by raising a finger. She dealt the next card smoothly, in the same sequence, and stopped. He turned over the six of diamonds.

"Most impressive," Roger said, meaning it sincerely. "How much more of that can you do?"

"There are many variations. I can deal from the top, the bottom or the middle. I can mark cards with my fingernail, so I can find them in the deck or recognize them in your hand. I can make you cut a deck where I want you to cut it, or I can put it back together uncut, as I did just now. It is only a matter of practice, many hours of practice."

"Is that what we're up against in Goestler? Our manipulation can beat his manipulation?"

"No. Goestler uses different methods. He and his partner communicate with a subtle series of body motions. A crossed leg, a certain position of the finger, a raised eyebrow, everything means something. They're so good at it that they can communicate virtually the entire content of their hand to each other in a few moments. They also use the same system during play, to direct the lead of a certain card or a given suit."

"How do we beat that?" Roger asked. "You don't propose to stack every deal do you? Besides, you only get to deal one hand out of four. Those are bad odds."

"We will manipulate only three hands during the entire evening," Suzanne said. "The trick will be to have the stakes raised at the right time."

"We're going to break him in three hands?"

"We are not trying to break him," she said. "We only want to beat him. He can't stand to lose. Also, we want to beat him in such a manner that he will know he has been cheated. That, and a few other hints during the evening, will cause him to investigate your background. His initial motivation will be revenge. When he finds out who you are, we are assuming that his need for a manager of the Bermuda operation will outweigh his desire to get even. He will still plan to punish you, but he is smart enough to wait until he's used you."

"And suppose his mind doesn't work exactly as you've programmed it?" Roger asked. "He may just send someone to break my legs, or worse."

"That's possible," she said, with a calmness Roger found unsettling. "Not even Paul can plan everything."

"That's fine," he said. "But they're my legs, not Paul's."

She looked angered.

"He bears more risk regularly than you would believe," she snapped.

Her rush to defend Paul only confirmed Roger's suspicion that their relationship went beyond business. Before he could frame a reply, Paul himself entered the room.

The Nova Affair

"I hope you two have got this mastered," he said. "We're due at the club in one hour." Casually, he turned to Roger and said, "Mister Courtney, do you feel up to playing tonight?"

"Of course," Roger answered.

Paul slapped his forehead in exasperation.

"Then who will Mister Forgeron play with? I warned you, once you assume an identity in this business, keep it at all times. Until I tell you otherwise, Roger Courtney does not exist only Roger Forgeron," he said, pronouncing Roger's first name in French.

"Okay, Coach. Point made."

"Where is the mustache?" Paul asked. "And your hair, you have washed out the gray."

"I couldn't see any sense in wearing it around the house," Roger said. "Besides, the mustache itches."

"At all times, even when you sleep," Paul reiterated, obviously annoyed.

"Okay, I've got the idea," Roger answered, equally upset at being dressed down in front of Suzanne.

"Let's discuss the game plan for tonight," Paul said. "I'll drop you two near the club about seven-thirty. Play starts at eight. This is the best-known Bridge club in France. They have a duplicate game every night for the tournament players. They also have a number of side rooms for private matches. Some of those games are just for good players who enjoy playing rubber Bridge with friends rather than playing in the duplicate matches. But most of the rooms are for money players, those who would rather play for cash than master points. It's important that you get into one of those games. It's also important that you bet big. Goestler pays the help to spot heavy hitters and new blood. Most of the old members won't play with him anymore it's too expensive. If you set the scene Thursday, you stand a good chance of getting an invitation from him to play on Friday. The invitation will come from the manager. If he approaches you before you leave, then we know we've set the hook."

"Remember, the key is to bet as much as you can talk your opponents into risking. Keep pushing the limits. It doesn't really matter whether you win or lose, although winning is better. Goestler doesn't care how good a player you are, he plans to win in any case, but he'd rather beat the best. It feeds his ego. He does care how much you're willing to bet. Any questions?"

Roger raised his hand, as if in the classroom. Paul looked slightly irritated.

"Who pays if we lose? Who keeps the money if we win?" Roger asked.

"Suzanne is the bank. We fund the game, win or lose," Paul said.

Roger pulled six of the ten fifty-dollar bills from his wallet.

"Here," he said, handing the money to a startled Suzanne. "I just bought in. Prorate that over the bank, win or lose."

Paul looked even more exasperated but shrugged his shoulders.

"That's not necessary, but as you wish," he said.

"One more loose end," Roger said. "If Suzanne is supposed to be my girlfriend from Chicago, doesn't she need both a false identity and an English accent?"

"My papers indicate that I am Suzanne Forgeron, your wife," Suzanne said, with a slightly irritated tone in her voice. "That is the way you will introduce me to Goestler and the others. And I can speak French as though I am from anywhere I wish." Even as she spoke, her pronunciation changed into a perfectly horrible English accent.

Roger smiled sheepishly.

"You simply won't believe that we know how to do these things, will you?" Paul asked.

"Just testing," Roger answered.

Abdul entered and announced that the car was ready. They left the room without any further conversation. Roger replaced his disguise before they left the house.

Suzanne was silent during the ride into town. She was apprehensive over the performance she must give in the next several days. She was also concerned with other aspects of the

The Nova Affair

situation. If the operation went forward as planned she would be thrown into a situation of great intimacy with her new partner. She was happy to find him reasonably good looking and intelligent. But she was as concerned as Paul that his lack of training would cause him to falter at a critical moment, not only risking the entire operation but also putting them into physical danger. Roger's Bridge skills were no longer a concern but his obvious difficulty in keeping an assumed identity was a problem. He seemed decent enough but he had not yet earned her respect or her confidence.

Of the many operations she had performed for Paul and the Agency over the years, this was by far the most complicated and the most dangerous. Usually, her job had been only to set up a mark by causing the person to lose more than they could afford in a rigged game of cards. Other times she had assumed some minor role in a greater scheme that she never understood, often completing her portion and leaving the scene to others to finish. In being forced to pose as the wife of someone she had never met, she was assuming both a professional and personal risk that went beyond her normal commitment. It was only Paul's promise to release her from her personal commitment to him if the operation was a success that had caused her to accept this assignment. The tips of her fingers tingled. She always had this sensation before the start of a game.

The limousine dropped them at the curb, about a block from the club, which was located in the Opera Quarter on a small dead-end street off the Boulevard Malesherbes. Paul was to meet them later at a cafe on the corner.

As they walked down the short street to the club, Roger held out his arm to Suzanne.

"We're supposed to be lovers," he said. "We ought to act the part."

She looked at him quizzically, then smiled and took his arm. Roger was acutely aware of her body next to his. He wished the walk were longer.

The club was named Le Bridgeur. Only a faded wooden sign hanging over the door announced its presence. They entered and approached a small, gray-haired man behind a desk next to the door. The man wore a faded, but neatly pressed, uniform. Roger produced a card, previously given him by Paul, which indicated that he was a member of the Chicago Whist Society. Although Roger was not a member, he knew this to be a genuine club.

"I am vacationing in France with my wife," he announced. "I understand that your organization grants guest privileges to certain American clubs. I hope that this will suffice." He handed the man his counterfeit membership card.

The old man took the card from Roger and referred to a well-worn register in the top drawer of his desk.

"Of course, Mr. Forgeron. We are happy to have you as a guest. You are just in time to join this evening's duplicate session."

"We prefer a private game," Roger announced. "Perhaps with someone who enjoys playing for stakes. Can you arrange something?"

"I may be able to locate another pair," the old man said. "Would you like to wait in the lounge?" The man escorted them to a small sitting room off the foyer. "Please help yourselves to the wine," he said, indicating a carafe on the sideboard. "Your French is excellent, for an American, Mister Forgeron."

"I teach French at a small college in Illinois," Roger answered, doling out another bit of his new cover. "I'm here for several months on a sabbatical."

"Then we are doubly pleased to have you sir." The old man exited with a gracious smile. Within ten minutes he returned.

"You are in luck," he said. "I have found you a game. Two of our regular members, Madame LaRouc and Mademoiselle Charbon, would like very much to play our two guests from America."

The Nova Affair

The old man ushered them down the hall and into one of the many side rooms. The room was equipped with a felt-top table, four straight-backed chairs and an overhead light. A small wooden stand by the side of each chair provided a place for ashtrays or drinks. Madame LaRouc and Mademoiselle Charbon were already at the table. The old man made the introductions and left the room. The two ladies, both in their sixties, immediately began to shuffle the two decks of cards which were on the table.

An amateur would have expected little opposition from the older women. Roger knew better. He had run into their type many times in the States. Away from the table they might appear somewhat addled and cranky. Once at the table, however, they turned into demons, giving no quarter and asking none. They rarely played with brilliance but they usually handled their cards with consistent skill and aggressiveness. Even worse, they usually played with each other regularly. This gave them a distinct advantage. Not only had they refined their bidding system to perfection, but also they were acutely aware of every subtle inflection and gesture by their partner. It was technically illegal to convey information in such a manner, but it was an inevitable result of a long established partnership. Roger had several times enjoyed a similar advantage with partners he had played with regularly in the States.

"What stakes?" Madame LaRouc asked.

"We enjoy a good game," Roger said. "Is a franc a point too high? Each, of course."

Madame LaRouc raised an eyebrow. This was obviously more than the normal wager. As it is not impossible for there to be a swing of up to five thousand points in the course of an evening's play, a franc a point meant each player was exposed to a loss of over a thousand dollars.

The two old ladies exchanged a glance and came to a decision.

"A half franc will do," Madame LaRouc said. "After all, it is a friendly game."

"Very well," Roger said.

"So there is no misunderstanding," Mademoiselle Charbon said, "we play until twelve. The club closes at midnight."

"That is understood," Roger acknowledged.

They began to play immediately. As Roger had expected, the old ladies played a technically perfect game and bid with an almost clairvoyant skill. To his surprise, Suzanne played poorly. She missed several obvious bids that landed them in poor contracts and she misplayed several key hands.

Every twenty or thirty minutes a waiter would stand silently in the doorway, not disturbing play but making himself available for an order of food or refreshments, if anyone asked. Roger ordered several cups of coffee and the old ladies went through a steady succession of pots of hot tea. Suzanne ordered nothing but soda water.

On several occasions, strangers walked into the room and stood silently in the corner, watching the play. The old ladies explained that it was the custom of the club to allow any game to be viewed by the other members, so long as they did not kibitz or disturb the players. The old man who had met them at the door and who apparently served as club manager also entered to watch several times.

Madame LaRouc had preempted the job of score-keeping. After each hand she would show the scoresheet to Roger and wait for his acknowledgment before the next hand proceeded. At the end of each rubber she would transfer the total points for both teams to a fresh scoresheet. Roger noticed that she always wrote the stakes at the top of each scoresheet, apparently both to eliminate any misunderstanding and for the benefit of the spectators.

At the midpoint of the evening they were down several thousand points. Suzanne complained of a headache and asked to be excused for a few minutes to visit the restroom and take an aspirin.

When she returned she was smiling and seemed more relaxed. She spoke directly to Roger in English.

"I feel our luck is about to turn, darling. I suggest we raise the stakes."

The Nova Affair

Roger explained Suzanne's request to their opponents and they readily agreed to a doubling of the stakes. By this time the old ladies smelled blood and were quite convinced that their winnings were to be blamed more on Suzanne's inept play than as a result of her headache. Roger felt quite sure he knew what was happening and saw no choice but to follow Suzanne's lead. He didn't relish setting up the old ladies but realized that they had to follow the script, even at the expense of innocent pensioners.

For the balance of the evening Suzanne performed brilliantly. When she and Roger enjoyed the better cards she bid and played flawlessly, often correcting Roger's bids in an almost psychic manner to arrive at unlikely, but unbeatable, final contracts. When their opponents held the superior hands Suzanne harassed them unmercifully with a series of defensive bids and sacrifice contracts.

As their lead dwindled and then disappeared the old ladies began to loose their composure. Several times they argued bitterly over failed contracts. In frustration, they made three ill-considered sacrifice bids that cost them many more points than it was worth to keep Roger and Suzanne out of their own contract. The fact that the old ladies were now playing for uncomfortably high stakes only aggravated their dilemma.

Roger did not enjoy what was happening to his opponents. He was sure they could ill-afford their pending losses. Nonetheless, he could not help but be impressed with Suzanne's tour-de-force. It was one of the finest displays of Bridge he had ever seen at one sitting.

By midnight Roger and Suzanne were almost six thousand points ahead, a fantastic swing in only two hours. Roger shuddered as Madame LaRouc wordlessly wrote out a check and handed it to him. The old ladies had lost almost three thousand dollars in total. He put the check in his pocket without looking at it and rose to his feet as the women silently and imperiously left the room.

The manager had reentered the room in time to see the final hand and the result of the evening. He looked at Roger and Suzanne with mixture of respect and scorn.

"I congratulate you on your play," he said. "You know, of course, that they cannot afford such stakes. They live on small pensions. This is their only pleasure."

Roger almost pulled the check form his pocket and gave it to the old man. Instead, he played his part.

"We were very lucky," he said. "We had no intention of taking anyone out of their depth. Is there perhaps someone more, well, more suited to our style of play? We do not wish to offend our status as your guests."

"There is one pair who plays with your skill and style. Perhaps, if you can return tomorrow night, I might arrange another game. Where can I reach you tomorrow?"

Before Roger could think of an answer, Suzanne said: "We will be between hotels tomorrow. Can we call you? Say, perhaps, in the late morning?"

"Of course," the manager said. He produced a card from his vest pocket and gave it to Suzanne. She, in turn, insisted that the old man take a thousand-franc note for his efforts and inconvenience. The manager protested only mildly before he pocketed the money.

As they left the club Roger let out a huge sigh of relief.

"We did it. It's surely Goestler that he intends to match us with tomorrow."

"Probably," she said. "But nothing is certain yet. We will have to wait."

"About the winnings," Roger said. "Why don't we just not cash the check? I don't want the old ladies' money."

"Of course we will cash the check," she said, looking at him suspiciously. "In the first place, we won it fairly. In the second place, not to cash the check would arouse suspicion. Remember our goal. To stop a man like Goestler is worth the savings of many old ladies."

"Maybe we played fairly," Roger said, "but we definitely sucked them in. In the States we call that a 'hustle.'" He used

The Nova Affair

the English term, the French equivalent escaping him. "Don't tell me that the aspirin made the difference in your play the last two hours. You were setting them up, weren't you?"

She shrugged her acquiescence.

"We only had one chance to draw attention to ourselves. I had to do it as best I could."

"By the way," Roger said. "You were brilliant."

She looked up at him with genuine pleasure and gave him the first real smile he had seen from her. It made her seem even prettier. He swore that he detected a tightening of pressure from her hand on his arm.

Paul met them in the small cafe, as agreed.

"It went well?" he asked. "You both look pleased."

"We creamed two poor old ladies," Roger said. "They'll probably eat dog food for a month. But we were invited back to play tomorrow. I'm sure it's Goestler. We're to confirm by phone in the morning. Suzanne won player of the game honors. Incidentally, here's the evidence."

Roger handed the old lady's check to Paul. Paul glanced at it and did some arithmetic on a pocket calculator.

"We owe you ninety-eight dollars and fifty-one cents as your share of the pool," Paul announced.

Roger had forgotten his heroics of the afternoon. He did some mental arithmetic of his own. If Paul's computation was correct, it meant that Suzanne had carried a bank of about $9,000 or over 35,000 francs. They had had plenty of cushion.

"I'll donate it to an old age home," Roger said. "There's blood on that money."

Paul finished the cognac he had been drinking and rose to leave without offering to buy Roger or Suzanne anything.

"Abdul is waiting around the corner," he announced. "Now that the plan is on, we should not risk being seen together. Tomorrow we enter a new aspect of the game, Mister Forgeron. We will learn to play Goestler's version of Bridge."

5

Roger called the manager of the Bridgeur at 11:30 the next morning. Suzanne and Paul waited expectantly at the dining room table. The manager advised Roger that he did, in fact, have a match for them that evening, a game with "two German gentlemen" who very much enjoyed playing for "significant stakes." Roger's smile announced the results before he could give a thumbs-up sign to the waiting pair.

"8:00 PM sharp. Thank you, Monsieur."

Roger hung up the receiver and let out a yell.

"We're in!. They bit," he shouted.

"Control yourself," Paul said. "We haven't won anything yet. This just gets us into the casino.

"Here's what we're going to do," Paul continued. "We've managed to hide a video recorder in the light fixture of Goestler's game room on two occasions. By comparing his gestures with the cards he held we have deciphered some parts of the code he uses. We'll teach you that code this afternoon. Your ability to pick up the same signals will somewhat cancel Goestler's advantage. Goestler and his partner are good players but they've become sloppy. You and Suzanne should be able to regain some advantage from the quality of your play."

"Why don't we just invent our own system of signals?" Roger asked.

"It might work too well," Paul answered. "When we're done we want Goestler to be absolutely sure that he's been cheated but have no way to prove it.

The Nova Affair

"We want you to lose during most of the evening, just not too much. About 11:00 you should be behind, but not more than two or three thousand points. Incidentally, you should double the stakes at mid-evening, just as you did against the old ladies."

"What happens at 11:00?" Roger asked.

"We have to wait until you have the deal," Paul said, looking at Roger, "then we substitute three hands in a row."

"Wait a minute," Roger cried. "I don't do any manipulation. What's this 'we' stuff? And what hands do we substitute? What happens to the real cards?"

"It's been worked out already," Paul said calmly. "Picture the way the cards move around the table. As one player deals the first deck, let's call it deck A, his partner shuffles the second deck, call it B, and lays it to his right."

Roger nodded impatiently. The two deck system had been worked out years ago as a method of speeding play. The use of two decks meant that play did not have to stop while the cards were shuffled. One player dealt one deck while his partner shuffled the other. The player shuffling then put the cards to his right so that they were to the left of the next player, as the deal progressed clockwise. That person, on the next deal, then moved the cards over and offered the player on his right the chance to cut the deck. By custom, the deck was cut only once, towards the dealer. The whole process becomes so routine for experienced players that the cards are dealt, shuffled, moved and cut with no conscious thought by any of the participants.

"Here's the sequence," Paul continued. "After your deal your team has three consecutive chances to manipulate the cards. First when you cut deck B which Suzanne shuffled while you dealt deck A. Secondly, when she deals deck A after deck B has been played and, finally, when she cuts deck B for the opponent on her left."

"You forgot something," Roger said. "No matter how she sets up deck B when she shuffles, the next player to deal will pass them to me to cut. I can't substitute a deck or make a fake cut and I must cut naturally or it will arouse suspicion."

"No problem," Paul said. "Suzanne will pretend to shuffle the original deck B and then substitute a stacked deck which is marked where she wants you to cut it. All you have to do is feel for the mark and cut it there."

"It's very simple," Suzanne said. "I can teach you in few minutes. I just bend up one set of corners enough to make a small split in the deck. You feel for the split with your fingertip and divide the deck at that spot. Once you get the feel, it's almost automatic."

"Okay," Roger said. "That's substitution number one. But number two and three aren't so easy. Her second chance is when she picks up deck A to deal after her right hand opponent has cut. She can't set up that deck ahead of time, the other opponent gets to shuffle it, so where does she make the switch?"

"That one's tricky," Suzanne said. "I must palm a stacked deck, transfer the real one to my left hand and drop it inside a special pocket in my jacket, then proceed to deal the substituted cards. It only takes a second and the slightest distraction covers the critical move. It's routine slight of hand."

"Here's where you come in again," Paul said. "Just as she's ready to deal, you light a cigar. Goestler doesn't smoke. He'll tolerate cigarettes but he abhors cigars. I guarantee you that until he gets you to put out the cigar he won't be paying any attention to Suzanne."

"I ought to tell you that I can't stand cigars either," Roger said, "but anything for the cause. That's two. How does she do number three. She only gets to cut the deck, not handle it."

"That one's easy," Suzanne said. "I just palm the third stacked deck, flip it to the bottom and cut in the same motion. I come away with the original deck palmed. Again, I need a moment of distraction to get the palmed deck into my jacket."

"One more time," Paul said, looking at Roger. "This time you pull out a pipe. Goestler will go berserk. By the time he calms down it's too late. Two deals in the bag and the third one's on the table."

The Nova Affair

"How will you know in advance what brand of cards we'll be using? The decks are supplied by the club."

"That's our advantage," Paul said. "All the decks are the same pattern with either blue or red coloring. It's a unique design used by the club for years. We've managed to steal a few. Suzanne will have to be sure she pulls the decks in the right order. She'll have each deal duplicated in both colors as we can't be sure in what order the two decks will be played at that point. We could play the red deck twice and the blue once, or vice versa.

Roger leaned back in his chair and smiled.

"Once again, you've thought of everything--or at least everything I can think of. What about these stacked decks? Who makes them up and what do they look like?"

"I'll leave you two to work on that," Paul said. "I've got other obligations to attend to. You will leave at seven. Be sure you stay in your new identity at all times from here on, Mr. Forgeron. And keep that equipment I gave you last night with you. Abdul will give you a cigar and pipe along with the requisite paraphernalia tamper, tobacco pouch and so on. But don't pull any of it out until the right moment."

As Paul left the room Suzanne reached into her handbag.

"I have already made up three deals," she said. "I have duplicates here. We should review each hand carefully so we're prepared for any deviation in the anticipated bidding or play." She lay all three deals out on the table, face up and with each deck segregated into four hands.

Roger examined each deal separately, his smile growing into a malicious chuckle by the time he reached the third. Each hand was a cleverly arranged trap. Two of the hands were designed so that any normal partnership would bid game or more. The bids were, however, unmakeable. The third hand was set up so that Goestler or his partner, expecting substantial penalty points for setting the contract, were almost certain to double a bid by Roger and Suzanne. Conversely, the bid was makeable, thanks to freakish distribution. Doubling a contract had the effect of substantially increasing the points won or lost on a given hand.

Roger and Suzanne spent almost two hours with the hands. They tried to anticipate any possible line of play that would negate the intended result. Roger suggested several small changes in the distribution, but the hands stayed essentially as Suzanne had designed them.

When they had finished, Suzanne spent another hour working with Roger to teach him to cut a doctored deck. Suzanne was right. There was really no trick to it. After a half-hour, Suzanne blindfolded him and he quickly cut ten decks in a row, exactly where Suzanne had intended.

As they had the previous afternoon, they finished their work session with a light dinner prepared by Abdul. Roger tried to pick up the conversation where it had ended the previous day but Suzanne was largely unresponsive. She did not seem nervous. More accurately, Roger thought, she seemed preoccupied. He wondered what she could have on her mind that would weigh more heavily than their imminent performance over the evening ahead.

When they arrived at the club they were met at the door by the manager. The man personally escorted them directly to one of the playing rooms, slightly larger and more lavishly furnished then the one they had played in the night before. The manager was obsequious, asking again and again if they would like any refreshments or special accommodations. His interest was even more than Suzanne's tip of the previous evening would justify. Roger decided that the man was simply preparing the lambs for slaughter. Goestler obviously had a reputation for taking no prisoners.

A few moments later, the manager escorted Goestler and his partner into the room. Goestler was an impressive figure. He was of average height, but well muscled and graceful in movement. Roger knew that the man was in his mid-forties but he looked much younger. He had an angular face with high cheekbones and a jutting chin. His full head of short-cut hair

The Nova Affair

was a mixture of blond and white that Roger had never seen before. His most striking feature was his eyes. They were a pure, azure-blue. Goestler exuded arrogance as he briskly went through the introductions and took his chair.

His partner was introduced as Monsieur Zimmerman. Zimmerman was short, almost squat, dark-haired, dark complected and ugly. Despite his German name he appeared to be of middle-eastern origin. He had heavy features and fat, ruby-colored lips. He looked like a man with many appetites and the habit of indulging them all.

"Stakes?" Goestler asked as he sat down. "I am advised that you appreciate a good game."

As they had previously agreed, Roger suggested ten francs a point. This put the potential swing for the evening into the thousands of dollars. To Roger's surprise, Goestler looked irritated.

"Rather meager for a team who did so well at their first sitting," Goestler said. "May I suggest twenty francs each?"

Roger nodded and smiled at Goestler.

"That should suffice to maintain our interest." Suzanne's bank was starting to look thin.

Goestler smiled back contemptuously and Zimmerman suppressed a humorless laugh. Like Madame LaRouc before him, Goestler had preempted the scoring duties. He carefully marked the stakes at the top of the blank scoresheet and picked up one of the two decks on the table to shuffle.

As they began play, Roger had trouble picking up the signals between Goestler and Zimmerman. He realized after a while that they had refined the system since Paul had taken the videotapes. Their movements were now more subtle, almost a shorthand of the originals, and they proceeded with lightning speed. The two men were able to disclose the basic elements of their hands to each other in no more than ten or fifteen seconds. It was an impressive display.

Suzanne and Roger pulled no punches. They played as skillfully and aggressively as they could. Nonetheless, they were almost two thousand points behind at the end of the first hour. The effectiveness of Goestler's scheme was obvious. A number of hands that normally could have gone either way had been won by Goestler and Zimmerman as a result of their illegally gained knowledge of the lay of the cards. Roger noticed that they were careful, however, not to make a play so bizarre as to raise anyone's suspicion.

From that point on, Roger and Suzanne held their own. They were fortunate to be dealt several hands in a row that were "lay downs," that is, hands in which their cards were such that no defense could beat them. Goestler and Zimmerman knew what cards Roger and Suzanne held but could not do anything to alter the outcome of the hand.

Spectators lined the walls of the room throughout the evening. Goestler's reputation apparently always attracted a crowd. This worried Roger. The switch of decks planned later depended on distracting Goestler's and Zimmerman's attention for a few moments. Now he would have to be sure that he distracted everyone else in the room also.

Several times during the evening Roger made attempts at small talk. Although Goestler mostly ignored him, Roger had managed to put out the same shell of a cover that he had provided to the manager the evening before. After Goestler scored one of the rubbers Roger asked to see the scorecard, questioning the arithmetic. While going through the motions of verifying Goestler's addition, he pulled out the ball-point pen given him by Paul. He made the motion look absent minded, an automatic habit. He let the pen lie on the table when he was done. Goestler's eyes immediately fell on the monogram and then back to Roger's face.

"You are satisfied that I don't cheat, Mister, Mister Forgeron, was it not?"

"You are correct on both counts. My apologies," Roger answered.

Goestler gave Roger another of his patronizing smiles and the play proceeded. Roger watched Goestler as much as possible, trying to get some clue to man's inner workings. He was struck by Goestler's self-control. The man never appeared

The Nova Affair

rattled or at a loss. He bid and played with deliberate speed, even allowing for the fact that he knew the layout of the hands. His most striking character feature, Roger decided, was a total lack of empathy. Goestler ignored everyone in the room, even Zimmerman, except for the minimum conversation necessary to the bidding and play of the cards. His expression hardly ever changed. When it did, it was usually to activate his arrogant and patronizing smile. He reminded Roger of a man playing a game with small children, going through the motions to amuse them but with his mind on totally different matters.

The closest thing to an emotional reaction Roger ever saw was an almost imperceptible tightening of the jaw muscles after the relatively few hands that Goestler and Zimmerman lost.

Roger remembered reading an article on the psychological profile of mass murderers. Their one common trait was the total inability to sympathize with others. They suffered a lack of empathy so deep that the murder of another human being was a matter of no emotional significance to them. Roger decided that Goestler must be of the same mold. As such men gained power, their ability to do damage to others increased to frightening proportions. Up to now, he had regarded Goestler simply as a thief and a murderer. He began to realize that the man was much more dangerous than that, which meant that he was taking a far larger risk than he had originally bargained for in Chicago. He shuddered involuntarily and forced his attention back to the cards.

Shortly after 10:00 they bid and made two games in row, giving them a rubber score and lowering their deficit to about 2,500 points. By this time both he and Suzanne were picking up the signals between Goestler and Zimmerman so well that the advantage was actually turning in their favor. They each knew the specific contents of both Goestler's and Zimmerman's hands and by adding this information to what they knew of their own hands they could then deduce what the other held. Goestler and Zimmerman, on the other hand, might know that either Roger or Suzanne held a critical card but had no way of knowing in which hand it lay. More importantly, neither suspected that their cheating had become an open book.

Suzanne gave Roger an almost imperceptible nod and he turned to Goestler, trying to imitate the man's arrogant style.

"The cards have been all yours tonight. I feel our luck is changing. Shall we double the stakes?" Goestler's only display of surprise was a momentary hesitation.

"Luck indeed," Goestler said contemptuously. "Forty francs a point each," he confirmed and corrected the notation at the top of the fresh scoresheet. Zimmerman gave another of his humorless laughs. Despite the rules, a slight murmur rose from the dozen or so spectators in the room. This meant that each 1,000 point swing translated into about $20,000 per team.

Over the next hour Roger played the best Bridge of his life. Only the experience gained from his many years of tournament play let him control his anxiety as he concentrated on the cards. The tension in the room was palpable. No one spoke a word not necessitated by the play. Roger and Suzanne gained slowly. On several occasions they were forced to lose hands they might have won, given their knowledge of the opponent's hands. However, to do so would have involved a line of play so unusual that Goestler and Zimmerman would surely have suspected something. With full knowledge of the lay of the cards, Suzanne repeatedly interjected defensive bids that disrupted Goestler's and Zimmerman's normal smooth bidding and forced several errors in judgment. Once, Zimmerman failed to pick up a signal by Goestler that required him to either raise Goestler's bid over an intervening bid by Roger or to double Roger's bid for penalties. As a result, Roger and Suzanne stole a hand that belonged to Goestler and paid a cheap penalty for the privilege. Roger watched the muscles in Goestler's jaw work furiously as the hand ended. Zimmerman avoided Goestler's gaze. A small furrow appeared between Goestler's eyes. A chink in the armor, Roger thought. The man was capable of some emotion after all.

A few moments after eleven, Goestler, sitting to Roger's right, took the deal. Another slight nod from Suzanne cued

The Nova Affair

Roger that their switch would begin on the next hand. By this time they had narrowed the deficit to 1,500 points. Given the increased value of the last one thousand points gained, they were actually slightly ahead. Roger tried frantically to think of some way to call off the scheme. They could win without the substitution of the cards and avoid the risk of discovery.

Roger's hands had broken into a sweat that made it difficult for him to hold his cards. He felt a rumble in his bowels and was afraid for a moment that he would lose control. He realized that there was nothing he could do to stop Suzanne from carrying out the switch. He was even afraid to reach for the cup of coffee at his side for fear that his shaking hand would betray his state of mind. He automatically reached for a cigarette and stopped himself just in time, remembering that he must light the cigar in a few minutes.

The hand that Goestler dealt ended with a part score in Roger and Suzanne's favor. This meant that they had to bid less on the next hand to get a game, but that they could lose most of the benefit of the points if Goestler and Zimmerman bid and made a game first.

As the hand ended, Roger reached for the extra deck to his left, already shuffled by Zimmerman, and slid it to his right for Goestler to cut. Goestler, his attention on the scoresheet, cut the deck towards Roger without looking at it. Roger could not take his eyes off the loose cards in the center of the table. Suzanne calmly gathered them together and shuffled. After mixing the cards three or four times she evened the deck with her left hand and straightened the scarf that hung over the front of her blouse with her right hand. Roger knew that in that moment she had palmed one of the stacked decks stored in the pockets of the heavy, mohair, Cossack jacket that she was wearing. In the next few seconds she had to reach for the deck on the table with her right hand, flip the palmed deck to the bottom and then slide the combined decks to her right. After she withdrew her hand she had to deposit the original deck back inside her jacket.

Roger realized that by staring at the cards in front of Suzanne he had drawn the gaze of several of the spectators to her hands. He had to do something instantly. He turned and spoke loudly to Goestler.

"I believe you have made an error in the score, sir," he said.

Goestler, obviously irritated, shoved the scoresheet in front of Roger.

"Two spades, bid and made, sixty points," he said. "What error do you detect, Mister Forgeron?"

"My apologies again," Roger said. "It looked to me that you had given us ninety points. I wouldn't want anything we hadn't earned." The scoresheet quite clearly read sixty and Goestler looked at Roger in disgust.

All eyes had turned to Roger and Goestler during the exchange. Suzanne had quickly slid the cards to her right and again nervously adjusted her scarf. The stacked deck was now on the table and the legitimate cards had been safely hidden in her jacket. Roger breathed slightly easier. The first hurdle had been cleared.

He quickly dealt the next hand. He and Suzanne competed on the deal to the five level, more than they needed for a game, even without their partial score. Roger played the hand and managed to make it using a dummy reversal, a seldom-employed technique that turned the weak hand into the master in order to take advantage of distributional values.

This meant that they had scored one of the two games necessary for a rubber, the basic scoring unit in Bridge. It also meant that should they fail to make any future bid during that rubber that the penalties were increased, particularly if their opponents doubled them.

The furrow between Goestler's eyes was now readily apparent. For the first time in the evening, he stared at Roger and then at Suzanne with some interest. His frustration was obvious. Despite their cheating, he and Zimmerman had been losing steadily for well over an hour. It was probably the first time he had ever been at a disadvantage since he and Zimmerman had concocted their scheme. It was 11:20. There was time for only a few more hands.

The Nova Affair

"We have played all evening to no purpose," Goestler said, indicating the scoresheet. "Shall we double the stakes again, to make the last few hands more interesting?"

Goestler obviously refused to accept the possibility that he could lose. The timing could not have been better if Paul had written it into the script. Roger looked at Suzanne. She shrugged, feigning indecision, and played with her scarf.

"Of course," Roger said, forcing a relaxed smile. A single thousand-point swing now translated into over forty thousand dollars, well more than their entire bank. If anything went wrong, it could be very awkward.

Zimmerman slid the next deck across the table for Roger to cut. Distracted by the conversation, he almost forgot to feel for the upturned corners of the cards. After a moment's hesitation, he found the spot marked by Suzanne and finished the cut. He almost held his breath until he could pick up the hand and be sure that it had been dealt as planned. He was sure that his sigh of relief was audible as he stared at the first of the planned hands:

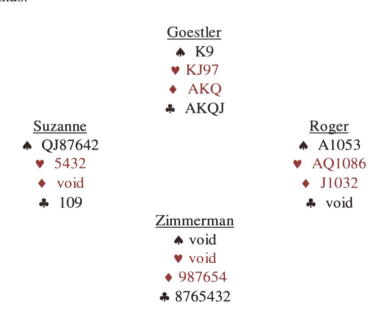

Roger could barely contain a smile as Zimmerman frantically signaled his bust to Goestler. Goestler hardly responded. He was staring at a hand that held twenty-six points out of a total of forty in the deck. Roger thought he could detect a smile on Goestler's lips.

Zimmerman, as dealer, opened the bidding with a pass. Suzanne bid three spades. This was a defensive bid, dependent on her long spade suit, and was designed to deny the opponents bidding room. Her hand was at the minimum point count for such a bid but it was not so unusual as to be questionable, particularly after a passed hand by one of her opponents.

Goestler bid four spades. A bid in the opponent's suit at this level was absolutely forcing on partner. Goestler wanted to know what Zimmerman's longest suit was and he demanded him to bid it. Goestler knew that Zimmerman had a bust and Zimmerman knew that he knew. By using a forcing bid at this level, Goestler was also announcing his intention to proceed to at least game, if not to slam.

Roger bid five spades. As everyone at the table knew that Zimmerman was being forced to bid next, this was a free bid. It announced spade support and some strength.

Zimmerman dutifully bid six clubs, his longest suit. A simultaneous signal by Zimmerman announced to Goestler that he held seven cards in the suit just bid. Goestler signaled back a query about Zimmerman's diamond holding, planning to ask for each suit in turn. When Zimmerman indicated a holding of six diamonds Goestler could barely suppress his grin. All thirteen cards in Zimmerman's hand were accounted for. Zimmerman's point count was immaterial. Goestler could see two lines of play for a slam bid of seven clubs, obligating him to take all thirteen tricks. If the opponent's trumps split evenly, he would draw them in one round and trump every one of his hearts and spades in Zimmerman's hand. Or, by leading the ace, king and queen of diamonds from his hand, after drawing two rounds of trumps, he could set up the diamonds in Zimmerman's hand. If the opponent's diamonds split four-zero, he could still set up the suit with one ruff of a diamond in his hand.

The Nova Affair

Suzanne calmly bid six spades. This was a sacrifice bid. The assumption was that Goestler had a good chance of making a slam bid. If Goestler could be lured into doubling the sacrifice, the points he would gain from setting the bid would still be less than he would gain from bidding and making his own slam.

Goestler briefly debated doubling but decided that the score for a grand slam would exceed the potential he might realize by setting Suzanne's spade bid, particularly considering that Roger and Suzanne held eleven of the spades between them and that the hand obviously contained unusual distribution.

Goestler confidently bid seven clubs. Roger hesitated as long as he dared and then bid seven spades. Goestler was now visibly agitated. The only higher bid was seven no trump, an impossibility for him given the distribution and the fact that he was missing two aces. At no trump he was sure to lose at least one spade and several hearts. If Roger and Suzanne could clear the spade king, they could run the whole suit on him, a disaster. Goestler resignedly doubled, planning to make Roger and Suzanne pay a substantial penalty for their apparently overly aggressive bidding.

As the original spade bidder, Suzanne would play the hand and Goestler would lead. Goestler selected the diamond king. When Roger laid down the dummy the furrow on Goestler's brow increased noticeably. His hand was neatly neutralized. The ace and ten of spades set behind his king and nine. Roger's heart holding exactly covered his own. The board was void in clubs, indicating that Suzanne could trump her club losers with Roger's spades. The diamond suit offered no hope as Roger's hand held every missing card in the suit, meaning that Suzanne was void in diamonds and could trump them in her hand.

As expected, Suzanne trumped the diamond lead in hand. No other lead would have helped Goestler. Suzanne would have trumped a club lead on the board and she could overtake any heart or spade lead in Roger's hand. Zimmerman had no trumps with which to ruff.

Next, Suzanne led a low spade. Goestler smoothly played the nine of spades. Normally, Suzanne's best play would be the ace from the board, hoping to drop both trumps. In this case it was obvious that Goestler held all the missing points and she finessed the ten of spades. Then she played the ace of spades, dropping Goestler's king.

The rest was automatic. She led diamonds from the board, trumping in her hand, and returned hearts through Goestler's hand. Whatever he played, she covered. After the fourth heart finesse, it was over. The board held nothing but a good trump and a good heart.

Goestler threw his remaining cards into the center of the table in disgust. Zimmerman looked pale, even his ruby lips were drained of blood. Roger wasn't sure if Zimmerman's concern was over the money lost or in anticipation of Goestler's ire. Roger watched Goestler total the score. They received 1,500 points for bidding and making the grand slam, 420 points for the seven spades doubled and made, a fifty point bonus for making a doubled contract and another 700 points for finishing the rubber. Altogether, they had gained 2,670 points on the hand. With the new stakes they had just won over $100,000. Roger had never heard of anyone playing Bridge for such amounts.

By this time, word about the game in progress had spread throughout the club. Spectators lined the walls two deep and another group craned their heads in the hallway to get a view. Despite the strict rule against conversation a low buzz had risen from the group when the size of the loss on the hand became known.

Goestler demanded silence and the group instantly fell still. The number of bodies in the room had raised the temperature uncomfortably. Roger realized that his shirt was soaked with perspiration. He desperately wanted to take off his jacket but to do so might make the fact that Suzanne could not remove hers all the more suspicious.

The Nova Affair

"Please deal, Madame," Goestler said to Suzanne. "Our time is running short."

As Suzanne passed the cards to Zimmerman to cut, Roger realized that this was his cue. As soon as Zimmerman had completed the cut he removed the cigar from his breast pocket and began to peel off the wrapper.

"Mien Gott," Goestler cried. "Are your filthy cigarettes not sufficient. I cannot allow you to smoke that, Mr. Forgeron. Cigar smoke makes me violently ill."

Out of the corner of his eye Roger saw Suzanne's hand fall away from her blouse. The second switch was done.

"I'm sorry, Herr Goestler. I did not realize. Of course I can wait to celebrate." Roger put the cigar back in his pocket.

"The match is not over, Mr. Forgeron." Goestler could not resist reacting to his barb.

Roger did not reply. Instead, he picked up the second of the planned hands.

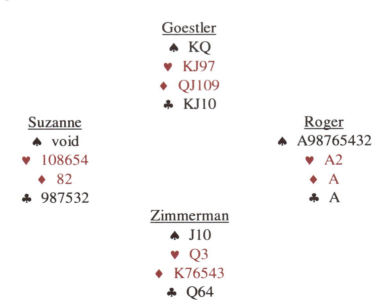

Goestler
♠ KQ
♥ KJ97
♦ QJ109
♣ KJ10

Suzanne
♠ void
♥ 108654
♦ 82
♣ 987532

Roger
♠ A98765432
♥ A2
♦ A
♣ A

Zimmerman
♠ J10
♥ Q3
♦ K76543
♣ Q64

Suzanne, as dealer, passed her bust hand. Goestler was looking at a perfectly normal hand. He still had no reason to suspect a setup. He held sixteen points and normal distribution. The hand met all the requirements for a one no trump opener in most systems, except for its lack of aces. However, the intermediate values compensated for this. In any case, Goestler was in no mood to temporize. He bid one no trump.

Roger's hand was too unusual to fall under any rule. Many players would jump to game at four spades, a few would even risk slam at six spades. Roger bid three spades, which was justifiable following a partner who had passed and an intervening no trump opener. It was a preemptive bid, promising spade length and some outside strength. The jump to the three level was designed to cut off some of the opponent's bidding room. None of the spectators would consider the sequence unnatural.

Zimmerman and Goestler were signaling madly. By now Roger was so attuned to their system that it seemed impossible to him that the spectators were not picking up the exchange. To the rest of the room the two seemed only to fidget for a moment. The crossing of a leg, the infinitesimal change in the position of the fingers holding the cards, the casual pursing of the lips, all this seemed natural to an unsuspecting observer. Goestler asked Zimmerman for his point count and was told it was eight. That left Goestler only slightly short of the amount generally needed for a game. He also asked Zimmerman if he held any spade honors and must have been pleased to find that Zimmerman had two. He failed to establish two critical things. First, that Zimmerman held only two spades and, second, that their side was missing all four aces.

Roger and Suzanne had discussed the next bid at length. It was entirely reasonable that some conservative players would pass out the hand, leaving Roger in three spades, or simply double three spades on principle. Roger could easily make his bid but they had better things planned.

Goestler finally decided that although three no trump was probably not a sure thing, he could not get hurt seriously. Down one seemed the worst possibility. Goestler signaled Zimmerman to go to game. The bid looked much more natural

The Nova Affair

if Zimmerman bid it then if Goestler went to the three level unsupported. Zimmerman dutifully bid three no trump.

Suzanne and Goestler passed the bid to Roger. Goestler had every right to expect Roger to push the bid to four spades, in which case he would double for penalties. He seemed a little surprised, but unconcerned, when Roger doubled his bid. From Goestler's perspective, the double was chancy also.

Zimmerman and Suzanne passed in turn. Before Goestler could bid Roger threw in something that wasn't in the script.

"You have been losing so consistently, Herr Goestler, that I am counting on you finishing the evening in the same style." He concluded the statement with his best supercilious grin and a forced laugh.

For the first time, Goestler lost his composure.

"Redouble," he said. The stakes, already at a ridiculous level, had been quadrupled. Zimmerman looked sick.

Goestler had bid no trump first, so he would play the hand and Roger would lead. Roger hesitated over the opening lead, playing the moment for all it was worth. Finally, he led the ace of spades. When Zimmerman laid down the board Goestler's furrow reappeared. Roger had the pattern down pat now. The jaws worked when he was mad and the brow knit to indicate anxiety. The furrow was very deep now. Goestler had just realized that his spade holding was duplicated on the board. He did not have the minimum of two spade stoppers that he had counted on, but only one. Further, he did not hold an ace, which meant that he could control no suit.

Goestler helplessly played the ten and queen of spades on Roger's ace. Goestler visibly blanched when Suzanne failed to follow to the spade lead. He could have expected Roger to hold six or seven spades, but nine was a statistical improbability. Goestler's only hope now was that Suzanne held one or more of the missing aces and would not be able to lead back to Roger's spades. But, of course, that was not to be. Roger led a small spade from his hand, conceding a trick to the king. He then glanced at the clock. It was 11:45. They had one more deal to play. He briefly considered playing the hand out and not risking the final switch. But he had his confidence back now and, instead, he simply fanned his cards face up on the table. No matter what Goestler led, Roger would take the ace, play his other two aces and the remaining good spades.

"I concede a heart," he said. It was possible for him to play the heart last, hoping that Goestler would fail to save a heart in either hand, but the odds were two to one against and he wanted to be sure that the last hand was played.

Goestler had taken only two tricks after contracting for nine. He was down seven, doubled and redoubled a total of 2,600 points. Their winnings had just doubled. Goestler and Zimmerman now owed them well over $200,000!

Zimmerman looked positively ill. The spectators in the room were transfixed. The last two hands were as exceptional as any they had ever seen played. To have also seen the hands played for the highest stakes in the club's history was a momentous event.

Goestler was staring straight ahead, his eyes not focusing at all. His jaw worked methodically. His face was flushed for the first time and a small drop of sweat glistened on his upper lip. His right index finger tapped an irregular tattoo on the felt tabletop. It was a gesture Roger had not seen before.

It was Goestler's deal, but he was ignoring the deck of cards, previously shuffled by Roger, that lay at his left elbow.

"Herr Goestler," Roger said politely, pointing at the cards. "The last deal."

As Goestler slid the cards over to Suzanne to cut, Roger pulled out the pipe and tobacco pouch given him by Abdul.

"You would not mind a pipe, surely?" Roger asked. His tone was almost pleading.

Goestler looked at the pipe and tobacco in amazement. Without warning he reached out and grabbed the pipe from Roger's hand. Silently, and while staring Roger directly in the eye, Goestler broke the pipe stem in two, using only his left hand. Then he dropped the broken halves in front of Roger.

Despite himself, Roger laughed. The act looked as if it had been lifted from an old Laurel and Hardy routine.

The Nova Affair

"A simple 'no' would have sufficed," he said graciously, as he deposited the broken pipe back into his jacket pocket.

During the exchange, Suzanne had cut the deck and was waiting patiently for Goestler to begin to deal. Her eyes told Roger that the switch had been successful.

In a few moments he was looking at the last of the planned hands:

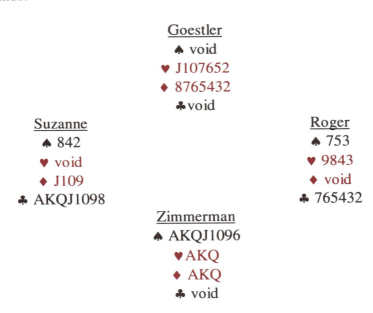

Roger watched Goestler's eyes as the man examined his cards. The German's face mirrored a series of emotions in rapid succession surprise, puzzlement and then a dawning comprehension. Goestler now realized that he was being had. The extraordinary distribution, three hands in a row, was beyond any statistical possibility. Goestler glared at Roger and Suzanne and his jaw muscles worked furiously.

Goestler's eyes darted around the room, from the cards on the table, to the players, to the bystanders against the wall. Goestler was trying to deduce how they had done it. He could not complain openly. There were fully twenty spectators in the room who had watched every deal.

Goestler let one of his cards slip from his grasp and fall to the floor. He quickly bent over to recover it and Roger knew that he had checked the bottom of the table in the moment that his head was lowered. Goestler continued his examination of the room. Roger could see his gaze focus on Suzanne's jacket, then fall on his own sport coat and go back to Suzanne. They were the only two people in the room still wearing jackets. A hint of a smile crossed Goestler's lips. He rose suddenly and stood behind Suzanne. Roger's stomach felt as if he had been hit. They were discovered!

"It is unbearably hot in here, Madame. Let me help you off with your jacket." Without waiting for a reply, Goestler reached over the back of Suzanne's chair and started to slip the jacket off her shoulders. Suzanne smiled calmly and leaned forward to accommodate the motion. Roger sat frozen in fascination. As Goestler raised the short jacket above the chair he flipped it open to expose the lining. Nothing was visible. The cards had disappeared!

Goestler hung Suzanne's jacket on the back of her chair. His gaze immediately turned to Roger.

"And you, Mr. Forgeron, may I hang up your jacket?" Again, without waiting for a reply, Goestler moved behind Roger. Roger stood nonchalantly and shrugged off the jacket. He had nothing to hide but was afraid, nonetheless, that the cards had somehow materialized in his pockets.

Goestler quickly ran one hand down the jacket, feeling for bulges. Finding none, the furrow reappeared between his eyes. Goestler casually handed the jacket to one of the bystanders, who had no choice but to stand and hold it. As Goestler retook his seat his fingers began to drum the table again. The whole scenario had taken only a minute. It was now 11:50. This would be the last hand. The attention of the room returned to the cards.

Goestler was now sure that the hand was a setup, but from his cards he had no way to tell where the trap lay. Nothing in the complicated set of signals between Goestler and his partner

The Nova Affair

allowed him to communicate such a warning. Zimmerman was still oblivious to the situation.

The bidding began with Suzanne, who had a difficult bid under normal circumstances. Because of her one strong suit she could open with a preemptive bid of three or even four clubs, but the hand was slightly too strong for that treatment. Roger and Suzanne played short club opening bids in which a bid of one club announced only an opening hand and stated nothing about the quality of the club suit. Therefore, a one-club opener would require several re-bids of the suit to establish her length. If the hand were passed out, she would lose a good chance at game. Also, a one-club opener would easily give the opponents time to find a fit in hearts or spades.

After a proper pause, Suzanne opened five clubs. To the spectators, this was a reasonable gamble. She would have to find four tricks in Roger's hand in order to make the contract. On the other hand, it was very possible that the opponents had a game in the major suits. By preempting at this level Suzanne would severely cramp the opposition's ability to find their correct contract. It was not an unusual bid. Other players might have opted for a different line, but no one could find the bid questionable.

Goestler passed, all the while sending every negative signal in his repertoire. Zimmerman was oblivious. He was mesmerized by his hand. With spades as trump he had thirteen tricks off the top. Even a six-zero spade split could not hurt him. He was almost sure to get a club lead, which he could trump. At that point, the hand would be a laydown.

Roger quickly passed. Zimmerman bid seven spades without skipping a beat. Goestler winced and his shoulders slumped. He seemed to shrink in his chair. His jaw muscles began to work again, rhythmically, and sweat beaded his forehead. He stared fixedly ahead at his cards, in resignation.

Suzanne passed and Goestler looked slightly relieved. He had expected a double. Goestler passed in turn and then looked in surprise as Roger calmly doubled. Roger's bid was a convention, an artificial bid. It demanded an unusual lead from his partner. In context, it told Suzanne not to lead a club but instead a heart or a diamond. The only possible reason for such a bid in these circumstances was the expectation of a ruff, as Zimmerman obviously had every suit stopped. No one looking at Roger's hand would question the bid for a moment. It was a textbook situation.

Zimmerman looked confused and irritated. He understood the bid as well as everyone else in the room. It was the one contingency he hadn't foreseen. Finally, assuming that the odds of Suzanne finding the right lead were no better than fifty-fifty, Zimmerman redoubled. His level of frustration probably had not helped his logic. Everyone passed. Goestler looked cadaverous the color drained from his face.

Roger stole a glance at Goestler. The man's pale face under his white hair gave him a spectral look. Goestler's eyes met his and Roger could not help flinching. Goestler's face was frozen but his eyes spoke rage.

Suzanne, of course, could have no problem with the lead as her hand was void of hearts. She lead the jack of diamonds, which Roger ruffed. Zimmerman cursed in German. Suzanne's lead was also a convention. By leading the highest possible diamond she was telling Roger to return the highest of the two side suits, in this case, a heart. Roger led a small heart that Suzanne ruffed. They continued the cross-ruff until each was out of trumps. Zimmerman was down six before he got the lead. In disgust he fanned the rest of his cards and claimed.

Zimmerman looked at Goestler in terror. He thought he had risked down one at the worst. Six down, doubled and redoubled, was a disaster 2,200 points. This added another $100,000 or so to the damages already accrued.

The spectators, likewise, stood in shock. Not only had they witnessed the highest stakes game ever played at the club, but also they had seen a champion thoroughly trounced. The game would go down in history, to be talked of and replayed for decades to come.

Roger glanced at his wristwatch.

The Nova Affair

"Five after twelve," he announced. "We have finished the evening."

With admirable self-possession Goestler computed the score of the last hand, added it to the previous total and, in a barely audible tone, announced the results.

"You have won 1,296,300 francs. A very good night for you, sir," Goestler said, staring straight at Roger as he spoke. "We shall have our revenge another time."

Roger knew beyond a doubt that Goestler was not referring to a rematch. Nonetheless, he went along with the game.

"We would be happy to play again sometime," he replied.

Goestler looked at him contemptuously and reached inside his breast pocket. For a moment Roger expected Goestler's hand to emerge carrying a gun, but it held only a checkbook. The German calmly wrote out a check and handed it to Roger. Goestler took one last shot.

"Your playing methods are truly extraordinary, Mr. Forgeron. I look forward to the opportunity of discussing them with you in the future."

This time Roger responded in kind.

"We will be busy traveling, Herr Goestler. We may be hard to locate. I will call you in a day or so if you will give me a number where we can reach you. Perhaps you would allow us to buy you dinner?"

Goestler snorted at the patronizing remark and, without further comment, rose and walked through the crowd to the door. An obviously terrified Zimmerman followed at his heels. The spectators drifted from the room amid a buzz of conversation. They would replay the last three hands for months to come.

The manager was the last to leave. He stood in the doorway staring at Roger and Suzanne in disbelief. As the broker for Goestler's matches he must have known something about the man and his methods. He undoubtedly received a fee for his services. He would probably not receive a fee for this match. Worse yet, he must have feared that some of Goestler's rage would be directed at him. If Goestler ever suspected that the manager had set him up, he would have more to fear than a lost tip.

"This is a private club established for the pleasure of its patrons," the manager announced. "In only two nights you have considerably aggravated several of our oldest and more prominent members. I think it best if you do not return. Your extraordinary luck is beyond our normal experience." The last remark was obviously intended to let Roger and Suzanne know that the manager suspected something also. Roger nodded graciously.

"As you wish," Suzanne said. "We meant no harm. Here is something for your trouble." She handed the man a thousand-franc note. The manager hesitated, torn between his greed and his fear of appearing to be in league with them.

"No, no, that is not necessary." The man pushed the money back and left the room.

As soon as they were alone, Roger felt the tension began to drain from his body. He realized that he was totally exhausted. His limbs felt so limp that he was not sure that he could stand. He leaned over the table and grabbed Suzanne's right hand in both his own. It was partly a congratulatory handshake and partly an act of reverence.

"The cards," he whispered. "Where on earth did you put the extra decks?"

She smiled and pointed at her lap.

"I stuck them down my pantyhose. I have a crotch full of cards. I'm not even sure I can walk. Goestler was obviously getting suspicious so I took advantage of the little scene with the pipe to take them out of my jacket and stuff them down the front of my slacks. Even Goestler didn't have the guts to check there."

Roger laughed under his breath. Her quick thinking had averted a disaster. His respect for her grew by the moment.

"Let's get out of here before they think of doing a strip search," he said.

Roger put on his sport coat, which the spectator who had been holding it had carefully left hanging on a chair back.

The Nova Affair

Suzanne took her own jacket and hung it in front of her waist, over one arm. This allowed her to stand and still hide the bulges made by the decks of cards under her clothing. They made their way directly to the street. A few of the spectators were standing about, presumably still discussing the game. The conversation stopped as Roger and Suzanne approached each group, then picked up again as they passed by.

"I think we're being talked about," Roger said. "Perhaps it's best that we resigned. I think that we'd have trouble finding another game anyway. Where are we meeting Paul?"

"We're not," she answered. "We're into this now and we must operate on the assumption that we are being observed at all times. We have a room at a local hotel, in the name of Mr. and Mrs. Forgeron. We will stay there and hope that Goestler tracks us down after he has had a chance to check you out."

"We haven't given him much to go on," Roger said. "What makes you think he will make the connection with Roger Courtney of Chicago?"

"He's resourceful," Suzanne answered, "and at this point he's certainly motivated. He knows that you're a crook, even if he can't prove it. He also suspects that you're traveling under an assumed name. He certainly noticed the initials on the pen you used. We've also given him a direct tie to Chicago. Remember the fake membership card in the Chicago Whist Society? Also, your cover as a professor in an Illinois college is a confirmation. It's logical that you'd pick a familiar area as background for your cover."

"Okay, that will put him on the track," Roger said, "but how can he be sure? He's not going to recruit me unless he's quite positive that I'm his man. I'm not just worried about the plan, mind you. The alternative is the broken leg option. Now that I've met the man I think that broken legs would be the best we could hope for. He isn't a good loser. A bullet in the head would be much more likely."

"I agree with you," Suzanne said. "We've arranged one other confirmation. We will have among our things in the hotel a copy of today's European Edition of the *Wall Street Journal*.

The paper contains a small article concerning your flight from the authorities Roger Courtney's, that is. That article will be circled. Goestler's sure to have the room searched. That should give him his confirmation."

"Suppose he just decides to shoot us before we can get to the bank Monday morning to cash his check?"

"Too obvious," Suzanne answered. "He knows the authorities are watching him. He wouldn't do anything to give them an excuse to apprehend him. His style would be to wait until he could make our deaths look like an accident. In the meantime, we are gambling that he'll discover your 'past' first."

They had exited the small dead-end street and turned right on the Boulevard Malesherbes. Suzanne stopped by a dented, dirty Renault parked by the curb.

"This is our car," she said. "Our luggage is in the trunk. Abdul left it for us earlier. We will have no direct contact with Paul or the Embassy until this is over."

"Suppose we need to communicate, or just need help?" Roger asked.

"That is what your radio beacon is for," she reminded him.

"Paul, or someone working for him, will always be near. In addition, I have a special number to call. Whoever answers, you are simply to identify yourself and leave a message. Paul will get the message in minutes. Here, memorize this and then throw it away." She handed him a small slip of paper with a local number written on it. Roger repeated the number to himself several times, until he was sure that he could recall it, then tore the strip of paper into small pieces and let the scraps float off in the breeze.

"Here, you drive," she said, handing him a set of keys. "Go south and cross the Seine on the Pont de la Concorde."

As Roger drove he had time to consider two facts. He was obviously not being told anything more about the operation than was absolutely necessary. Paul had entrusted Suzanne with all the information concerning the car, the hotel and their contact number. He wondered how much more she knew that she hadn't shared with him. Secondly, it had suddenly struck him

The Nova Affair

that Suzanne had not mentioned rooms at the hotel, but a room. That was only logical, he conceded. They were traveling as husband and wife. However, the implications started a train of thought that he fought to control. He could not help stealing a glance at Suzanne as she fished the cards from her underwear. After she had all six decks in hand, she removed two large rubber bands from her purse and wrapped the cards in one large stack. As they crossed the Pont de la Concorde, Roger slowed the car and Suzanne threw the bundle of cards over the railing and into the Seine.

"Why not just leave them lying around the hotel room?" Roger asked. "If Goestler does search it, that will only confirm the scheme."

"That's too obvious," she answered. "We have to do the logical thing. Besides, we have already confirmed it by disposing of the extra cards. The black Peugeot, two cars back, we're being followed. Goestler's even quicker than I thought."

With a start Roger stared into the rearview mirror. It had never occurred to him that they would be followed so soon. He could make out the car in the lights of the oncoming traffic, but he could not see any occupants.

Suzanne guided him to a small hotel on the Rue de Sevres, near Montparnasse. They left the car in an interior courtyard, reserved for guests, and were shown to their room by an aged porter. They had one small bag each, only several changes of clothes. Roger took this as a clue that Paul did not expect this stage of the operation to last long.

Roger was acutely aware of the fact that the room held only one, rather small, double bed. If that fact held any significance for Suzanne, she did nothing to show it. The room was otherwise furnished with a small desk and with an armchair and settee separated by a coffee table.

Suzanne produced a bottle of wine from her bag. They sat next to each other on the settee.

"Let's discuss stage two," she announced, as she poured them each a glass of wine in the dusty tumblers she had retrieved from the bathroom. "Assume that Goestler follows the trail we have laid for him and contacts you with an offer, what will be your terms to go to work for him?"

"Will I have any choice?" Roger asked. "It may be that, or the bullet in the head."

"You can't let him intimidate you," she said. "If he doesn't think you're strong enough to run the Bermuda operation then he will simply even the score now. Remember, he needs someone like you like Roger Courtney very badly."

As they talked Suzanne had kicked off her shoes and tucked up her legs on the couch. She had also removed her scarf, unbuttoned the top of her blouse and then reached behind her back to unclasp her bra. She was close enough to Roger so that he could clearly smell a mixture of perfume and perspiration that, under the circumstances, he found exceptionally provocative.

The wine began to relax him. In his already fatigued state he felt a curious numbness seep through his muscles. He was acutely aware of an aching in his groin. He wanted to take Suzanne in his arms but he didn't know how to begin. They were not lovers, they were not even dating, they were only working together and she had given him no hint of encouragement. He was certainly not inexperienced with women but in this situation he felt no confidence in his ability to control events.

She leaned forward to refill their glasses and her blouse fell open enough to expose the fullness of her breasts. Roger decided that it was time to address the issue.

"I need to rest," Roger said, glancing at the bed. "The room offers little choice as to sleeping arrangements. I don't want to appear presumptuous, but it seems we must share the bed."

She smiled. "We are supposedly lovers traveling together as a married couple. We are being watched. Of course we must share the bed. We may have to share one for some time. Does that bother you?"

"Of course not," Roger blurted. "On the contrary, I find the thought extraordinarily attractive. It's just that it seems we need

The Nova Affair

some transition. Our relationship has been nothing but business."

"Well then, transit," she said and smiled affectionately.

Shit, Roger thought. I'm handling this like a schoolboy. He walked to the door and turned off the light. The room was bathed in a weak glow from the streetlights below the window. He sat his own glass down and then took Suzanne's from her hand and sat it next to his.

He gently slid her feet to the floor with one hand and pulled her closer with the other. He kissed her. She was passive, not resisting but certainly not responding. This wasn't going to work, he thought. There's no spark.

Suzanne had decided to let the situation develop naturally. She was more comfortable with Roger now. He had passed the first test. She could have told him to sleep on the floor but that seemed ridiculous under the circumstances. On the other hand, he had to earn the privilege. She was not going to make it too easy for him. How he handled the situation would be another test.

Instinctively, his hand slid up under her loosened brassiere and cupped her breast. He caressed her nipple until he felt it began to turn harder. Slowly, she started to respond. Her lips began to move against his and her hand ran up and down the small of his back. Their embrace took on energy of its own. She leaned back and sideways and he rolled over until she could feel him, hard and ready, against her thigh.

They moved to the bed and left their clothes in a single jumbled pile on the floor. She lay on top of the bed and pulled him down to her. He entered her easily. She was now fully aroused. She raised her legs and locked them behind his back. They rocked in unison until each was satisfied.

Later, they lay under the covers and smoked while they finished the wine.

"I thought for a while that it wasn't going to work," Roger said. "What did I do right?"

"Nothing," she answered. "It's what you didn't do wrong. I was waiting to see if you were gentle. When I found that you were, then I felt right about it."

In a few moments, she fell asleep in his arms. He lay awake for awhile, pondering the fact that she must have known from the beginning that this situation would develop if their plan against Goestler were successful. No wonder she had seemed so distracted earlier in the day. Had she done it for him, or for Paul, he wondered. How much did she owe the man from the CIA?

6

The next morning Roger and Suzanne went sightseeing. It had been many years since Roger had lived in Paris and he wanted to visit the sights and see how the city had changed since he had been there last. They went to Notre Dame, Montmartre and ended the day strolling through one of the many galleries of the Louvre.

They walked hand-in-hand and acted and felt like lovers. Once relieved from the strain of her role, Suzanne became more open and cheerful. She told him about her childhood and her family. She had grown up on a small farm in Brittany with a half-dozen brothers and sisters. Her parents were retired and all her family still lived in the area where she was raised. She visited them regularly, but could not tolerate for long the drudgery of the farm or the dullness of the small village.

Officially, she worked as an interpreter and guide in Paris and tutored English, German and French for extra money. Unofficially, she spent much of her time working for Paul. She

The Nova Affair

offered no explanation as to how she and Paul had met or how deep their relationship had grown. Roger had to fight the desire to query her in more detail. He remembered her remark when they first met: "I owe Paul a debt," she had said. He wanted very much to know what that debt was and when it would be repaid.

Before they had left their hotel room they had carefully memorized the position of the folds in their clothes as they lay in the drawers and the exact location of the few objects that had been left in the room.

After returning, they examined the room in detail and decided that it had indeed been searched.

"Goestler's right on schedule," Suzanne announced. "That should have done it," she said, pointing to the *Wall Street Journal* lying open on the desk with the short article concerning Roger's disappearance circled in pen. "He's run with the bait, now the question is whether or not he'll swallow it."

They made love in the pink light cast by the setting sun. As the shadows darkened in the room they lay quietly in the bed and talked of nothing. Suzanne had promised to take him to one of her favorite restaurants for dinner. She finally left the bed to bathe and dress. Roger listened as the sound of her bath water filled the tub. He reached for a cigarette, finding only an empty package on the nightstand. He remembered seeing a vending machine in the lobby. Not wanting to disturb Suzanne, he dressed quickly and slipped out of the room, planning to be gone for only a moment.

The lobby was deserted. He found the vending machine in the corner and retrieved a package of cigarettes. As he walked to the stairwell, a frail, middle-aged man approached him and spoke in poor French with a heavy accent. The man held a faded map of Paris in his hands.

"Pardon, excusez-moi, Monsieur. I am looking for a friend and I cannot decipher these directions. Could you help?"

Roger took a step towards the man and craned his neck to look at the map. The muzzle of a pistol suddenly appeared from under the folds of the map and pointed directly at Roger's forehead.

"Please turn and walk down the hallway to the rear," the man said. His French had improved immensely.

At first Roger thought he was being robbed. Then it occurred to him that this must be Goestler's next move. Once again, the German had acted with a speed he had not anticipated. He entered the dimly lit corridor to the rear of the lobby. A pang of guilt struck him as he remembered Suzanne, alone and defenseless, in her bath upstairs. Not a smart move, he thought, not good at all. Paul was sure to give him a bad grade on this one.

"Stop here. Face the wall," the man ordered.

Christ, he's going to shoot me right here, Roger thought. Goestler hadn't swallowed the bait. This was pure revenge. He heard a heavy step behind him and braced for a blow, or the shock of a bullet. Instead, he was suddenly grasped around the waist by a huge arm and jerked backwards and down. His arms were pinned to his sides in a grip of unbelievable strength. His legs hung at an angle in front of him. He could not rise or kick backwards. The small man obviously had an accomplice. Roger was not a weakling, but he felt helpless in the grasp of the unseen attacker.

A hand holding a handkerchief appeared in front of him and then firmly clasped his mouth and nose. He was aware of a pungent, biting odor. He had a vision of a white-smocked man wavering before his eyes. Ether! He hadn't smelled it since high school chemistry class. As his consciousness faded he remembered that his jacket, with the special pen, pencil and lighter, was draped over the chair in the room upstairs.

He awoke to find himself lying on a leather couch and staring at a dirty, white ceiling from which the paint was peeling in patches. His head hurt and his mouth felt like it was filled with cotton. At the foot of the couch, staring intently at him, stood a huge, broad-shouldered man with heavy Arabic features. The man was dressed in a lumpy, poorly tailored suit.

The Nova Affair

He had thick eyebrows and greasy, black hair combed straight back. This was, presumably, the second, unseen, attacker. Roger dubbed them Mutt and Jeff.

He turned his head and saw the small man sitting in a straight-backed chair before a desk. The desk had a flexible-necked reading lamp on it. The light was turned so as to shine directly in Roger's eyes. He could just make out the outline of a man sitting behind the light. The figure was tapping the desk with his right index finger.

"Please sit up, Mr. Courtney, we have several matters to discuss." Goestler's voice was unmistakable. Roger was as frightened as he had ever been, including any time in the service. He rose slowly and felt the throbbing in his temples increase proportionally. He tried to analyze the situation. Suzanne had said that Goestler would not try anything serious so quickly after the Friday night confrontation. But that certainly hadn't stopped Goestler from kidnapping him. If Suzanne was right, that left two alternatives. Either Goestler wanted his check back or he had taken the bait and was going to offer Roger the Bermuda job, or both. Or all three, in reverse order, Roger thought wryly.

"I could use an aspirin," Roger said, as he sat straight up on the couch.

"Later," Goestler replied. A pack of cigarettes flew over the lamp and landed in Roger's lap. "I believe you were looking for these when we were so fortunate as to find you alone in the lobby," Goestler said. "You enjoy your tobacco so much, please feel free to have one." Goestler laughed maliciously.

Roger opened the pack and extracted a cigarette. The big man lit it for him with a butane lighter.

"So?" Roger asked. He blew a cloud of smoke towards the lamp.

"We have been looking into your background, Mr. Courtney-Forgeron," Goestler said. "We find that you are not what you pretend to be in person or at the Bridge table."

"Very clever of you," Roger answered. "Interpol's been trying to crack this for years."

"I suggest you don't provoke me," Mr. Courtney. "This time I hold the pat hand."

"So you do," Roger said. "What do you want?"

"First, I want my money back," Goestler said. "We have put it all together the jacket with the pockets, the extra cards thrown into the Seine very clever. Your 'wife' is an accomplished cheat. Where did she put the cards before I searched her jacket?"

Roger decided there was no purpose in lying about the situation. "She stuck them down the front of her slacks," he replied. He was tempted to ask Goestler about his own ethics at the table, but that was information he had obtained from Paul and he didn't need to point any fingers in that direction.

"And where is the check?" Goestler asked. "We've searched your room and we've searched you but haven't found it."

"In an envelope in the hotel safe," Roger said. "We thought it best not to leave it lying around. We planned to visit the bank Monday morning."

Goestler spoke very calmly. "I assure you, Mr. Courtney, it would be worth your life to cash that check. We will make arrangements for its return later. Now, to the second matter. Do you deny that you are the Roger Courtney of Chicago who recently fled the authorities while under indictment?"

"You know that I am," Roger answered calmly. He hadn't realized until that moment that his mustache had been removed. He'd become so accustomed to its presence that his upper lip felt strangely bare. He lit a new cigarette from the butt of the first. He felt much better. Goestler obviously had something on his mind other than pure revenge.

"And the woman?" Goestler asked. "We know she is not your real wife."

"No," Roger confirmed. "She is an old friend. Coincidentally, she needed to leave Chicago under circumstances somewhat similar to mine. It seems that she

The Nova Affair

dropped a card at the wrong time. Someone was looking for her. She was born in France and immigrated to the United States with her parents when she was in her teens. I speak French also because I lived here as a child. We thought we could blend in here better than someplace else. We are broke. The Bridge games were just a way to raise some money to live on."

"Two cheats, running from justice," Goestler said, a note of scorn in his voice. Roger had to bite his tongue to keep from blurting out that at least they did not kill people.

"You are an incredibly fortunate man, Mr. Courtney," Goestler said. "I might have simply had you killed for what you did to me. But I have discovered that your background is such that you fit into another plan of mine. I am looking for a man with a particular set of attributes."

Roger had to bite his lip again. Those were almost exactly the words that Kronovich had used during their first meeting in Chicago. He answered as though he were reading the lines of a play.

"What attributes would those be?"

"I need someone who knows the reinsurance business, someone with some acting ability, someone who wishes to remain incognito indefinitely and, most of all, someone with no scruples, an established thief."

"Bingo," Roger said. "What's in it for me?" He had a mental image of a bobber disappearing under water.

"Your life, first of all," Goestler answered. "Secondly, enough income to live comfortably during the operation. Finally, if you carry out the assignment as charged, enough money to disappear for a long time."

"Should I classify this as an offer I can't refuse?" Roger asked.

"I suggest that you do," Goestler said.

"Okay," Roger said. "What's the deal?"

"I control a French company which in turn owns a company called Mayberry Reinsurance, Ltd. in Bermuda. You have heard of it perhaps?" Roger nodded his head slightly. "It is my intention to use Mayberry as a vehicle to enter the American insurance market. I then intend to write as much, how do you say it in English? long tail business as possible. When we have accumulated as much money as we can, and before the claims start to accumulate, we will pass the cash upstream to France, split the take and disappear."

"And you need someone with insurance experience to run Mayberry and get it into the American market," Roger said.

"Precisely."

"I repeat," Roger said. "What's in it for me, besides my life and living expenses?"

"Ten thousand a month, tax free of course," Goestler said. "Plus expenses. If we carry it off you get a one million bonus at the end."

"Forget the million," Roger said. He was on familiar ground now. He made his living brokering. "I'll take ten percent of the gross. If we can't get at least ten million out of this it's not worth doing. Besides, that gives me an incentive. One other condition Suzanne stays with me and she gets five grand a month. I'll need at least one other person I can trust anyway."

"That will be acceptable," Goestler said.

Goestler's quick acquiescence to his conditions only confirmed Roger's suspicion that the man had no intention of keeping his part of the bargain.

"Very well then, Mr. Courtney, we have a bargain. Plan to check out of your hotel by 10:00 AM tomorrow and wait in the lobby. My associates will pick you up and take you to the airport. You leave for Bermuda at once. We will supply you and your friend with new papers. Mr. Zimmerman, who I'm sure you remember, will accompany you. He will be my liaison. I expect daily reports from you and I expect every dime to be accounted for. I will not tolerate another crooked shuffle."

"Understood," Roger said.

"One more thing," Goestler said. "I expect the check back when we meet tomorrow."

The Nova Affair

"For sure," Roger answered. "We'll need an advance on our wages then. We're a little low on funds at the moment."

Goestler snorted. "I'll see that you get enough to cover expenses. By the way, stay clear of the tables. I don't want this deal screwed up because you two get caught with an ace up your sleeve, or down your slacks." He chuckled at his own crude joke. "We will return you to the hotel now. You must be blindfolded, I'm afraid. This location will be my secret."

The big man extracted a dirty linen napkin from his pocket and tied it tightly around Roger's head, covering his eyes. He then grasped Roger by the back of his shirt collar and half-led, half-carried him out the door and down a flight of rickety, wooden steps. Roger smelled an oily, musty odor and sensed he was inside of a large, open building. He presumed that it was an abandoned warehouse or manufacturing plant. They walked across a few feet of concrete floor and Roger was pushed face downward into the back seat of a vehicle.

Someone threw a blanket over him. The small man spoke into his ear.

"Do not move until we tell you to," he said. Roger remembered an old detective story he had once read in which the hero, in a similar situation, had memorized the turns made by car in which he was held and had also counted the number of seconds between each turn. By reversing the process from the point at which he was released, the hero had back-tracked his route to the criminal's hideout. Roger decided to try the same procedure.

He heard the sound of a large overhead door swing open. In a few moments they were on the street. It took only a few minutes for Roger to become totally confused. The car made turn after turn and he quickly lost track of the timing or sequence. So much for detective stories, he thought. He could hear heavy traffic around him at all times and he had the general sense of going in circles. He decided that they had never left the inner city.

After what seemed almost an hour, the car stopped, the blanket was pulled back and his blindfold was removed. They were sitting in a deserted alley. The big man was driving and the small man was leaning over the back seat.

"Get out here," he said. "Go forward to the end of the alley, then turn left. Your hotel is two blocks away."

Roger got out of the back seat and walked past the front of the car. He stole a glance over his shoulder as the car reversed out into the street. It was a new, cream-colored Mercedes 360SL. No front license plates, Roger noticed. The car was gone before he could see anything more.

When he entered their room he found Suzanne sitting in the armchair in the corner.

"My God," she cried. "We thought they had killed you." She left the chair and embraced him. Over her shoulder Roger saw Paul step out of the bathroom. He held a pistol in one hand and a small radio transmitter in the other. He was dressed in a pair of heavy, dirty coveralls. He looked at Suzanne in Roger's arms with a very pained expression and then turned to speak into the transmitter. Across the back of the coveralls was the name of a plumbing repair service. Roger could not hear what he was saying.

"Quickly," Paul said. "Tell me what happened. I cannot stay here any longer than necessary."

"Goestler bought it," Roger answered. "He had me abducted from the lobby by some Mutt and Jeff pair. They anesthetized me and took me to a hideout of Goestler's, some kind of abandoned factory or warehouse. I can't tell you where it is, except I think it's in Paris. Goestler wants me to run the Bermuda operation. Suzanne and I leave tomorrow, with Zimmerman. He also expects me to return his check. He was quite open about the fact that he'd have killed us if he hadn't discovered some other use for me. If he ever finds out that we're plants, I figure we've got a life expectancy of about sixty seconds."

"The transmitter," Paul said. "Why didn't you have it with you? It's exactly the type of situation we intended it for."

The Nova Affair

"I screwed up," Roger said. "I left my coat with all the James Bond stuff in the room. I was only going to be gone a few seconds."

"Amateurs," Paul said with distaste. "You must never let your guard down, not for an instant. We were all lucky. If Goestler had decided to kill you, we could not have helped. Perhaps you have learned a lesson."

"You can't say anything I haven't already told myself," Roger said. "What's the plan now? We're on our way to Bermuda. How do you want me to play it? How do we stay in contact? I've got to go through the motions of setting up the operation, but I don't want to get so far into it that I actually start hurting people."

"You won't have to," Paul answered. "We only have to accomplish two things. Take the operation far enough along so that a felony is established and then get Goestler into the jurisdiction. We've agreed to cooperate with the British. If we take him in Bermuda then they prosecute first and we get extradition rights after he's served his time there. Vice-versa if we get him in the States. Naturally, I'd like first crack."

"Is that enough?" Roger asked. "If the man's really a mass murderer, he ought to be tried for that."

"We have to take what we can get," Paul said. "If the French or the Germans could prove the murders they'd already have him. Our only hope is to try and turn one of his accomplices into State's evidence. First, we have to get enough on them to have a long prison term to trade."

"Why doesn't someone just terminate him?" Roger asked. "Isn't that the term you guys use? He's obviously a menace."

"Such things are much more common in novels," Paul said. "Besides, the French have decided not to take such action. They have a highly developed sense of justice. Now that he's being watched, the chance of his taking any more action in France is remote. For us to commit such an act on French soil without their permission would be very bad form. There are understandings about such things."

"How is a felony established?" Roger asked. "Exactly what does Goestler have to do to convict himself?"

"Get someone else's money in his hands and convert it to his own use," Paul answered. "Preferably, at least several hundred thousand dollars, enough to get the court's attention."

"It won't work that way," Roger said. "If we write the logical kind of business for this scheme, business on which the losses take years to develop, we could go on indefinitely before Goestler decides its time to renege on a claim. In the meantime, we'll accumulate a lot more that several hundred thousand dollars. I told Goestler I could do at least ten million the first year and, frankly, that's conservative." Roger gave Paul the same lecture he'd given Craigwell and Kronovich on the structure and cash flow peculiarities of the insurance business.

"But Goestler won't wait years to take the money out," Paul persisted. "He'll make some kind of move relatively soon."

"True," Roger said. "But there're legal ways to do it. He can understate his estimates for future claim payments, which creates artificial profits, and then dividend the profits upstream to the French holding company. Or, he can just take out the cash and replace it with a surplus note from the parent company."

"What's a surplus note?"

"Just a promise by the parent to replace the cash if the subsidiary ever needs it."

"That's legal?" Paul asked, incredulously.

"Sure," Roger said. "It's done every day. Many offshore companies don't have any assets to speak of at all except for surplus notes."

"That's a rather loose procedure for a company holding monies due other people years in the future," Paul said.

"Others have made the same observation," Roger replied.

"Well then, how do we get him to make a move?" Paul asked. "We're prepared to fund the operation up to several hundred thousand dollars, but ten million, or more, is out of the question."

The Nova Affair

Roger thought a moment. "There's one way," he said. "We blind-side him on the claims. We'll set up some fictitious losses that have to be paid at once. That will force his hand. He'll have to take whatever's in the pot and run."

Suzanne had been listening to the exchange in silence. At this point she rose and stomped her foot with surprising vehemence.

"No!" she shouted. "That's like signing our death warrant. Goestler surely intends to kill us when this is over. If we blow the scheme while we're still involved we'll be easy targets. He'll take us for sure."

Roger surprised himself. "It's not impossible," he said. "It will just take some close timing. We'll go out the back door while the claims come in the front. Goestler will assume we ran because we botched the scheme. He might never suspect our real involvement. If Paul does his job, Goestler will be in no position to worry about us."

Suzanne sat down, obviously not satisfied.

"How do we force Goestler to come to Bermuda, or the States?" Paul asked.

"We'll have to leave the situation so muddied that he'll have no choice but to come over himself to try and salvage it," Roger answered. "Let me work on that as we go along."

"Okay," Paul said. "I can't stay much longer. Here's the routine. As soon as you know where you're staying in Bermuda, call this number." He handed Roger a slip of paper. "That's your lifeline. Memorize it and throw it away. Tell whoever answers where you are and what's happened up to then.

The message will get to Craigwell and Kronovich. They'll establish themselves as close to you as they safely can. I'll continue to direct the operation from here. If and when I'm needed, I'll come. You start up the scheme exactly as Goestler intends you to until we can agree on how and when to spring the trap. As long as Goestler thinks you're performing as expected, he'll leave you alone. We'll have to depend on you to structure the arrangement so that we can act relatively soon. Any questions?"

Roger and Suzanne both shook their heads. Paul exited without a further word.

When they were alone, Suzanne turned to Roger and said "I'm afraid, Roger. There are so many things that can go wrong. There's something else I must tell you. Paul and I were once lovers. I ended the relationship but I know he still cares for me. He can be a very vindictive man. It would not upset him if his excuse to get Goestler were your murder. That would, how do you say, kill both birds with one stone. He would never plan such a thing, but he might let you make a mistake that would let it happen."

Roger took her in his arms. He felt elated. It was the first time she had opened up to him.

"Then you must help me to not make a mistake," he said. He debated asking her what the debt was that she owed Paul but decided that that, too, would come in time. It felt right to have her in his arms. Despite the danger, he felt for the first time since his involvement that he was in a position to control future developments. Later, he would shudder at how naive he had been.

Suzanne had not realized until Roger was missing how strongly she had come to feel about him. She had contacted Paul in panic. Her concern was not just for the success of the operation or for a colleague in trouble but it was personal. She had found the thought of Roger in trouble to be deeply distressing. It seemed that she had hardly breathed until he walked back into the room, hours after she realized that he must have been taken. She tried to sort out her thoughts and emotions. Did the fact that he had become her lover lead her to display the appropriate emotions or was this something different, something spontaneous? It put the situation into an entirely different context. She now had to react on two levels, one professional and one personal. It was, she thought, only going to make the next few weeks only that much more complicated and stressful.

7

As a result of Roger's agreement with Goestler, two unusual communications originated from Paris before the day was over.

Paul Sullivan sent a coded message to his superior in Washington and copied a liaison in both Paris and London.

RE: NOVA

OPERATION PROCEEDING AS PLANNED.   ACTIVITY MOVING TO BERMUDA. WILL ADVISE.

Later that day, Zimmerman drove alone to a public telephone that he picked at random from a bank of booths alongside the Gare St. Lazare. He placed a station-to-station call to Bonn which was answered at a pay telephone by a military attaché of the Iranian Embassy.

Roger and Suzanne, accompanied by Zimmerman, arrived in Bermuda the afternoon of the following day. Roger had now assumed the identity of Louis Monieux, a native Frenchman with a long and totally fabricated history of employment in the French insurance industry. Suzanne was given the name Brigette Pavalone and was traveling as his executive assistant.

They took a cab to a small villa on a bluff above one of the many small bays that ringed the island. The villa had two bedrooms and a bath upstairs. The lower level contained a large living room, a kitchen with a dinette and a one-car garage. The Villa offered a beautiful view of the bay, which could be reached by a flight of steps cut into the stone face of the bluff. A small dock extended into the bay from the foot of the steps. A Honda Accord sat in the garage. The villa was comfortably furnished and the kitchen had recently been stocked with provisions, fresh fruit, beer and wine. Someone had apparently prepared the home for their arrival.

Roger was impressed with the quality of the accommodations and the efficiency with which the transfer had been handled. Goestler obviously had many resources at his command, including access to forged documents that looked as good as those with which the CIA had originally provided him. He was not at all excited about sharing the villa with Zimmerman, particularly if the alternative was to be alone with Suzanne. Finding time alone, to make love or to conspire, was going to be difficult.

Zimmerman had thrown his bags into one of the bedrooms and returned to the ground floor.

"You two start work tomorrow. I'll take you into town and introduce you to the staff. You can keep the old manager on if you can convince him to take a demotion. Otherwise, fire him. If anyone questions any of your orders fire them immediately. If you have any trouble with anyone let me know. I'll be reporting to Herr Goestler daily. I expect a full report from you by 5:00 PM every afternoon. You are to go nowhere except the villa and the office without my permission. If you need anything tell me and I will see that it is provided. Understood?"

"What about travel?" Roger asked. "As soon as things are organized here, I'll have to make several trips to the States."

"We travel together all three of us," Zimmerman said. "Herr Goestler has ordered that I watch both of you at all times."

"That won't work," Roger said. "It wouldn't look normal for me to make some of the calls I'll be scheduling with two assistants in tow."

The Nova Affair

"We will wait at a discrete distance," Zimmerman replied. "By the way," he continued, switching to surprisingly good English, now that we're in Bermuda we should speak the Queen's language. It's more natural and I need the practice."

"Wow," Roger quipped, "a trilingual trio." He could have kicked himself immediately. Zimmerman had no way of knowing that he spoke German. He tried to cover the slip. "Among the three of us three languages."

Zimmerman looked at him suspiciously. "I speak five languages," he said, a hint of pride in his voice. "Add Arabic and Farsi. Now, it's time for dinner. Madame Miss Pavalone, would you please prepare something."

Zimmerman was obviously of the old school. It never occurred to him, with a woman in the room, that he or Roger would do any cooking. Roger could tell by the look on Suzanne's face that she was about to advise Zimmerman of her liberation. He caught her eye just in time and shook his head.

"I'll pitch in," he said. "Steaks on the grill in no time." Zimmerman gave him a contemptuous look and retired to his bedroom. "We need all the time alone we can get," he said to Suzanne as soon as Zimmerman was out of earshot.

"This will give us a good excuse. Besides, maybe he'll feel guilty and do the dishes."

They ate a silent dinner, after which Zimmerman immediately returned to his room. After doing the dishes, Roger and Suzanne walked down to the water and sat on the steps, watching the moon rise.

"We should call our contact as soon as we get a chance," she said. "Kronovich and Craigwell need time to get situated. If you still intend to sabotage Goestler's plan as soon as possible, we may need them at any time."

"Don't worry," Roger said. "They're probably already here. Besides, at the best, it will be several months before I can arrange to pull the plug."

Roger changed the subject. "Do you find it strange that Zimmerman speaks five languages? Do you know anything of his history? He doesn't strike me as being that well-educated. Where would he have learned both Arabic and Farsi?"

"You forget that most Europeans are multi-lingual. Many of us grew up in a home where a second or even a third language was spoken. Paul told me nothing of Zimmerman except that he is an immigrant to Germany and that he has been with Goestler since he surfaced after being sacked by the Bonn Government. I would agree though, five languages, including Arabic and Farsi, is a little out of the ordinary. But he doesn't look German. He looks like he was born in the Middle-East. I think it might help us to learn more about him."

"I agree. Let's pressure the Bobsey Twins for more background after they show up. Also, the first time we can lure him out of the room, I'm going to go through his things."

"If he even suspects we've done that it could be bad for us. Goestler won't need much of an excuse to kill us."

"It's worth the risk," Roger said. "We may need some leverage on him someday."

"Do you have a weapon?" Suzanne asked.

Roger was surprised. He hadn't even thought of carrying a gun. "Just that pop-gun lighter that Paul gave me."

"I have a small pistol in my suitcase," Suzanne said. "Paul gave it to me some time ago. It's not much, but it's better than your one-shot lighter."

"You keep it," Roger said. "I haven't fired a pistol since the service. Just knowing it's there helps, though."

They opened a bottle of wine they had brought from the villa and sipped it in silence as they watched the moonlight illuminate the surf breaking on the reef in the distance. If Roger hadn't had so much else on his mind he would have realized that it was one of the most beautiful and peaceful scenes he had ever witnessed.

The next day Roger began work. Zimmerman took him and Suzanne to a small, second-story office in an older building in downtown Hamilton. It was on the fringes of the area populated by the many insurance offices on the island.

The Nova Affair

Mayberry Insurance Company Ltd. occupied a crowded suite of offices at the rear of the building. It employed about twenty people, including the resident director, or manager, an assistant manager, several underwriters and a gaggle of clerks and typists.

Before Goestler had acquired control, the company had specialized in reinsuring the many Bermuda-domiciled captives of American companies. Its leverage came from the access it had to various European reinsurance markets, with which it shared the risks it wrote in Bermuda. That access had been provided by the English owner of the company who worked in London but who had many contacts on the Continent. When that gentleman had wanted to retire Goestler had offered him a price for the company he could not refuse.

Zimmerman simply introduced Roger as the representative of the new owner with complete authority to manage the company as he saw fit. Zimmerman described himself as the "transatlantic messenger boy" who would report to Herr Goestler, the new owner. True enough, Roger thought.

Roger retired with the manager to his office, along with the assistant manager and Zimmerman. Suzanne left, ostensibly to shop, actually to call the number of their local contact given them by Paul in Paris. The German sat as unobtrusively as possible in a corner chair and let Roger conduct the meeting. Roger asked the manager for a complete review of the company's condition and its current marketing plan. It quickly became apparent that the company had been foundering since Goestler had taken over. The contacts in Europe had been those of the previous owner and, without him, the company was becoming increasingly ineffectual. The manager was obviously very uncomfortable with Goestler's order that he began writing business directly in the American market. He was very nervous at the prospect of changing the entire marketing philosophy of the company. He was a good enough underwriter to know that he could not make any effective selection of risks dealing in a foreign market of which he had no personal knowledge.

The assistant manager was a zero. The man appeared to have no opinion on anything and was obviously waiting until he could deduce Roger's attitude on matters so that he could agree with him. He appeared to have acquired his position through a combination of longevity and the fact that the other underwriters in the office had even less to offer.

It was apparent to Roger that the manager must go. He was not the smartest insurance man that Roger had ever met but he was far too astute to stand by and let Roger do what was planned without making waves. Given Goestler's penchant for killing the witnesses, Roger figured he was probably doing the man a favor. The poor fellow would never see it that way though. The rest of the staff were classic mushrooms who could be left in the dark and fed large quantities of bullshit.

Roger did what had to be done quickly. He excused the assistant manager, informed the manager that he did not feel that he would fit into the company's new game plan, gave the man a very handsome severance and a letter of recommendation and sent him on his way. Zimmerman immediately complained about the size of the severance. Roger ignored him.

Next, he called a meeting of the entire staff. Using the best French accent he could muster, he introduced himself and repeated his spurious resume to give himself some credibility. He advised his new team that, with their lost contacts on the Continent, he felt it necessary to take up the slack by more aggressively pursuing business in the United States. To that end, he would shortly be making several trips to begin to identify potential sources of business in the American market. In the meantime, it was business as usual. As soon as the meeting was over, the assistant manager informed Roger that this was exactly the advice he had been giving the former manager for some time. Roger was taking an active dislike to the man.

It was eleven O'clock Monday morning. It struck Roger that it been exactly one week since his first encounter with Craigwell and Kronovich in Chicago. It seemed like months. He spent the rest of the day reviewing the books and records of

The Nova Affair

the company in detail and planning an itinerary for his American trip.

At the end of the day he gave Zimmerman a long list. He needed airline and hotel reservations for a one-week trip beginning in Boston, going on to Philadelphia, Chicago and Dallas and ending in Los Angeles. They would plan to leave on Wednesday. In addition, he would need a complete makeup kit, several business suits with accessories, luggage, cash or credit cards, a good briefcase, pens and pencils, a laptop computer, a calculator and several copies of various company files which he had set aside. Zimmerman read the list without flinching. He instructed Roger to leave him alone in the private office of the former manager. Roger waited at one of the underwriter's desks in the open office, now empty after the end of working hours. He watched the light on the desk phone go on and off three times, indicating that one of the several lines to the office was in use.

Three calls one was certainly to Goestler, but why the other two? When Zimmerman emerged he advised Roger that they had a date with a tailor at 9:00 AM the next morning. Everything else was being taken care of per Roger's instructions. Okay, Roger thought, call number two was to the tailor. The last call must have been to the unknown accomplice who had prepared the villa for their arrival. Zimmerman had delegated all the busy work. Roger needed to know the identity of the outside contact. He couldn't risk any missteps with someone looking over his shoulder, who would then report to Zimmerman.

The next day was spent accumulating the material needed for their U.S. trip. The tailor did wonders with several off-the-rack suits and had a complete wardrobe, with accessories, ready by the end of the day. From his seemingly bottomless pit of surprises, Zimmerman produced a complete set of identification in Roger's new name, including an American Express Gold Card. A nice touch, Roger had to admit. Zimmerman was unimpressed. "It's as easy to forge one as the other," he commented. Roger was given several hundred dollars of cash for pocket money. Beyond that, Zimmerman made it clear, he would act as bank. Suzanne was allowed to purchase several thousand dollars of clothes at the local boutiques. The briefcase and other supplies were waiting at the Villa when they returned, confirming Roger's suspicion that the unseen accomplice had received the bulk of the logistics burden. He still had no idea who that person was.

After a quick dinner, Zimmerman announced that he had to run an errand. Roger and Suzanne were not to leave the Villa until he returned. As soon as his car disappeared Roger headed for Zimmerman's room.

"Wait," Suzanne cried. "I'm sure it's a trap. He expects us to search his things."

"You're probably right," Roger answered. "But I intend to look without looking."

A pair of binoculars sat on the mantle in the living room and Roger took them up the stairs with him. He went into the bedroom being used by him and Suzanne and got out the penlight that Suzanne carried in her purse. There was a small bath between their bedroom and Zimmerman's. He entered the bath and removed the screen from the window over the stool. There was about a three-foot space between the ledge under the bathroom window and the closest of the two windows in Zimmerman's bedroom. The windows were of the casement type, opening outward from the center by the use of a small crank at the bottom of the frame.

Roger was immediately stymied. He could not exit the window without opening it but the open window stood perpendicular to the side of the villa and barred his potential progress to the end of the ledge. The back of the villa overlooked the stairs leading to the dock. It was a full twenty-foot drop to the concrete steps below the window.

Roger stood on the windowsill and tested the casement by grasping it at the top and raising his feet until the window held his full weight. It bent noticeably. No good, he thought, it could fail at any moment. It was never designed to take such a strain. In order to step around the window he would have to

The Nova Affair

grasp it at the top and swing around to the other side. If the hardware failed he would fall to the steps below. The sill only extended several inches beyond the open window, so that even if he managed the first part of the maneuver successfully he had very little margin on the other side. Also, he had a similar problem once he bridged the gap between the two rooms as Zimmerman had left his windows fully open. There had to be a better way. He searched for an alternative.

Glancing up, he saw a vent pipe extending through the roof about half-way between the two rooms. It was presumably the vent for the soil pipes in the bathroom and the kitchen below. He had seen an unopened coil of cotton rope in the kitchen, probably for a clothesline that had never been hung. He told Suzanne to bring him the clothesline and something small and heavy. She returned a few moments later with the rope and one of her high-heeled shoes. Roger tied the shoe to one end of the line and swung it up and over the eave in an arc so that the rope wrapped around the vent pipe and the shoe slid back down the tiled roof and over the eave.

Using the pocket-knife that Paul had given him, he cut off a twenty foot section of the rope and then repeated the process twice so that he now had a triple strand of line wrapped around the vent. He then tied the ends together so that the closed loop fell at shoulder height. He slid the loop over his head and then under his arms. He leaned back tentatively. The rope seemed to hold with no strain.

The rest was easy. Leaning back into the rope he stepped around the window on his sill, then across to the sill on Zimmerman's side and then around the projecting pane until he stood in Zimmerman's open window. With both hands free, it was easy to aim the penlight with one hand while he held the binoculars in the other.

Zimmerman's suitcase lay open on the end of the bed. He hadn't taken the time to unpack it. Roger could see nothing in the suitcase except clothes and an empty gun holster. He could see no sign of a gun anywhere in the room. There were two stacks of papers on the desk in the corner. One was covered with a white manila folder on which Roger could make out the word "Zorndorf." The word meant nothing to him. Roger could see nothing else in the room of any interest. He accidentally focused the light on the bottom of the closed door leading to the hallway. Zimmerman had left an empty wire coathanger leaning against the bottom of the door. He must have closed the door half-way, propped the coathanger against it, slipped out and then closed the door the rest of the way. Simple but effective. Anyone entering the room would have pushed the coat hanger aside. Even if they had realized its purpose, they could not have replaced it in exactly the same spot. Zimmerman had anticipated them searching the room.

"He's back," Suzanne cried across the open space.

"Oh, Christ," Roger said. "Close the bathroom door and stall him downstairs."

Roger could see the lights from Zimmerman's car swinging into the drive. He maneuvered back the way he had come as fast as he could. His weight had pulled the knots in the rope so tight that he could not free them with his fingers. Using the knife again, he sliced through all three cords and pulled them free of the vent. He stood in the center of the bath and tried to find a place to hide the cords and the single shoe. Seeing no other alternative, he stuffed everything inside the tank on the back of the stool. He hoped Zimmerman would not try and use the facilities until he could retrieve everything. The toilet could easily malfunction and prompt an investigation.

He ran water into the sink as loudly as he could and then went down to meet Zimmerman who was in the kitchen with Suzanne. He had their tickets for the trip planned to begin Wednesday morning. He also had a message from Paris. Goestler wanted a complete explanation of Roger's itinerary, who he intended seeing and what he intended to accomplish on each call. The reply was to be sent to Goestler in the morning, using Mayberry's fax machine. Roger spent the rest of the evening preparing the report and submitted it to Zimmerman for his review at midnight. After Zimmerman nodded his approval, Roger asked for permission to walk down to the dock in order

The Nova Affair

to clear his head before turning in. Zimmerman waved him from the room. Suzanne was already in bed.

Roger stood on the end of the dock, watching the surf splash against the pilings and smoked a last cigarette. He was lost in thought. He knew roughly what he wanted to accomplish, but was not at all sure he could pull the various pieces together in the right order. He had to set up several genuine deals in the States to allay any suspicion Zimmerman and Goestler might have. At the same time, he didn't want any real premiums flowing to Bermuda right away, as he could not guarantee that the money could be recovered. Further, he had to make arrangements for the CIA money to be worked into the system so that they could establish enough bait to get Goestler to Bermuda when he blew the whistle. That would require contact with Craigwell or Kronovich and he had no idea how to reach them.

As he considered this, a voice came up at him out of the sea.

"Don't look down," the disembodied voice said.

Roger could not have been more startled. He literally jumped in his tracks. The voice was familiar.

"Craigwell?" he asked tentatively.

"Right on buddy. Sitting down here in my little yellow submarine waiting for you."

"How long have you been watching us?"

"We've got a villa across the bay. The stucco one with the tile roof." Craigwell chuckled. Most of the buildings in Bermuda were stucco with tile roofs. The bow of a small aluminum rowboat had edged out past the end of the dock. Craigwell sat alone in the center seat, the oars in his hands. We've been on your tail ever since you called. Didn't think we'd let you go into the cold alone, did you? Incidentally, your tail is as crowded as a bitch's in heat. There's a Mutt and Jeff pair following you when you're not with Zimmerman. Skinny guy with a mustache and glasses, about fifty, and a Neanderthal type who needs a new tailor. Familiar?"

"Yeah. They're the two that picked me up in Paris. Why would Goestler send them when Zimmerman's already glued to my ass?"

"Beats me," Craigwell said. "Maybe he doesn't trust Zimmerman. Guys like Goestler never trust anyone. They figure everyone's as devious as they are. Besides, I think they're working for Zimmerman. They show up when he disappears. They were out front while Zimmerman was in town. Tell me what's up before you're missed."

Roger hurriedly filled Craigwell in on his activity since arriving in Bermuda and on the plans for the next week. The man groaned. "You mean we have to follow you in and out of five cities in as many days? Shit. I was looking forward to some time in the sun. Make things easy on me. Leave a copy of your itinerary under a rock at the end of the dock. I'll pick it up tomorrow. Incidentally, that Zorro routine on the windowsill was stupid. You could have killed yourself, or gotten caught."

"You saw that?" Roger said with surprise.

"I see everything," Craigwell answered. "I'm like your mother, I always know what you're up to. What did you see in there, anything?"

Roger told him about the file and the empty holster.

"'Zorndorf,'" Craigwell repeated. "Doesn't mean a damn thing to me. I'll check it out."

"How do we contact you in the States if we need to talk?" Roger asked.

"That's why we gave you the beeper, remember?" Craigwell replied. Roger had forgotten about the pen/radio that he had been carrying since Paris. "If that doesn't work, wear a handkerchief in the breast pocket of your coat. We'll get to you as quick as we can. You better get back now, before Zimmerman comes looking for you. See you in Boston, sweetheart. And no more dumb stunts you don't have our 'hero' contract, just regular day labor."

As Roger ascended the stone steps, he could hear Craigwell chuckling to himself as he rowed into the darkness.

The Nova Affair

8

They landed at Logan airport slightly before noon the next day. Roger had not had time to set up any confirmed appointments. Instead, he had faxed several companies in Boston with which he had previously done business, and had advised them that Louis Monieux would be in the city on that day seeking business for a Bermuda carrier in control of a certain amount of unused European reinsurance. Further, that Mayberry was interested in building its book of American business. It would be a sufficient hook to get him in several doors.

He had elaborated on the disguise he had used as Roger Forgeron in Paris. The hair had become grayer and he had added some lines around his eyes and mouth, using makeup putty. He had shaved a widow's peak into each side of his forehead. These changes, along with his tinted glasses, would conceal his identity from anyone not previously intimate with Roger Courtney. The hardest part would be the accent. If he slipped just once and fell into American slang he could blow the whole thing.

He made several calls from the airport. By the time he left the booth he had both a lunch and a dinner appointment and another for mid-afternoon. Not bad, with only a couple of day's start, he thought. Zimmerman announced that he and Suzanne would dine at the same restaurants in order to maintain contact. While Roger kept the afternoon appointment they would check into their hotel.

Roger's first appointment was with a large multi-national conglomerate on Batterymarch Street in downtown Boston. He found his brokering job to be easy. Because he was not really interested in making a long-term profit he could give away much more than he normally would have been willing to consider. He could sense the wheels turning in the mind of the underwriter on the other side of the desk. He had instantly been categorized as representing the "innocent capacity" that had entered the U.S. market in recent years. This was the term used by seasoned American underwriters to describe the huge amount of foreign capital that had been committed to the U.S. insurance industry because it was perceived as a quick and easy way to put money to work in the United States. The owners of the capitol had no appreciation for the problems inherent in the U.S. tort liability system. Much of that innocent capacity was being manipulated by the American market to its own advantage. It would be several years before the foreign investors began to realize how seriously under-priced was much of the business they were writing.

In the eyes of his American contacts, Louis Monieux was just another lamb asking to be led to the slaughter. Before Roger left, a tentative deal had been arranged, contingent on the receipt of certain letters of authority from Mayberry attesting to its good standing in Bermuda.

Roger had a few minutes to kill before his afternoon appointment and he stopped in a coffee shop for a pack of cigarettes and cup of coffee. Purely by chance, he glanced into the mirror behind the counter and saw Mutt and Jeff in a doorway across the street. They were obviously waiting for him to emerge. Apparently Zimmerman did not trust him out of sight at all. Mutt and Jeff had obviously been assigned to follow him when he was not with Zimmerman. Roger decided to have some fun.

He left the shop and walked a half block toward his next appointment. He stopped by an alley and pretended to consult an appointment book in his coat pocket. He looked around as if confused as to his whereabouts. He then darted into the alley,

The Nova Affair

as though intending to take a shortcut to the next block. The alley was filled with dumpsters, trash-cans and a few parked vehicles. As soon as he was a few steps into the alley he ducked behind one of the dumpsters and waited. Within thirty seconds Mutt and Jeff passed him, their eyes fixed on the other end of the alley. When they reached the next street they looked in both directions and then began yelling at each other in obvious consternation. They stepped back into the alley, Mutt consulting a city map and Jeff looking at a sheet of paper he had pulled from his breast pocket, presumably a copy of Roger's itinerary, which they could have obtained from Zimmerman. Roger was ready to step back out of the alley and leave them to their own devices when another figure passed him. At first he paid no attention, assuming the person to be on some legitimate errand. It was a man, middle-aged, slightly taller than average, dressed in a business suit, expensive topcoat and carrying a leather briefcase. The man blended into the local business scene.

To Roger's surprise, the man stopped as soon as he saw Mutt and Jeff at the end of the alley and stepped behind a parked car. He hesitated a moment and then lay his briefcase on the hood of the car and flipped it open. He reached in to raise some object in front of him. Of course, Roger thought, it was Craigwell's man and the object was a radio. He was reporting in. The man took a furtive look over his right shoulder. As he did so, Roger could see that the object in his hand was not a radio but a handgun, with a silencer on the end of the barrel.

Their eyes met. The man's face expressed both surprise and recognition. He knows me, Roger thought. The man stood frozen with indecision. Roger was also immobilized, with both shock and fear. Why would Craigwell's man want to draw on Mutt and Jeff? And if it wasn't Craigwell's man who was it and how did he know Roger, particularly in his disguise as Louis Monieux? Before he could do anything, a cry arose from Jeff. The man had been spotted and Mutt and Jeff instantly disappeared behind a truck parked at the end of the alley.

The man turned and fired at Roger. The shot struck the brick wall of the building next to him, about four feet above his head. The man closed the briefcase and with gun still in hand raced back down the alley toward Roger.

Roger was terrified. He was backed into a corner between the dumpster and the building. He had no place to hide. He pulled out the lighter Paul had given him in Paris and held it in front of him, his thumb on the lever that would fire his single round. As the man passed him he raised his pistol to fire again. Roger pulled the lever all the way back on his lighter. He was surprised at the recoil. Without the normal mass of a weapon to absorb the shock, his wrist was bent back as though he had fired a 45-caliber handgun. The shot had no visible effect. His target fired again, once more hitting the building above Roger's head. The gun made only a low "phifft" sound. He was showered with fragments of brick. As quickly as it began, he was alone. There was no sign of Mutt and Jeff. His assailant had disappeared. He waited for someone to react to the shots but the traffic in the street seemed to be proceeding normally. He extracted the second of Paul's devices and activated the pen/radio. Assuming that it was the last place that Mutt and Jeff or his unknown assailant would look for him, he returned to the coffee shop and ordered another cup of coffee. He kept a weather eye on the street through the mirror in back of the counter.

Five minutes later Craigwell slid into the seat next him. "Trouble, sweetheart?"

"We told you that your tail was crowded," Craigwell said, after Roger had told him the story. "We picked this other guy up earlier today. We were still trying to identify him when the action started."

"You mean that you're following him, while he follows Mutt and Jeff, while they follow me?" Roger asked incredulously. The scene was taking on a comic opera overtone.

The Nova Affair

"Something like that," Craigwell answered. "Actually, we're not doing much following, in that we know where everyone's going. It's more wait in the bushes and see who goes by."

"So someone is tailing Mutt and Jeff someone who apparently wanted them dead. Why would he shoot at me if he wanted Mutt and Jeff? Who the hell is who?" Roger asked in frustration.

"We think your friend in the alley is a pro. He only shot at you to keep your head down. If he wanted you, he'd have gotten you. Both shots that missed were within an inch of each other. No one's that good of a bad shot. The question isn't just 'who is who' but who's working for whom?

"What's the motivation?" Roger asked. "Besides, 'who is working for whom,' what is everyone after? The cash they hope I might generate, or is it something else altogether?"

"My guess is that it's something else. This thing seems too far along to have just gotten started with you," Craigwell replied. "Remember, there have been several hundred million dollars disappear in Goestler's various schemes. We have no idea where it ended up. Maybe they're fighting over the spoils. Let me fill you in on some of the things we've learned since we talked last in Bermuda.

"First of all, Mutt and Jeff are really two old PLO operatives linked to Zimmerman, not Goestler. We're starting to get the picture that Zimmerman is an Iranian agent, which only confirms everyone's theory that Goestler has strong outside backing. Reading between the lines, Zimmerman, working for the Iranians, apparently did turn Goestler when he was with West German intelligence. Zimmerman was born in Iran but has been in Germany since his teens. We think Iranian intelligence recruited him some time ago. He apparently got to Goestler with the promise of big bucks and the full backing of the Iranian government.

After Zimmerman recruited him, they set Goestler up in the business of ruining the Western economy, one company at a time. Zimmerman was assigned to watch the Iranians' money and make sure Goestler played by the rules Iranian rules. Mutt and Jeff came along with Zimmerman. That raises the question of whether Zimmerman works for Goestler, or vice versa. Goestler is the brains and the front but Zimmerman must control the logistics and the money. Understandably, the Iranians don't trust Goestler to operate alone. That could also explain how Goestler and Zimmerman can produce things like perfect passports on a moment's notice, they have the whole Iranian intelligence apparatus behind him."

"That all fits," Roger conceded, "and it explains where all the papers and supplies came from in Bermuda, probably someone with the Iranian Consulate. But why the scenario in the alley. Who, besides us, would be after Mutt and Jeff?"

"We haven't a clue, at the moment," Craigwell said. "There could be another party involved, or maybe there's some kind of rift developing in the Goestler-Zimmerman partnership."

"What could cause that, after all this time?" Roger asked.

"What else money," Craigwell replied. "We know enough about Goestler's character to know that he wouldn't play fair with his own mother. The man's an habitual cheat. If he's squirreled away some of the money from his company-wreaking operations, it could get him in big trouble with Zimmerman and the Iranians. If he wanted to weaken Zimmerman's position, it's only logical that he'd want Mutt and Jeff out of the way first."

"That's pretty wild," Roger said. "What else?"

"Remember 'Zorndorf,'" Craigwell asked, "the name on the file you saw in Zimmerman's room in Bermuda? Well, we've done some research. Zorndorf is a small town in Poland, formerly part of Germany. It's where Zimmerman's grandfather lived when he immigrated to Germany, before World War Two. After the war he moved to West Germany and brought in his son, Zimmerman's father, and the rest of the family. Zorndorf has some special meaning to Zimmerman,

The Nova Affair

maybe something to do with the fact that it's changed hands a half-dozen times over the years."

"Christ," Roger exclaimed. "I thought we were going to have a breathing spell until we pumped some money into Bermuda. This is starting to look like something out of Abbott and Costello. No, it's worse than that, no one got shot in Abbott and Costello."

"Try Birth of a Nation." Kronovich slid into the seat on his other side. "The number of players is about right, too."

"Well, what next?" Roger asked.

"Go about your business," Craigwell said. "See if Zimmerman acts like he knows anything. Mutt and Jeff are sure to tell him someone's on their tail. We'll check with you in Philly. In the meantime, we'll see if we can ID your friend in the alley. We got a couple of good close-up photos of him."

"Great plan," Roger said, as he rose from the stool. "Really original. You get the coffee."

His afternoon appointment turned out to be a dud. The only man he could get in to see had no authority. His dinner appointment, on the other hand, was a true winner. The man had not only taken the bait, but he was running with it faster than Roger could keep up. By dessert Roger had the promise of a contract on his desk by the time he returned to Bermuda. The man obviously took Roger to be a complete fool and he intended to take every possible advantage of him.

Suzanne and Zimmerman were seated in a booth across the room. Roger had a hard time keeping his eyes off them. Zimmerman was ignoring Suzanne and trying to read a paper in the dim light of the restaurant. Roger felt sorry for her. It had to be a very dull and uncomfortable situation. If Zimmerman had any knowledge of the events of the afternoon, he gave no indication of it by his demeanor.

Later, Roger joined Suzanne in their hotel suite. They made love and talked into the morning. Suzanne was of no help in deciphering the events of the afternoon. They arose at 6:00 AM to catch the plane for Philadelphia.

9

Philadelphia turned out to be a waste. His one good prospect had left the company and the man's replacement had no interest in Roger's proposal. They all took a nap that afternoon and then caught an evening flight into Chicago. By ten that night they were registered at the downtown Hyatt, on the north side of the loop. Roger had not seen anyone involved in the affair except Zimmerman and Suzanne during the whole day.

Zimmerman had given them no acknowledgment that he knew anything was amiss. On the other hand, he seemed very distracted and was not particularly interested in Roger's progress reports. He spent a lot of time doodling on yellow legal pads and muttering to himself. Something was obviously on his mind, Roger concluded, beside the present operation. Presumably, he was still reporting to Goestler every day but because he always took his own room Roger had no way of verifying this.

On Friday morning Roger took particular care with his makeup. He knew hundreds of people in the insurance community in Chicago and was almost sure to be seen by someone who had done business with him previously.

Many of the insurance offices in downtown Chicago had gravitated to a string of new high rise office buildings along Wacker Drive on the west side of the loop. It was convenient for everyone involved, as the many agents, brokers, insurance companies and reinsurers who had occasion to do business with each other could meet face-to-face while expending a minimum

The Nova Affair

of time and effort in the process. Roger had made a half-dozen appointments that day within this complex.

Twice during the day he doubled back on himself to see if he could spot any tail. He saw nothing unusual on either occasion. He had been careful to schedule his appointments with people he knew of, but with whom he had not dealt closely before. He did not trust his disguise to fool anyone he had worked with regularly. He did have one scare when a woman he had dated before his marriage got into an elevator with him, carrying two paper cups of coffee from the convenience stand in the lobby. She had hardly given him a glance. He had seen several other persons from a distance that he recognized, but was thankful he had not had to bluff through an encounter at close quarters.

By the end of the day he had made two more good contacts. Both were with small managing underwriters. These were persons who operated as independent contractors and combined contracts to underwrite on behalf of several different small insurers into a package that allowed them to compete with some of the larger players. Conversely, this arrangement allowed the smaller company to enjoy more market penetration than it could achieve otherwise. Managing underwriters were always hungry and were particularly anxious for arrangements that allowed big commission payments on the front end, something Roger was in a position to offer. In both cases, the managing underwriters had agreed to feed business to Mayberry, subject to its approval as a reinsurer by their principals. The fact that Roger had offered to set up U.S. trust accounts to guarantee payment of reinsurance claims would make this approval much easier to obtain. The fact that these trust accounts would be totally inadequate, given the nature of the business being written, was a matter left unsaid by either party.

Roger met Zimmerman and Suzanne at the Hyatt cocktail lounge at 5:30 that afternoon. Zimmerman was agitated and hardly listened to Roger's report on his successful day.

"The rest of the trip is off," Zimmerman announced. "You have succeeded in doing what we came for. You can handle the rest by telephone or fax. There have been some developments in Paris that require my immediate attention. We will return to Bermuda tomorrow. I have already made the reservations. Two of my colleagues will stay with you there while I return to France."

Roger was quite sure who the "two colleagues" were. He did not know what had spooked Zimmerman. It could have been the attack on Mutt and Jeff or it could be something entirely different. He had not had a chance to talk to Suzanne to see if she could throw any light on the situation. His mind was racing. They would have to get word to Kronovich and Craigwell. There were dozens of details to clear up on the several tentative deals he had initiated. Once again, things were moving faster than he had anticipated.

Roger tried to pump Zimmerman for more information but the fat, enigmatic man would not discuss the situation further. They had a hurried and silent dinner in the lobby cafe and were instructed by Zimmerman to return to their room and not to leave it until their planned checkout time at six the next morning. Zimmerman was in a position to monitor their activity, as his room was immediately adjacent to theirs and shared a common door between the two sleeping areas.

During dinner, Roger had withdrawn his radio-pen on the pretext of doing some calculations. When he returned it to his breast pocket he had flipped the clip into its upright, transmitting position. He had also made a great production of blowing his nose and then casually returning his handkerchief to his breast pocket.

As soon as they were alone in their room Roger turned on the television and took Suzanne into the bath, closing the door behind them.

"What in the hell happened today?" he asked. "I haven't seen Zimmerman in such a sweat since the Bridge game."

"I don't know. We spent all afternoon in our rooms. I could hear him on the phone several times. Once he raised his voice until he was almost shouting, first in English and then in something I couldn't understand. It could have been either

The Nova Affair

Arabic or Farsi, based on what he told us. It was nothing I could understand. Then I heard him go out, about three, I think. He didn't come back until just before we were due to meet you."

"The only people he could be meeting here, as far as we know, are Mutt and Jeff," Roger said. "I wonder if there was more trouble like they ran into in Boston. Maybe the guy in the alley has shown up again. We've got to get hold of Craigwell. If we don't warn him, they could be on their way to Dallas tomorrow while we're going in the other direction. I've got the beeper on, let's hope he or Kronovich is close enough to pick it up."

"I don't like this at all," Suzanne said. "I think we're getting mixed up in something that goes much deeper than the Bermuda thing. I wish Paul were here. Maybe he could explain what's going on."

Roger saw an opening. "If he knows what's going on and hasn't told us, then why should we trust him anymore? How well do you really know him? Is it possible he's just using us in this thing?"

Suzanne hesitated. "Everything I've told you about him is true, as far as I know anyway. There are a few things I haven't told you. Remember I said that I owed him a debt?"

At last, Roger thought, the rest of the story. He nodded.

"It has to do with my father," she said, after hesitating again. "You must give me your word you will never reveal it to anyone." Roger nodded his assent. Suzanne continued:

"In the process of working on another case, Paul came across some evidence implicating my father as a German collaborator during the war. It is not such a terrible thing. In a sense, the whole nation collaborated. Only those who lived through it can understand how it was. My father did it to protect his family. I don't know exactly what he did and I never want to know. After the war, some of these things looked very bad. If the evidence came out, my father could lose his pension and his reputation, perhaps worse. He is in his eighties now and very frail. I did not want him to end his life under a cloud. Paul promised me he would see to it that the information was suppressed if I would work for him for the Americans. I had done a few things with the cards for the Paris police and he had heard of it."

"Hell," Roger exclaimed loudly, "that's not a favor, that's extortion."

"Yes," she replied. "But at the time I was so grateful that I did not see it that way. Besides, at first he asked me to do only a few small things set up a few marks and take their money, so that they could be blackmailed that kind of thing. I felt I was helping a good cause."

"Where did you learn the card stuff, anyway?" Roger asked.

"My father," she replied. "It was the same skill that got him involved with the Germans. It has perhaps caused my family more trouble than it is worth," she said with a wry smile.

"What about the rest of your relationship with Paul? You said you were lovers. Did he blackmail you into that too?"

"That was voluntary, in the beginning," she admitted. "I was very taken with him when we first met. He was so intelligent and so much in control of everything. I was younger then, of course. After a while I started to see some of his other side, his cruelty and his temper. He can be very ruthless if he feels that he's been crossed. Remember the story I told you about the man that betrayed him in the Middle-East?"

"You said 'in the beginning,'" Roger prodded.

"I tried to break it off after a while both the work and the relationship. At first, he wouldn't let me. He said I was committed to both. He became enraged when I refused to sleep with him. That's the only time he ever struck me. Finally, we worked out an arrangement. I would continue to work for him if he promised to keep the secret about my father and to not expect anything more from me. He has kept the bargain, but every once in a while he tries again, just to see if I've changed my mind."

The Nova Affair

"Christ, what a bastard!" Roger said. "That's rape and blackmail. So our Paul isn't all hero after all. What else do you know about him?"

"Very little," she admitted. "He never really let me in on the whole story of anything I worked on, just enough to do my job. He's never let me know anything at all about his life outside of his job."

"What about weaknesses, bad habits, that kind of thing?" Roger queried.

"Nothing. He is very controlled. I have sensed that he wants money. He likes fine things and enjoys playing the rich roles. I assume his real salary doesn't allow for much of that."

"And Abdul?" Roger asked.

"Just as I told you. Totally loyal."

"Well then, it's not impossible that Paul would use us, particularly if he's got a grudge against you. The fact that you enjoy my company probably doesn't help any either. But what the hell could be going on?"

Suzanne shrugged. They left the bath and Roger walked to the nightstand for an ashtray. He noticed that the red message light was blinking on the phone. Odd, he thought. He was sure that it hadn't been on when they entered the room and, even with the door closed, they would have heard the phone ring. He dialed the operator and asked if there were any messages. After a moment's pause, she connected him to another phone.

"Where've you been, sweetheart? I've been trying to get you for ten minutes. And turn off the beeper. You'll wear out the battery." It was Craigwell.

"Where are you?" Roger whispered. It had been a clever ploy. By not ringing his room, Zimmerman had not been alerted.

"Just one floor below you, listening to the bedsprings squeak." Roger blushed. He and Suzanne had caused some squeaking the night before.

"Hal's downstairs, watching the lobby and convincing the manager that it's okay if we play games with his phone system. I've got news but you rang me first."

"We're heading back to Bermuda tomorrow," Roger announced. "The rest of the trip is off. Something's up. Zimmerman's in a sweat and he has something heavy on his mind. What have you got?"

"Something's up, all right," Craigwell replied. "Zimmerman had a skull session with Mutt and Jeff this afternoon. Those two left for Bermuda in a panic right after the meeting. Plus, we've spotted your friend from the alley in Boston. But this time he's following Zimmerman, not the hired hands."

"Has Zimmerman been in contact with anyone?" Roger asked.

"Funny you should mention it," Craigwell replied. "We don't have a tap on, no time to get the court order. But we checked the hotel's billing records. Two calls to Paris, one to Goestler and the second to a number we haven't tracked down yet. Plus one call to Bonn a payphone. All very mysterious, huh?"

"Look Craigwell," Roger said, with all the conviction that he could muster, "this thing is obviously getting more complicated than we bargained for. Why don't you let Suzanne and me off here. It looks like the Mayberry thing is going to get lost in the shuffle and that's all I can really help you with. Suzanne's just along for the ride. She's already done her part. Someone's going to get hurt before long and, like you said, I don't have the hero contract."

"Sorry, sweetheart. In for a penny... Until we figure out where this is all going it's business as usual. In your case, the insurance business. We've kept you from harm's way so far. Trust in your government. Remember, you're a wanted man and you stay one until we clear you."

"Have you talked to Paul recently," Roger asked, changing the subject. He detected a slight pause before Craigwell answered.

"As often as necessary. Why do you ask?"

The Nova Affair

"Just curious. Zimmerman said he was needed back in Paris. Is that at Goestler's request, or is it on business of his own?"

"When we know, you'll know. If you need to, that is. We all do our own part here Courtney. You don't have our management contract either. You signed on to follow orders, not give them. Your present orders are to proceed back to Bermuda tomorrow with Zimmerman and continue to set up the Mayberry thing. We'll check in with you there. Bon Voyage."

The line went dead before Roger could reply.

"He knows more than he's telling us, I can sense it," Roger said to Suzanne. He briefly summarized the conversation for her. "Something's going on in Paris and everyone's getting up tight about it."

"Let's just do as we're told," she replied. "Maybe by the time we are back in Bermuda everyone will forget about us."

On a hunch, Roger assembled the pistol that Suzanne had brought to Bermuda. They had smuggled it into the states by disassembling it and splitting the parts among their two suitcases. By packing several coathangers, blowdryers and other metal objects next to the parts they had made it nearly impossible to discern in any X-ray examination, a procedure rarely performed on checked luggage anyway. They took a small chance going through customs but had been waved through after only a few cursory questions.

The pistol was a small, .30 caliber automatic with a clip in the handle that held six rounds. Roger had also reloaded his lighter with a single .22 cartridge given him by Craigwell in Boston.

"You will just have to take it all apart tomorrow, before we go to the airport," she protested.

"I know, but I'll feel a lot better tonight, knowing it's within reach. Craigwell said the guy from Boston is around and he's on Zimmerman's tail now. That's too close," he said, motioning to the door that led to Zimmerman's room. "We also know he's not afraid to fire into a crowd."

They retired without any lovemaking. With Zimmerman in the next room and Craigwell immediately below them they had lost the sense of privacy. Besides, neither was in the mood, given all the other news of the day.

Roger lay awake a long time, listening for anything unusual. He could track Zimmerman's activity by listening to the man shower and then watch television for a few minutes. In a while, the German's room was also quiet.

Roger had developed a habit from many years of sleeping in strange hotel rooms. He always left the bathroom light on and the door slightly ajar. More than once, he had awakened in a dead black hotel room, in which he might have spent only a few minutes before retiring, not always sober. He had bruised more than one shin trying to find a light switch in the dark. Without really thinking about it, he had done the same that night.

He was not terribly worried about their security in the room. They were on the fifth floor. The inside latch was locked and the safety chain was attached on the door. The door to Zimmerman's room was locked on their side. He did not feel they could be surprised. Craigwell and Kronovich were nearby. Nonetheless, it was a long time before he fell asleep.

Suzanne woke him with an elbow to the ribs.

"I heard something in the hall," she whispered.

Roger heard nothing. In any case, it was a busy hotel. People came and went at all hours. He glanced at the clock radio on the nightstand. It read 3:02 AM. He got out of bed and went to the outside door. He placed his ear flat to the door and listened again. Still nothing. He glanced through the peephole in the door. The fisheye lens gave him a view of the hall for several feet in both directions. He saw nothing and was about to return to bed when a man's figure suddenly rose into view. The man had been kneeling or crouched next to the wall between their door and Zimmerman's. The man turned and walked hurriedly past their door toward the elevators. Roger had just enough time to tell that it was the man from the alley in Boston.

The Nova Affair

His first instinct was to contact Craigwell. But he realized that he did not know the agent's room number. In any case, he had to find out what the man in the hall had been doing.

Roger moved fast. He flipped up the antenna on the pen-transmitter, then slipped on his pants and shirt. He grabbed the pistol off the nightstand and stuck it in his waistband.

While buttoning his shirt, he turned to Suzanne, still in bed. "The guy from Boston. He was messing around in the hall. I'm going to check. We're in 518. Try 418 and see if you can raise Craigwell or Kronovich. Tell them to check the lobby. Maybe they can get the guy on the way out."

Without waiting for her to reply, he opened the door and went into the hallway. He heard the exit door to the stairwell at the end of the corridor close just as he opened his door. Damn, he thought. The guy's not taking the elevator. He looked on the floor next to Zimmerman's door. There was a food tray sitting immediately adjacent to the door, covered by a large, white linen napkin. It was a common sight in the hotel. It looked as if someone had finished their room service and set the tray outside, to be picked up some time later when the maids came on duty.

He saw a small, rubber tube running from the tray to the crack under Zimmerman's door. He pulled up the napkin and found a metal cylinder, about three inches in diameter and twelve inches long under the linen. The rubber tube was attached to the cylinder and the control valve on the top of the cylinder was opened. A barely discernible hissing sound came from the tube. He turned off the valve and the hissing stopped. He used his passcard to reopen the door to their room. He shoved the cylinder inside and yelled at Suzanne.

"Show them this. I think they were trying to get Zimmerman. Wake him up and make sure he's okay. I'm going to see if I can tell where our friend went."

Another dumb move he thought as he ran down the hall. But he was tired of not knowing what was happening. Besides, he did not like people who tried to kill other people, particularly when he was in the line of fire. If the cylinder contained what he thought it did, the gas might have easily crept under the common door and killed both him and Suzanne in their sleep.

He ran to the end of the hall, where the stairwell exit was located. It was not until he hit the cold concrete of the staircase that he realized he was in his bare feet. Too late, he thought. He was already well behind his quarry. He could hear footsteps, moving rapidly down the stairs several flights below him. He had no real idea what he was going to do if he caught the man. There was no doubt that the assailant was armed. He moved down the steps, trying to look down the stairwell to see if he could see anything.

He approached a door on the second level marked "employees only." It was just swinging shut as he a reached the landing. Of course, the man would not do the expected. He would not leave the building through the lobby.

Roger realized that he was in over his head. He proceeded anyway. He drew the small pistol from his waistband and slipped through the door, holding his weapon at the ready. Nothing. He was in a long, bare corridor that ran for a hundred feet, or more, in both directions. There were a number of doors off the corridor. It was an access hall to service the various meeting rooms and banquet facilities that were situated on the second level. At this time of night it was not in use.

On instinct, he turned to his right and walked rapidly down the hallway. Each door had a small window in it so that the room beyond could be observed from the hallway. He stopped to check each room as he went by. They were all dark. He could see or hear nothing. The hallway ended with double doors, closed, with no windows. The doors swung in both directions. Probably the kitchen, he thought. From the kitchen there would be some access to the outside, so that supplies could be brought in to be stored. He pushed the right hand door open slowly. The kitchen was lit and occupied. Several persons in chef's uniforms stood before a large counter strewn with meats and vegetables. Work starts early in a hotel that must serve several thousand meals each day.

The Nova Affair

The chefs were all looking away from Roger, toward a door at the opposite end of the kitchen. Bingo, he thought. His quarry had probably just rushed through. One of the chefs heard the door swing shut behind Roger and turned toward him. The man's face blanched. Roger realized that he still held the gun extended in front of him. He had no time to explain and did not know what he would have said, anyway. He rushed to the other end of the kitchen, ignoring the chefs.

The outer door led to a loading dock that, in turn, faced a concrete ramp that ran down to street level. At the bottom of the ramp a single bulb illuminated the area. There was a large overhead door at the bottom of the ramp and a small access door next to it. Both were closed. The man he had first seen in the alley in Boston, and then again in the hallway, was at the bottom of the ramp, fumbling with the handle to the access door. Roger could see that the access door had a double cylinder lock in it. The door had apparently been locked from the inside, as a security measure, and his quarry was trapped. The controls to the overhead door were by the exit leading back into the kitchen. The only way out was back up the ramp and past Roger.

Oh shit, Roger said to himself. The guy's got no choice but to come through me. He considered going back into the kitchen and guarding the door from that side. But that would leave the controls to the overhead door free and the man could then exit that way. He might shoot the man now but knew he could not do that except in self-defense. Besides, he did not trust his aim. It was a good seventy feet to the outer door. As the man turned to come back up the ramp he saw Roger. Roger could not believe how fast the man reacted. The gun seemed to appear in his hand after no apparent movement. There were some crates of vegetables sitting on the loading dock and Roger dove for cover. He was splattered by debris as two shots rang through the confines of the enclosed area. He reached around the side of the crates and fired twice, not even seeing his target. He could hear the man's footsteps racing back up the ramp. Realizing he had only one chance, he rolled out from behind the crates and aimed down the ramp. The man was now about twenty feet away, running hard. He fired twice more and missed both times. The bullets ricocheted off the concrete walls and pinged into the overhead door. The man dove for the base of the loading dock and disappeared.

Roger was terrified now. He had two shots left. His opponent was obviously better at this then he was and the man had no choice except to attack him. He heard a sound to his right and turned instinctively in that direction. Nothing. He turned back in time to see the man come over the edge of the loading dock to his left, gun in hand. The man must have thrown something to distract him. Roger was still on his belly. He tried to squirm around to keep the crates between him and the man but was not fast enough. His gun was on the wrong side of the box. He could not bring it to bear. The man raised his weapon and pointed it directly at Roger's head. A shot rang out. Roger was sure that he was dead. But he felt nothing and watched in astonishment as the man's forehead suddenly burst into a bloody mess. As the man fell, Roger could see Craigwell standing in the open doorway to the kitchen, revolver in hand.

Craigwell walked over to the body, his gun still pointing at the man's head. He kicked the man's gun out of his hand and down the ramp. He then knelt and felt the side of the man's neck. Roger had seen what had happened to the man's forehead. There was no question that he was dead.

Satisfied, Craigwell turned to Roger and said: "Well, it's a pretty mess you've gotten us into this time, Ollie. How about I go back to Bermuda and you explain this to the hotel staff and the Chicago police."

"Shit," Roger said, exasperated. "The asshole tried to kill us. It's the same guy I saw in Boston. I thought you wanted him. Anyway, I'm tired of being shot at and not knowing who or why. By the way, thanks."

"Don't mention it. Your field skills leave a little to be desired, sweetheart. I keep telling you to leave the hero stuff to the guys that get paid for it. Here's what we do. You take off this poor slob's shoes and get out of here. Go outside and back

The Nova Affair

through the front door and then directly to your room. I'll have to make up some bullshit for the locals. I'll tell them the two of you attacked me, I shot this guy and you got away. Fortunately, my mess of credentials will keep them from asking too many embarrassing questions. But you have no idea how much paperwork I'm going to have to do for Washington. Remember, my types are not supposed to be operating in the U.S. We'll let the locals figure out what happened to the victim's shoes. Hurry up, before the crew in the kitchen get their nerve back and come out to see what happened." Craigwell pushed the button to open the overhead door.

Roger did as he was told.

A few minutes later, when he knocked on the door of his room and Suzanne let him in, he received another shock. Paul was in the room with Suzanne! It was the second surprise of the evening the first being to find himself still alive. It was also the second time he had returned from some misadventure to find Paul and Suzanne waiting for him. This time, Paul was dressed in a suit and did not look to be in a hurry.

"I understand you played James Bond again, and almost lost again," Paul said, a slight sneer in his voice. "We can't keep dragging you back from the brink forever."

It had been only minutes since the scene in the lower level. Roger had no idea how Paul had learned of it so quickly. This time he struck back.

"If you guys would have been doing your job, that creep would never have gotten so close to us. Anyway, you have him now. If it hadn't have been for me, he would have gotten away with it."

"Touché!" Paul responded.

"Who the hell is he?" Roger asked. "Who is he working for? Why are you here?"

"Good questions, all," Paul said. "We're working on who he is. Naturally, he has no identification that means anything. We've got some theories but nothing solid. I'm here because things seemed to be falling apart. We didn't factor in someone going after Zimmerman's boys, or tailing Zimmerman. It puts a whole different complexion on things. It could be Goestler, over some grudge we don't know about. It could be the Iranians, for the same kind of reason. It could be related to some other problem we know nothing about."

On a hunch, Roger asked: "When did Zimmerman last talk to Goestler? Or anyone else on the continent, for that matter?" Paul's eyes narrowed and he hesitated.

"Why do you ask?"

"Because something spooked him yesterday. It was more than just finding out someone was gunning for him, or Mutt and Jeff. He was in a panic to get back to Paris. He'd lost interest in my mission altogether. I think he got some other information that set him off."

"Kronovich told you that there was a call we could not trace. That must have been it."

"Speaking of Zimmerman," Roger said. "Where the hell is he. Is he all right?"

"Out cold, but still breathing. We decided not to call anyone for him. With all the other activity, if we called an ambulance for him it would raise too many red flags. You got the gas turned off before he got much of it. That's why I can sit in here with my feet up he's not going to interrupt us. After I leave, see if you can get him into a cold shower. Just tell him you scared someone off. Let the scene in the service area be our little secret."

"Okay, what next?" Roger asked.

"We'll stick with the game plan. You two go back to Bermuda tomorrow with Zimmerman. We'll follow him back to Paris and see what he's up to. Remember, the quarry here is still Goestler. Zimmerman may be pulling the strings but it's Goestler that's doing the dancing. We still have to stop him. If we can compromise Zimmerman and the Iranians in the process, all the better."

"Paul, are you telling us everything?" Suzanne asked. "This has turned out to be much more dangerous than we bargained for in Paris."

The Nova Affair

Paul's head shot up. "We? What we?" Paul responded, clearly angry. "I didn't know I was bargaining with a union. Courtney made his deal and we're going to hold him to it. You're here as a volunteer. You can quit any time. I'm leaving now. We'll contact you in Bermuda. Watch your tail."

After Paul left, Roger went into the next room to begin waking Zimmerman. Suzanne started to pack their bags.

Roger decided he would never have a better chance to go through Zimmerman's things. He was sure that some one of Paul, Craigwell or Kronovich had done the same. He did not trust them to share with him whatever they might have found.

Zimmerman was still out cold. Someone had propped him up on the bed with two pillows behind his back where he lay breathing with a labored intensity. He was wearing only a pair of boxer shorts and his fat, hairy paunch hung over the waistband in rolls.

Roger started with the suitcase and the clothes still hanging in the closet and scattered on the floor. Zimmerman was in no danger of winning a good housekeeping award. Nothing. He then checked both the bedroom and the bath for anything suspicious, looking in every drawer. Still nothing.

It wasn't until he passed the outer door, as he was leaving the bath, that it struck him. The safety lock on the door was still closed and the chain above the lock was still attached. How the hell had Paul gotten into the room? Zimmerman always locked the access door between his room and the one Roger and Suzanne were in so it could not have been through their room. He checked the lock on the window. It was latched. Anyway, they were on the fifth floor and there was nothing but a straight drop to the street below.

He called for Suzanne and explained the mystery. She told him that Paul had knocked on the access door between the two rooms a few minutes after she had reached Craigwell on the phone. It hadn't occurred to her to ask Paul how he had gained entry to Zimmerman's room.

The more Roger thought about, the more he was driven to a single conclusion. Paul must have been in the room when the attack occurred! But if that were true, why had he not succumbed to the gas as did Zimmerman? And why had Zimmerman admitted him in the first place? What reason would Paul have to meet privately with Zimmerman when the Agency was supposedly going to great lengths to conceal its presence from the man? Most of all, why would Paul risk such a meeting with both Craigwell and Kronovich in the immediate area and Roger and Suzanne next door? Zimmerman must have recognized Paul, even expected him, or he never would have let him into the room. The fact that the attack occurred at precisely the same time was too much for coincidence to bear. Nothing made sense. Except that there was obviously much more going on then he and Suzanne knew about. Worse, Paul was not only not telling them everything, he was purposely lying to them about what he was doing. Was Paul up to some scheme of his own or were Craigwell and Kronovich in on this too? He did not believe that Craigwell would have shot his unknown assailant earlier if he were in on whatever game Paul was playing.

In frustration, Roger continued his search. He checked all the contents of Zimmerman's pockets, which the man had emptied onto the dresser top, and found nothing out of the ordinary. That left only the briefcase.

He emptied the briefcase onto the floor. He found pens, pencils, a small calculator, a copy of that day's *USA Today*, a copy of the *London Times* several days old, a schedule of their itinerary in the United States and several files and papers Roger had given him to document the brokerage arrangements he had made in the previous days. The only things left were an unlabeled manila folder and a small, leather-bound address book. The manila folder contained two typewritten sheets on plain bond paper. The first was headed with the single word: "Zorndorf."

Bingo! Roger said to himself. He was immediately disappointed. The rest of the two pages were typewritten in Arabic script

The Nova Affair

Roger went on to the address book. It contained nothing but sets of numbers in some code Roger could not fathom. The numbers were arranged in groups of twenty or so, with five or six to the line. There seemed to be one entry for each letter of the alphabet.

He gave the two typed sheets to Suzanne and asked her to copy them. He was working on the code numbers in the address book when Zimmerman began to stir. He had gotten only as far as the "P's." He hurriedly replaced the contents of the briefcase and began to slap Zimmerman in the face.

They told Zimmerman as little as possible. Only that Roger had frightened the attacker away without getting a view of him. They also led the man to believe that only several minutes had passed since the attack. Roger killed two birds with one stone by telling Zimmerman that when he returned to their rooms after losing sight of the attacker in the hallway, he had found Zimmerman's door ajar, closed but not quite locked. That would both explain how he and Suzanne had gained admittance and, for Zimmerman's benefit, how Paul had exited.

Zimmerman grew increasingly agitated as he regained his senses. He insisted that they leave for the airport at once, even though their plane was not scheduled to depart for several hours. As they packed, Roger quietly called the desk and asked for room 418. The phone rang with no answer. They had obviously checked out. Roger had to talk to one of the CIA agents to establish what they knew. If they were in on this, he was in deep trouble. If they were not, he had to warn them of Paul's duplicity and get himself out of the line of fire. He would have to wait for Bermuda.

10

By that Saturday afternoon they were back in the bungalow in Bermuda, with Mutt and Jeff as their house-mates. Zimmerman had left for Paris as soon as he turned custody of Roger and Suzanne over to his henchmen. Mutt and Jeff turned out to be nominal Germans and were introduced by Zimmerman under two obviously false names, which Roger immediately forgot. Zimmerman had given Roger permission to travel to the offices of Mayberry and nowhere else. If they needed anything, Mutt and Jeff would provide. He was to tend to the insurance operation until advised otherwise. Zimmerman indicated that he would return in a few days. In the meantime, one of the two men would stay with Roger and Suzanne at all times. Suzanne was to stay in the second bedroom. They didn't want to give Roger and Suzanne a chance to conspire. Mutt and Jeff would use the couch and hide-a-bed in the living room.

The two men spoke in French, the smaller one quite well, as Roger remembered from the scene in the hotel lobby. The larger one had a heavy accent, but not German.

Roger had pumped Zimmerman on the sudden change of plans but the man had been totally uncommunicative. As far as Zimmerman knew, Roger was unaware of either the attack in the alley in Boston or his meeting with Paul the previous night. Zimmerman, himself, did not know about the shooting of the mysterious attacker in the hotel the preceding night unless Paul had told him.

Roger called the assistant manager at his home and made arrangements to be present the following Monday. He was advised that there were a number of e-mails, faxes and overnight packages from the States already waiting his attention. The staff was duly impressed with the results of his few short days of activity.

After dinner, Roger sat at the small desk in his room and reviewed the material he had gathered at such risk in Chicago.

The Nova Affair

He lay the sheet of paper on which he had copied the coded entries from Zimmerman's address book on the desk and stared at it. Each entry was a set of numbers or letters, in Arabic script, five or six to the line and grouped in units of five lines each. There were sixteen entries in all. Roger remembered that he had gotten as far as the "P's" in the book. There had been another ten entries that he had not had time to copy. Each section of the address book had contained only one entry one set of figures per letter. Upon closer inspection, Roger noted that each set of entries contained exactly 26 letters, made up of four lines of five letters and one of six. Further, some of the entries were in black ink and some in red. He was struck by the fact that each entry contained the same number of letters as the English alphabet. Beyond that, he could make nothing of it.

Next he looked at the text that Suzanne had copied, the one labeled "Zorndorf." In that it was also written in Arabic script, he could make no more of it, except to note that it seemed to be a straightforward text.

He carefully copied each set of entries onto a clean sheet of paper, using colored pens to remain faithful to the original. He planned to walk down to the dock later, hoping that Craigwell would meet him there as he had before. There was still an hour or so to kill until it would be completely dark. He and Suzanne were forbidden to see each other unless one of the two men was present. For lack of anything else to do, Roger opened his suitcase to unpack his few things. A few minutes later, he was left with everything put away except the pair of shoes, which had belonged to the dead man in Chicago. He had not dared leave them in the room so he had thrown them into his suitcase with his other things.

They were a nondescript pair of dark brown dress shoes with leather laces. Roger tried to find a label inside the shoes to indicate what brand they were but he could see nothing no label, no logo, not even a size. Odd, he thought, they were not so well-worn that the normal manufacturer's information stamped inside the shoe would have disappeared. He examined them more closely. They were well-made, with quality leather and heavy stitching. He found to his surprise that the laces were redundant. The shoe was really a loafer with eyelets and laces added over an elastic inner tongue. Why would anyone make such a shoe, he wondered. The sole was extra thick and was made of a hard rubber material, not leather. He noticed several small indentations in the toe of the sole. There seemed to be something wedged between the two layers of the sole but he could not make out what it was. He pried at one of the soles with his penknife and was startled to see a small knife blade snap out of the toe of the shoe. It was about an inch long and razor sharp. More carefully, he found the release in the other shoe and achieved the same result. The toe of each shoe held what was, in effect, a small switchblade knife. Roger could imagine the damage such a thing could do in a fight, particularly in the hands, or rather on the feet, of someone trained to use it. The reason for the strange design of the shoe was now obvious. If the owner ever had to use the equipment hidden in the soles of the shoe, he would not want to risk the shoe slipping off his foot in the middle of the action.

Fascinated now, he examined each shoe more closely. He found that each toe was steel encased. As the shoe was obviously not meant for construction work, it only confirmed its design as a weapon. He remembered hearing somewhere that spies always carried their secrets in the hollow heels of their shoes. He tried twisting each heel. Nothing. He returned to examining the inside of each shoe more closely. He noticed that one of the nail heads in the heel area on the inside of the shoe was considerably larger than any of the others. He pushed on it with the point of his penknife. It depressed with a well engineered "click." He twisted the heel again and it pivoted outwards, revealing a hollow interior. Roger was pleased with his cleverness but disappointed to see that the secret compartment in the heel was empty. Quickly, he repeated the exercise on the other shoe. This time he was rewarded with several sheets of folded paper.

The first sheet was a complete mystery. It was a piece of onion skin, blank except for a single inked line that began at one

The Nova Affair

end of the page and ran in a curious back and forth fashion to near the other end of the page, where it ended in a circle containing a large X. Each change of direction was marked by either a square corner or a carefully drawn angle, the only exception being one shape in the middle of the page, which looked like a half circle. Roger was baffled. The sheet must have some significance or the man would not have so carefully preserved it. It struck Roger that it was meant to be used as an overlay above a page, or a map.

He looked at the other sheet, hoping to find that it complemented the first, but saw that it contained only two addresses:

17 Eiderstrasse
424051

73 Rue de la Chandelles
46 15 91 00

The first address meant nothing to Roger except that it was obviously in German. There was no clue as to whether Germany, Austria or elsewhere. The second address he recognized as a street in Paris The Street of the Candles, so named because at one time its principle occupants were vendors of that product.

There was one other entry on the page just a seven-digit number. Presumably a phone number but with no hint as to location.

Roger copied both sheets and then added the originals to the material he intended to give Craigwell. He took one of the shoes and carefully dropped it onto the steps under his window. The steps led down to the dock. He would pick up the shoe on the way.

James Craigwell set at in the small rowboat, bobbing gently in the light surf under the dock of the bungalow, waiting for Roger Courtney to appear. He was deeply troubled. What had started as a clean-cut case was rapidly turning into a pile of shit, and the pile rested, at the moment, in his lap.

There was no explanation for the attacks by the unknown assailant either the one in the alley in Boston or the one on Zimmerman the night before. The shooting in the hotel would be hushed up, given the Agency's clout in Washington, but he would be subject to severe censure by his superiors for allowing the situation to get out of control. What bothered him most of all was the sudden appearance of Paul on the scene in Chicago. There was no justification for it. It violated every operational procedure. The thing that threw him completely was the fact that Paul had been in Zimmerman's room under circumstances that indicated that Zimmerman had let him in voluntarily. Paul's excuse had been that Goestler was on to the fact that they were after him and that he had been forced to come and make a deal with Zimmerman. If the Iranians gave him Goestler along with enough evidence to convict him, the Americans were prepared to ignore the Iranian involvement. Zimmerman and his two thugs would be promised safe conduct out of France.

Paul claimed not to have had time to present the deal, as the intervention of Roger and Suzanne had interrupted him, and probably saved both his life and Zimmerman's in the process. His only explanation for not also succumbing to the gas was that he was in much better physical condition than Zimmerman and that he had exited Zimmerman's room, into Roger and Suzanne's next door, as soon as he heard Roger discover the attack. His explanation for not pursuing the attacker was that he had been too woozy from the gas to function. As Suzanne had already alerted Craigwell, there was nothing more he could have done. He had not explained how he had convinced Zimmerman to let him into the room in the first place or why he had not alerted Craigwell or Kronovich of his presence in the hotel. A better question, thought Craigwell, was why Paul hadn't let him make the approach to Zimmerman if one was necessary. He had been on the scene and, supposedly, was fully cleared on all aspects of the case.

The Nova Affair

Craigwell was not satisfied with Paul's explanations. A big piece was missing from the picture and it had Paul's name written all over it. This put him in a very awkward situation. Paul was his direct superior. He had no authorization to go around Paul to anyone else in the Agency while the operation was in progress. To do so would violate every operational standard. On the other hand, if Paul were involved in some kind of double-cross, he would be at the man's mercy without some other leverage.

Craigwell had never worked with Paul before this operation. Like most CIA operatives, he lived a strange and dangerous life in the shadows. Between assignments he returned to Virginia where he worked on repairing a bad marriage and tried to get to know his two children. Once assigned to a case, he could disappear for weeks or months at a time, his family never knowing of his whereabouts or even if he still lived. It was impossible to maintain friends outside the Agency, and he was discouraged from trying. The only reason his wife had not divorced him was because her Catholic faith took precedence over her own desires. She wrapped herself up in her children and community work and explained to her friends that her husband worked for the State Department and was sent on many overseas assignments only half a lie.

Craigwell had been recruited by the Agency upon graduation from college. He had joined out of a combination of ill-defined patriotism and a quest for adventure. Like most of his fellows, once he was into his career far enough to realize the price he would pay in his personal life, it was too late to change. The thought of taking a routine business position, after the challenge and exhilaration of his Agency duties, seemed out of the question. He still retained enough of his original dedication to know that his work was essential to the survival of his country, even though it involved activity that, for the most part, was directly contradictory to every concept of fair play and all the democratic principles for which the United States stood.

He had never before, though, been in a position like this. Neither his training nor his experience had prepared him for a situation in which his control was part of the problem. Either Paul had been turned by the enemy or he was engaged in some private campaign, the goal of which Craigwell could not discern.

A few minutes after the evening had become completely dark, he heard soft footsteps coming down the dock above him.

"Craigwell?" He heard Roger's voice whisper above him. "Are you out and about my friend? I've got news."

Craigwell let the boat drift out past the end of the dock. "Good evening sweetheart, tell me your story."

Roger reviewed the conversation with Paul, told Craigwell about the search of Zimmerman's briefcase and his discovery of the documents in the shoe of the dead man. He tossed the shoe containing the packet of material down to Craigwell in the small boat.

"Good work," Craigwell said sincerely. "We'll get on this right away. In the meantime, stick with the plan. I'll be in touch in a day or so."

"Just a goddamn minute," Roger hissed. "Something's going on here that has nothing to do with Mayberry. What the hell is up? Who was the guy you shot last night? Who was he working for? Why was Paul in Chicago? How did he get into Zimmerman's room? What's going on in Paris? There's a lot that's happening here that you're not telling me."

"There's a lot happening here that I don't understand either," Craigwell whispered back. It was the first time Roger had seen the man admit that he was not in full control. It was also the first time that Craigwell had not spoken to him in a patronizing manner. "Just stay cool for a couple more days," Craigwell continued. "When I get the pieces put together, I'll be back to you. Maybe part of the answer is in here," he said, holding the packet up in front of him.

"Look," Roger said. "I don't care about the indictment any more. If you can't tell me what's happening and where this goes next, I'll just go down to the American consulate and turn myself in. I'd rather face the charges in Chicago then stay in the middle of this. It's not worth it to me and I refuse to ask

The Nova Affair

Suzanne to risk her life anymore. I'll give you two days understood."

"Fair enough, sweetheart. I'll see you day after tomorrow. Until then, stay alert."

Craigwell's warning turned out to be good advice.

Roger spent the following day in the Mayberry offices. The scheme was reaching a critical stage. He had proceeded far enough with the Americans he had visited so that he would soon be in a position where they actually began to write business on his behalf, trusting in Mayberry's pledge to accept most of the real risk as reinsurance. This would mean that innocent insureds would start receiving paper for which there was no real backing, other than the assets of the issuing companies, who would be left with far more of the exposure than they had any intent or ability to retain. It was not certain that anyone would be hurt, but it could get very messy. Roger managed to delay the whole matter several weeks by purposely mishandling the paperwork concerning Mayberry's authorization by the Bermudan government, which was the last step left in the transaction. By the time the paperwork made another round trip he hoped the situation would have resolved itself so that he could call off the scheme.

That night Suzanne had cooked a simple meal for the four of them. She and Roger ate on the steps of the dock while their two guards took their meal in the house, watching them from an open window. It was the first time since they had returned to Bermuda that they had been alone. Roger related his conversation with Craigwell the night before and told her about the discoveries found in the shoe.

"I won't let you turn yourself in," she cried. "These people will abandon you and you will go to prison. Not a nice one like they promised you the first time, but one not so nice and for a long time. If they even let you live, that is."

"The alternative is to stick around until we get caught in the cross fire," Roger said. "It's not worth it. We don't even know what's going on. I'm not sure who does. We're being used, if not by the government then by Paul. You didn't bargain for any of this. It's not fair to you."

"But I did bargain for it," she protested. "When I agreed to come with you I knew there would be risk. Besides, I couldn't leave you now. Not now that...."

Her uncompleted sentence said what he had hoped to hear for a long time. She had made a commitment. It was his turn. He took her hand in his.

"Deal," he said. "Let's say we're married. When we can do it legally, we'll do it right."

She answered with a kiss. Had it not been for their unwanted companions they would have sealed the arrangement with something more passionate.

Roger never knew why he woke up later that night. Maybe some inner voice raised an alarm in his subconscious. Or, perhaps, he had heard a noise in his sleep that alerted him without his being aware of it.

In any case, he opened his eyes to find a black hulk standing at the end of his bed. He could not make out any details but it had to be Jeff. He started to cry out some objection to the man's uninvited presence when he saw the glint of steel in the man's right hand. It was either a knife or a gun and there could be only one thing the man intended to do with it after sneaking into his room during the dead of the night.

The gun Suzanne had given him was hidden inside some dirty clothes which were stuffed into a bottom drawer across the room. It still had two bullets left in it after his shoot-out in Chicago. He could think of no way to get to it. The figure started to walk around the side of the bed toward him. He remembered the lighter, lying on the bedstead next to him. "Last chance," he said to himself, as he suddenly stood up and threw the sheet which had covered him over the big man's head.

Jeff grunted in surprise and raised his hands to throw off the sheet. Now the darkness worked in Roger's favor. He

The Nova Affair

pawed in the dark until he located the lighter and then rolled to the floor at the side of the bed.

Jeff did the smart thing, which Roger had not counted on. The man backed toward the door, feeling for the light switch. Roger realized he had only a moment. He raised the flip top of the lighter, laid his arms across the top of the bed and aimed the weapon, as best he could, in the big man's direction. Ready for the kick this time, he slowly pulled the top of the lighter toward him. When the weapon discharged the room was momentarily filled with sound and flash.

Jeff cried out in pain and surprise and grabbed his chest with his left hand. The right hand still held the gun pointed toward the center of the room.

"Oh shit," Roger thought. "All I've done is arouse him." It takes a lucky shot to fell a three hundred-pound man with a .22 short bullet. Jeff's right hand was pointing the gun erratically around the room. Roger realized that the man had been momentarily blinded by the flash of the shell in the dark room. Knowing that he was a dead man if he were wrong, Roger stood silently and aimed a kick at Jeff's wrist. The man was not ready for the blow and, despite his size, the gun was knocked from his grip. It went smashing into the ceiling and then fell clattering to the tile floor. Jeff went for the sound of the gun striking the floor. Roger went for the dirty clothes. Both men got to their respective weapons at the same time. Roger fired his last two shots at the outline of the figure he could barely see in the corner of the room. Jeff fired at the sound of the drawer opening.

This time at least one of Roger's shots had a result. Jeff cried out, obviously hurt, and slumped forward. The big man had been kneeling before he was hit. He now lay with his knees under him and his forehead on the floor, his hands stretched before him, palms down. He looked like a Muslim at daily prayer. The gun had fallen from his hand.

Roger flicked on the light switch. Jeff did not appear to be breathing but Roger could not be sure. Roger glanced at the bureau. There were two bullet holes in the wall, only inches above where he guessed his head had been when Jeff had fired. His bowels involuntarily loosened. He thought he might foul himself before he got control. He considered a bullet to Jeff's head but before he could debate the matter he heard the sound of footsteps coming up the stairs.

It must be Mutt, he thought. He had no idea where Suzanne was by this time. She had to have heard the shots. He opened the door a crack and looked out on the landing. Mutt stood at the top of the stairs, one arm was around Suzanne's neck and the other held a pistol pointed straight at him. Suzanne was still in her nightgown.

For not the first time in this adventure, Roger realized that he was out of his element. His gun was empty. He would not have risked a shot in any case. If he did nothing, Mutt would have him. He had no place to run. He surprised himself.

"Let her go," Roger said, holding his empty pistol to his side, pointed at a spot that Mutt could not see. "Your friend's on the floor bleeding, I can finish him with a shot." Some flicker of motion in Mutt's hand, or perhaps some change of expression in the man's face warned him. He dove to his left and flicked off the light switch just as Mutt fired. The man obviously either did not buy Roger's bluff or did not care what happened to his colleague. The bullet tore through the doorframe. Roger grabbed Jeff's gun from in front of the fallen man's body and turned toward the door. Only now did he notice the silencer on the end of the pistol. That portion of the hall that he could see was empty and silent. He had one small advantage. The room was still dark but he could see out into the lit hall.

Suddenly there was a scuffle, a moan and then a full-throated scream, not Suzanne's. Roger leapt to the open door. Along the wall to his right Mutt was alternately pushing and pummeling Suzanne. She had sunk her teeth into the man's wrist, the one holding the gun, and was holding onto Mutt's arm with both hands. Mutt was trying to swing her loose by throwing his right arm in a circle. At the same time, working against himself, he was trying to strike the back of her neck

The Nova Affair

with his opened left palm. They pirouetted in a macabre dance down the hallway. Roger didn't screw around. He took two steps towards the pair, waited until Mutt's head came around, and put a bullet into the man's ear. Blood, bone and brains sprayed all over the hall. Whatever ammunition Jeff had been using, it wasn't for target practice. Mutt fell in a heap, leaving Suzanne standing with the side of her face and the front of her nightgown covered with gore.

Suzanne took a long time cleaning up. While he waited for her, Roger found two old tarpaulins in the garage and carefully wrapped each body in one. Then he found a mop and bucket and cleaned up the bloodstains and wiped down the walls in the hallway as best he could. His stomach was doing somersaults during this last duty. It would never fool a forensic team but at least the visual evidence was gone. He hadn't figured out yet what they would do with the bodies.

After Suzanne had showered and changed they sat at the kitchen table and talked for several hours. Suzanne made a pot of strong coffee. After several cups Roger switched to brandy. They outlined their options. They could turn themselves in, but that could leave them with the job of explaining the two bodies, not to mention the charges still pending in Chicago. They had no assurance that Craigwell, Paul or the CIA would come to their rescue if they went public, particularly as there was good reason to believe that Paul was mixed up in whatever what was going on.

They debated returning to Paris and confronting Zimmerman and Paul before one of them returned to Bermuda. That option had many disadvantages. They weren't sure where to find either man and didn't know enough about what was going on to know what to do if they did find them.

Finally, they decided that there only hope was to contact Craigwell and somehow force him to share with them all that he knew. Roger had no idea how to contact the agent. They were almost certainly too far away to use the radio-pen. He remembered that Craigwell and Kronovich were staying someplace from which they could observe the house. There should be some way to send a signal.

The next few hours they spent going over the documents that Roger had copied. They had the two pages of text and the sixteen entries from Zimmerman's briefcase. From the dead assailant's shoe they had the curious overlay, the two addresses with phone numbers and the seven-digit number with no explanation as to its meaning. They decided that they must have an Arabic dictionary with equivalents in English, French or German before they could hope to decipher Zimmerman's material. The overlay was useless without some clue as to what it was to be laid over. They debated calling the two numbers, but without an area code to go with the one in German they could not be sure of reaching the right phone. In any case, to call the numbers blindly could expose them to any number of dangers.

Suzanne solved the problem of the bodies. There was a freezer in the garage that had been stocked with various cuts of meat and TV dinners. They emptied it, putting as much of the food as they could in the freezer compartment in the refrigerator in the house and, after unwrapping the rest, threw it into the bay. The tide would take it far enough out so that no one could trace it to the house. They spent an hour carrying the two bodies out to the garage and forcing them into the freezer. Mutt was easy. Jeff was all they could handle. Their delay had allowed rigor mortis to set in and they had to force the two bodies into a fetal position to fit them into the freezer. By the time they finished it was dawn.

Roger drove to the office and dropped Suzanne off in a shopping district to find a dictionary. She would take a cab home. At noon Roger feigned illness in fact, his head was splitting and left for the day. When he returned Suzanne was still out. He went to his bedroom, stripped the bed and tied the sheet to the center post of his window so that it hung down the rear of the house, facing the bay. That done, he lay down on the couch in the living room and immediately fell asleep.

The Nova Affair

He awoke to find Suzanne shaking him, with Craigwell and Kronovich standing behind her.

"Up and at 'em, sweetheart," Craigwell said. "We've much to do."

Craigwell explained that they had suspected something was amiss when Roger and Suzanne had left unaccompanied that morning. Kronovich had followed them, eventually staying with Suzanne as Roger was obviously headed for his office. When Craigwell saw the sheet he had instructed Kronovich, by radio, to risk a direct contact with Suzanne. As soon as she explained the situation they decided it was time to meet.

Suzanne had spent all morning finding an Arabic-English dictionary. Craigwell could have saved her the time. Breaking procedure, he had gone directly to a friend in the Agency in Washington, faxed the man copies of all the material Roger had given him, and had received a translation back within a few hours. Craigwell removed several sheets of paper from his breast pocket.

"Get comfortable and hold on to your socks, kiddies, this gets pretty heavy. First, the text you found in Zimmerman's briefcase. It finally explains what this is all about. It's a copy of a report Zimmerman sent his control, someone in Berlin. He never should have saved it, but he's obviously documenting his file. It seems that a considerable amount of the money that was obtained from Goestler's various operations has disappeared, over one hundred million dollars, in fact. Goestler has been playing both ends against the middle. While he was sabotaging the West, he was skimming the proceeds and stashing the take in Paris. The Iranians finally caught on and challenged Zimmerman to account for the money. The problem is Zimmerman has no proof as to exactly how much is missing or where it is. We figure Zimmerman was instructed to play along until he found out what Goestler's done with the money."

"Why should that change our plan any," Roger asked. "We still want Goestler out of commission and prosecuted in the west. If the Iranians lose part of the take, so much the better."

"Patience, the plot thickens considerably," Craigwell replied. "How does this scenario strike you. Goestler discovers, or senses, that Zimmerman is on to him. He sends Zimmerman to America, with you, so that he'll be without Iranian support. Then he sends the hired gun to eliminate Zimmerman. The gun decides to take out Mutt and Jeff first, so as to have a clear run at Zimmerman, which explains the scene in the alley in Boston. First, you screwed that up by showing up at the wrong time. So, the gun decides to go after Zimmerman directly after all, which explains the bottled gas routine in the hotel in Chicago. You screw that up also. Do you know how much that guy wanted a piece of you when he had you on the loading ramp? Incidentally, the forensic report from Chicago identified this guy. He's a freelance pro from Europe. Used to work for French intelligence and then decided that there was more money on the outside. He's not political, just worked for whomever paid the most at the time."

"And how does this explain Paul's presence in Chicago," Suzanne asked.

"Now we get to the hard part," Craigwell replied. "The preceding is just normal cloak and dagger. According to Zimmerman's report, it seems that Goestler stashed the money in a curious place and in a curious way. With both the Iranians and the French watching him, he couldn't use the local savings and loan. The money's hidden someplace in Paris. It's in some kind of locked or keyed container and it's booby-trapped somehow. Turn the wrong key, or whatever, and it blows up. Now, the guy I shot in the hotel in Chicago also learned what Goestler was up to. He must have gotten a chance to go through some of Goestler's papers. Or, maybe Goestler needed his help in sequestering the money. In any case, I think the overlay you found in his shoe is the key to the location of the money. Maybe, and I'm just taking a stab here, the seven-digit number is the combination that let's you into the container safely."

"What about the addresses and phone numbers?" Roger asked.

The Nova Affair

"We think they're message centers where he could reach Goestler if he had to. This is low key stuff we run into all the time. Someone who needs a few extra bucks agrees to take messages for a fee. Normally, they never see or know anyone involved and the messages are usually so cryptic they don't make any sense except to the sender or receiver. The calls are always made from a pay phone and both parties use aliases. There's nothing to trace. We can apprehend these people but they almost never know anything and there's no law against taking a phone message. It's simple and effective."

"And the other notes, the ones in Zimmerman's address file?" Suzanne asked.

"That's the one we can't answer yet," Kronovich said. "It's obviously some kind of code, but we haven't the faintest at this point. We can't even be sure that it has anything to do with this situation. It could be a list of Zimmerman's girlfriends back home, although somehow I doubt that."

"Wait," Suzanne said, "if the hired gun had the overlay and the combination, why didn't he go after the money?

"That's why we think there's something more to getting the money than just the combination," Craigwell answered. "Otherwise, we would have to ask the same question. It's possible that the gun didn't know what the key to the overlay was. Presumably, the key is a map. But it could be a street map, a floor plan or even some kind of schematic."

"I wonder if the code that was in Zimmerman's address book could have anything to do with that," Suzanne asked.

"Maybe so, but if that's what it is, we don't have all of it. Roger didn't have time to copy all the pages."

"Now, the question we've all been waiting for," Roger said. "Where does Paul fit in all this?"

"That's the real tough one," Craigwell replied. "I think he's involved. I don't know exactly what he knows but I'm convinced that he figured all this out long before we did and that he's after the money. His actions don't make any sense, otherwise. I think he came to Chicago to make a deal with Zimmerman, he was telling the truth about that, but not the deal he described. I could have done that. He must have some of the pieces of the puzzle and he believed, or hoped, that Zimmerman had the rest. I think the deal would have been to combine their files, eliminate Goestler and split the money. Then Zimmerman could disappear and Paul could fade away at his leisure. As far as the Agency would be concerned he would have successfully completed the assignment Goestler dead and Zimmerman driven out of western Europe. He would wait a decent interval, resign his post and then go off to enjoy his gains, in a low profile fashion, of course."

"Wow! That puts you in a real spot," Roger exclaimed.

"That's the only reason I'm telling you, kid. We need help and we can't get it from Washington. Without proof they'd never accept our word on this. We'd just get pulled from the case and washed out quick."

"Okay, what next?" Roger asked. "We'll help up to a point but this is way beyond the original deal. If you've got a bad apple in the CIA's barrel it shouldn't be our job to clean it out."

"True, but we can't give you a clean bill of health until either Paul signs off on your contribution or until we can expose him. Unless you want to go back to Chicago and talk to the District Attorney, you'll have to see it through. We know that wasn't part of the deal. Sometimes life ain't fair, sweetheart."

"Fine," Roger said. "Two conditions. One, we're partners. Everything you know we know and we make all decisions jointly. Otherwise we walk. Second, you call me sweetheart one more time and I'll kick you in the balls. We may not be Agency, but so far we've done most of the work and taken most of the heat. We're sick of being treated like second class citizens."

"Fair enough....Roger," Craigwell answered, after a pause. "As of now, you do know everything we know."

"Then I say again, what next?"

"Well, the action's in Paris. We have to figure a way to flush out Paul, expose or eliminate both Goestler and Zimmerman and find the money."

"What about Mayberry and all the action I've started in the states, not to mention the two bodies in the freezer?"

"Leave the bodies where they are. Unless we get a power failure they're as well off there as anything else we can do with them at this point. Suzanne said you'd put a hold on the insurance deal for a couple of weeks by screwing up the paperwork. Let's hope that's enough time. We go back to Paris tomorrow. By the time we get there, we'd better know what we're doing."

They talked long into the night.

11

They arrived in Paris on separate planes and met in a seedy hotel near Montmartre. Roger went back to using the alias with which he had originally entered France Roger Forgeron. The paperwork was good and no one had any reason to be looking for him under that name, at least for a few days. Craigwell was working on getting them new identities.

They had decided that they needed to flush out their quarry, to make everyone reveal their hand. The way to start was to threaten Zimmerman with public exposure. That would force him to run for cover, probably into the Middle-East where his sponsors could shield him. Before he left, he would have to do something about Goestler and the money. As soon as a run for the money started both Goestler and Paul would have to come out of hiding or they would each risk Zimmerman getting to the stash first. Goestler obviously knew where the money was and how to get it. Zimmerman presumably knew that the stash existed, had some idea how to access it, but might not know the exact location. They had no idea what Paul knew but they had to assume that he was missing some of the pieces or he would have taken the money and ended his charade by now. They assumed that the meeting in the hotel room in Chicago had been for the purpose of offering to pool information with Zimmerman, so Paul obviously had at least some of the answers or he would have had nothing to trade.

They had the overlay, which would give them the location, once they found the map or diagram that it referenced. They also might have part of the access code in Zimmerman's notes, if they could figure out how to decipher them. All in all, everyone else was a little ahead of them. Their advantage was that none of the others knew they were here or knew that they were looking. That advantage was only temporary. It would not take either Zimmerman or Paul long to figure out they had left Bermuda.

They started the ball rolling by sending an anonymous letter to a number of the Paris papers. The letter included enough information on Goestler, Zimmerman and the Iranian plot to get everyone's attention. Once the first paper broke the story, things would start to unravel fairly quickly.

The major problem was surveillance. Craigwell and Kronovich could not rely on their usual Agency support as Paul controlled that resource. Roger and Suzanne were relatively useless for that purpose. All the players would recognize them on sight and, in any case, they were not trained for such work. Suzanne came to the rescue. In her various dealings with Paul over the years she had been exposed to a number of persons that made their living outside the law. She had put Kronovich into contact with several of them who would take almost any job for a fee. In this case, it was easy. These persons were asked only to establish a very loose tail on each of the three quarry and report back. No contact and no physical stuff. It was almost legal. Kronovich and Craigwell were to supervise the surveillance while Roger and Suzanne worked on the parts of the puzzle that were still missing.

The Nova Affair

They bought maps of France, Paris and the other major cities and spent hours trying to find a pattern of roads or streets that matched the overlay. Nothing came close. At the same time, Suzanne used the Arabic-English dictionary to decipher the strange arrangement of codes that Roger had found in Zimmerman's address book.

They found that all the entries were either numbers or letters, which could be translated into an English equivalent, but that they formed no words in Arabic, or any other language, as far as they could tell. The entries were laid out in a uniform pattern, five or six to a line, twenty-six to a group, and each group in either red or black ink:

3	9	J	2	5	
6	A	9	A	K	
7	Q	2	8	K	Q
8	6	6	J	J	
A	9	3	K	2	

or

A	4	5	6	J	
K	2	7	K	5	A
Q	3	J	4	8	
2	6	8	Q	7	
7	9	A	3	8	

There were a total of 16 such entries, distributed among the letters from "A" to "P", each letter having one entry. After staring at the entries for a while, Roger realized that each letter could represent a playing card in the standard Bridge notation of A = ace, K = king, Q = queen and J = jack. This theory was quickly supported by the fact that no other letters appeared. The reference was further heightened by the fact that the number of letters or numbers in each entry was exactly half the number in a normal deck of cards and exactly the number of cards in either the black suits or the red suits. Also, the number

"1" did not appear at all, there being no such card in a standard deck. Further, Zimmerman's and Goestler's exposure to Bridge was well known.

"It's unlikely Zimmerman would have constructed this code out of the blue," Roger commented. "He's not that smart. It's more likely that he copied it from Goestler. Now Goestler is a very devious and clever man. Let's look at the problem from his perspective. He's hidden a large sum of money someplace in France. It has to be in a location he can get to fairly quickly, which means it's probably in Paris or at least nearby. It has to be someplace he can get to without attracting suspicion, but it has to be hidden well enough so that someone won't stumble across it by accident. But someone else may know where the stash is, either because they helped him put it there or because he knows that he might have been followed. So he sets up an elaborate access code so that even if somebody locates the stash they can't get at it. According to Zimmerman's report to his superior in the Zorndorf file it's booby-trapped somehow. There is a code or combination of some sort required to open it. Use the wrong code and you're hamburger. We have to assume that this is the key to the code."

"He wouldn't have used any of his own property," Suzanne said. "If anyone suspected anything they would have looked there first. It's almost a sure thing that he didn't use a bank or any other public depository. He couldn't have risked leaving any kind of paper trail. I would guess it's in a public place, somewhere he went frequently but a spot where no one would suspect him of hiding money."

"Which means it must be very cleverly concealed. Otherwise he wouldn't have dared leave it where anyone could stumble across it."

"Assuming this code is his, and Zimmerman just copied it, why would he need it at all? It's hard to believe that Goestler would use a code so complicated that he couldn't keep it in his head."

"Unless that's his protection," Roger replied. "If the key's that complicated, he doesn't have to worry about anyone else

The Nova Affair

figuring it out. I can't imagine what the connection to cards, or to Bridge, could be."

    Having exhausted every road map they could get their hands on, they next tried all the public buildings in Paris. They spent several days haunting the Louvre, The Invalides, Notre Dame and other landmarks trying to find a floor plan that matched the overlay. It was late in the third day that they got lucky. Returning from the Sorbonne, they walked through the Luxembourg Gardens on the way back to their rented car. Halfway through, as they rounded a circular pond in the middle of the park, they both stopped dead. The walk around the pond matched the strange half circle on the overlay. Excitedly, they followed the path back to the entrance and retraced their steps. The pattern fit exactly. Trying not to attract any attention, they hurried on down the path to where the map ended. They were brought up short at a mausoleum containing the body of a long-dead and forgotten general of the Franco-Prussian War. The mausoleum was made of granite, with only a small entrance door in the rear, half-hidden by shrubbery. The door was secured with a rusty padlock. They copied the inscription above the door and the date of its occupant's death 3 October, 1903, in the European style, with the day of the month first. It wasn't until later that Roger matched this with the seven-digit number he had found in his dead assailant's shoe in Bermuda 3101903.

    Elated, they returned to their hotel to find Craigwell waiting for them. He had one of the Paris papers in his hand.

    "The fat's in the fire kids. They picked up the story." He handed them the paper.

    The story was expertly written, citing several unnamed sources and hinting at an official investigation, without actually saying that one was in process. No names were used, but reference was made to a West German expatriate and certain Middle-Eastern operatives who were working together to undermine the French economy. There was no question that Zimmerman and Goestler would recognize themselves.

Thomas Bloom

When Suzanne and Roger shared their discovery, Craigwell was all smiles.

"Fantastic, we go back tonight and check out the grave site. If the money's there, we don't have to follow them anymore. We can wait until they come to us. Incidentally, our tail picked up another tail on both Zimmerman and Goestler. Someone else is following our boys. I'd bet anything it's Paul. Assuming the gun in Chicago was working for Goestler, it's a safe bet that he might have helped Goestler set up the stash. That would explain how he came to have the map. He presumably intended to use it himself or to sell it to someone else. Goestler certainly wouldn't have needed to draw it for himself. Zimmerman must have gotten the code when he went through Goestler's papers looking for some proof of his double-dealing. We don't know what Paul knows but he must have most of the pieces by now."

"What happens next," Roger asked.

"Here's the way I see it," Craigwell replied. "Neither Zimmerman nor Goestler can stick around very long now that the story's in the press. Goestler will go for the stash, Zimmerman will follow him and Paul will follow them both. Except Goestler knows that Zimmerman's on to him, otherwise Goestler wouldn't have sent the gun after him. So, my bet is that Goestler goes after Zimmerman first, before he goes for the money. When Goestler finds out that you two have dropped out of sight he may figure he's been had, which will also clue him that someone else is after him. Likewise, when Paul realizes that Kronovich and I aren't checking in any more, he will figure we've made him. The problem then becomes that while the three of them circle each other they'll all be looking for us. It always gets so messy!"

"Suppose we stake out the mausoleum and one or all three shows up?" Suzanne asked. "What do we do next? We don't have any arrest powers. We can't just shoot them."

Craigwell looked at her with a mixture of scorn and pity. "You guys still don't understand, do you? We're playing this game off the court. There are no rules except don't do anything

The Nova Affair

to embarrass your own government. One way or another, someone's going to get hurt. It's even money as to whether Goestler or Zimmerman gets the other first. I'd bet on Goestler because Zimmerman wants the money and he can't finish off Goestler before he knows where it is. Paul is committed and he knows it. He won't hesitate to take any of us out if we get between him and the money. I would prefer to take Paul alive and turn him in to the Agency, but he won't go with a breath left in him. He's got a life sentence waiting for him and he'd rather die. By the way, remember that little guy that works for him, Abdul, he'll do anything that Paul asks of him, including slit any one of our throats. So, to answer your question, we shoot first, and if we embarrass the Agency or the French government, tough. By the way, have you still got that pop-gun pistol you had in Bermuda?"

Suzanne nodded her head.

"Well keep it with you and keep it loaded. I'll see if I can get you two something more respectable. It's a bitch not having access to central supply."

"Just a minute," Roger said. "If you're assuming that either one of us is up to cold-blooded murder, I think you're wrong. I'll fire to defend myself. But I won't lie in the weeds and just shoot the first one of these guys that comes along."

"That's why you're not on the varsity, kid. You'd better believe that they'll do it to you. You made your bones in Bermuda. Believe me, it gets easier every time."

"I hope it never gets easy," Roger answered, his voice tense.

The four of them returned to the Luxembourg Gardens after midnight. They were all dressed in dark clothes and carried flashlights and a small toolbox. Kronovich stayed hidden in the bushes about fifty feet away from the mausoleum, positioned so that he could watch the pathway from either direction. Both he and Craigwell carried small walkie-talkies.

Craigwell applied one of the tools he carried to the padlock and it was off in seconds. The door opened easily, without creaking, a good indication that something other than a long dead body was inside. They closed the door behind them and turned on their flashlights. The room had a musty, unhealthy smell. In the center was a granite podium on which rested a metal casket. That much was normal and expected. However, there was a metal box secured to the foot of the casket by several screws. On top of the box rested a long-dead bouquet of flowers. The box could have been placed there for that purpose, but a simple shelf would have sufficed. It was about two feet long and nine inches on each side. The top was hinged. Craigwell removed the vase of flowers and gingerly lifted the top of the box. Roger winced. They knew it was booby-trapped and he thought Craigwell was being more than a little careless.

"Not to worry," Craigwell said. "Whatever the trigger is, it has to be more complicated than that. Now, what's this?"

The inside of the box contained a complicated mechanism. A dial at one end revealed a counter with the number 23 displayed. The dial was attached by wires to a bank of lithium cell batteries and a set of electronic parts that appeared to contain several computer chips. Another set of wires ran from both the electronic array and the batteries to a series of switches that filled the rest of the box. There were thirteen switches in all, each with a lever that could be set opposite a number running from one to thirteen. At the bottom of the set of switches was a simple on-off switch, set to on, which was also wired into the maze. Several wires disappeared into the casket through a hole that had been drilled from the inside of the box.

"I think we found the end of the rainbow," Craigwell announced. "The stash is in the casket but if you open it without setting this gizmo to the right position you get to fertilize the gardens. I assume you set these levers in the right sequence and you can then disarm the booby-trap by turning off the switch."

"Is the body still in there?" Suzanne asked, with a small tremor in her voice.

The Nova Affair

"Could be," Craigwell answered. "But I'd guess the old general is pushing up flowers someplace else. Who would miss him? They don't take inventory in these places. Don't touch anything but look around and see if you can see anything else out of the ordinary. I want to get some pictures of this thing."

While Craigwell took a series of flash-lit photographs of the mechanism Roger and Suzanne examined the rest of the crypt, finding nothing.

They were out of the gardens within a half-hour of the time they had arrived.

That night they moved to a new hotel and registered under false names. It was assumed that all three of their quarry would be looking for them from this point forward.

12

Roger and Suzanne spent the next day in their flat. They had purchased a supply of large pads of paper, marker pens and tape. They started by drawing a diagram of the device in the mausoleum on one sheet of paper. Then they copied each one of the entries in Zimmerman's diary and hung them in sequence around the room.

"This has to be a fit," Roger said. "There are thirteen switches and there were twenty-six total entries which appeared to be evenly divided between red and black thirteen each. The sixteen entries we have include nine black and seven red, sequenced more or less at random."

"We can't be sure that there were exactly twenty-six entries or that they split evenly," Suzanne said. "If only you'd had time to copy the rest of the book."

"True," Roger replied. "But that's got to be our working assumption. Let's assume that the thirteen black entries are one set and that the thirteen red are another. Now match them against the possible settings on the device. There are only thirteen possibilities on each setting, yet we have twenty-six letters or numbers in each entry."

"Maybe that's where the counter comes in," Suzanne said. "The counter may tell you which of the twenty-six to use at any given time. The counter was on twenty-three yesterday. Maybe that means that you use the twenty-third item in each entry."

Roger puzzled over the entries. "But then what do you do with the letters? What's an ace or a king mean? Is there some kind of sub-code that establishes a number value for each letter. Also, how do you know whether to use the red set or the black set? And if you did know, do you use them in the order they appear, or backwards, or there could be some other pattern."

"The value of the letters could be the standard Bridge count," Suzanne replied. "Ace counts for four, king for three and so on."

"Possibly," Roger mused. But what about ones and zeros? The settings run from one to thirteen thirteen possibilities in all. There are no ones anyplace in the diary entries. It would be possible to have an ace equal one, that's what it's worth in some games. Then the face cards could equal ten. But why go to all the trouble of having four different cards equal the same thing?"

They debated any number of possibilities over the rest of the day but could come up with no better analysis than the original one. They decided that they had to watch the counter for several days. They had to verify how often it changed, whether or not it stayed the same color and, most important, if it recycled after it passed twenty-six.

For the next three nights they repeated the sojourn to the park. The first night they were elated to find that the counter had advanced to twenty-four and that the numbers showing on

The Nova Affair

the dial were in red. The next night the counter read twenty-five and was red again, which indicated that the red-black sequence did not alternate daily. The third night threw them for a loss. Fully expecting the counter to read twenty-six, they were astounded to see that it had cycled back to one, in black letters. The next day they returned to their charts.

"Look, maybe this isn't the end after all," Roger said. "We've been puzzling over the odd construction of the entries. Always twenty-six items with four rows of five and one row of six. We always have one letter or number that sticks out like it doesn't belong. Maybe it's just as simple as dropping that item, leaving twenty-five items in each entry."

"That just sounds too simple," Suzanne argued. "I think it's a trap of some kind. Goestler couldn't risk committing to memory twenty-six sets of numbers and letters so he had to write them down. But once he did he knew he risked someone finding the key. It's logical he'd build a trap into the code. Something that he could easily remember but which wouldn't mean anything to someone else."

Roger spent a half-hour studying the entries. Finally, something struck him.

"Look here," he cried. "Every one of the lines with six items contains a letter entry, standing for a face card, with a higher ranking card on the line above and lower ranking card below. The three cards are always either in order or can be put in order by moving the line one item to the left or the right. That could be the trap. In some cases you do drop the odd item. In other cases you have to move the whole line over, so the three face cards appear in order, and then drop the item that's been pushed out of the set."

"Let's see if the rest fits then," Suzanne said. "We know from the number on the counter which one of the set to use, the first through the twenty-fifth entry. We know from the color of the counter whether to use the black or the red entries. We assume there were twenty-six entries in all, one for each letter of the alphabet. So the simplest method would be to start with the entry under 'A' in the address book and use the twenty-fifth number if it matches the color of the counter. Then you move on to the next entry of the same color and so on until you get a number for all thirteen settings."

"That works," Roger replied. "But we've still got major problems. First we're missing the last nine entries so we don't have the whole key. We can't even be sure that there were twenty-six entries or that they were split evenly between red and black. Even if we had all twenty-six, we don't know for sure that you simply take them in sequence. It's possible you could start from the back of the alphabet and go toward the beginning, or start anyplace in the middle of the sequence. Also, we haven't figured out what to do with the face cards yet. The numbers in the entries we copied run from two to ten. But if our theory is correct, we need thirteen numbers. The logical way to work with ace and face cards would be to let the ace equal one, the jack eleven, the queen twelve and the king thirteen. Goestler must have thrown in the ace and the face cards just to make it that much more difficult. Or, maybe Zimmerman did it when he copied the code, for the same reason."

"Let's take the code and project the numbers as far as we can, using this theory," Suzanne offered. They spent the next hour working through various combinations of the code and ended up with a chart that seemed to contain a definite pattern:

Counter number	Color, if known	If red then sequence is:	If black then sequence is:
1	BLACK	6,8,0,0,5,1,3	8,9,10,11,12,13,1,2,3
2		7,10,4,2,2,1,0	9,10,11,12,13,1,2,3,4
3		10,11,12,13,1,2,3	6,0,3,3,10,8,2,4,5
23	BLACK	9,8,10,1,1,3,4	5,6,7,8,9,10,11,12,13
24	RED	6,7,8,9,10,11,12	4,7,8,8,3,9,0,2,1
25	RED	7,8,9,10,11,12,13	10,0,0,3,7,2,8,0,1

The Nova Affair

They had only seven of each red sequence and nine of each black. Nonetheless, a clear pattern was evident. The numbers in the color that did not match the key were always random. The numbers in the other color always ran in order and the first number was always one later in the sequence than the first number of the preceding entry, beginning with the number "8" opposite counter number one.

"Can it be this simple?" Roger asked. "Why go to all the trouble to set up this kind of code and then have every number run in sequence. Maybe it's a trap. You actually take the sequence of the opposite color, then you end up with a random code each time. Besides that, he wouldn't need the key to remember this. As long as he remembered that entry number one began with the number eight, he could figure the code for any other day very quickly."

"You're right," Suzanne replied. "But look at it from his perspective. He knows that if he ever goes for the money that he may be in a hurry and under pressure. He wouldn't have bothered with the code unless he needed it to decipher the key. If he went ahead and computed the key for each day then he risked someone finding that record. So he has to leave the code in its raw form. On the other hand, if he hurries through it and makes only one mistake, he blows himself up. By having the numbers run in sequence, he has a fail-safe check of his accuracy in deciphering. He knows he can't make a mistake in setting the switches."

"Something's still missing," Roger answered her, still poring over the numbers. "Look, we were able to solve this thing with hardly more than half the entries. It's just too simple and Goestler's too devious. There has to be something more to this. The simple fact is that all this technology just isn't necessary. With thirteen settings on thirteen switches, the odds of anyone guessing the right sequence are infinitesimal. He could have remembered one sequence with no problem. Why set this up at all? It only makes sense if Goestler was sharing the secret with someone. If each person has half the code, then you make it as complicated as possible so that you need both halves to get the full sequence."

"But who would he have been sharing it with, and why?" Suzanne asked.

"Who else knows what's going on?" Roger replied. "The Iranians, fronted by Zimmerman, and the CIA, fronted by Paul. Assume Goestler and Zimmerman were actually plotting together to steal the money from the Iranians. They set up the stash and each keeps half the key, knowing that the other can't get to the money in the meantime. Then they have a falling out for some reason, maybe when the guys in Teheran get wind of the plot. Then Zimmerman does an about face and leads the guys he reports to to believe that it's Goestler's plan alone and that he's about to end it and recover the money. Goestler finds out he's been double-crossed and sends the gun after Zimmerman. Someplace along the way the gun gets his hands on part of the plan. That explains the bits and pieces he had in his shoe. Zimmerman figures out that Goestler's on to him and high-tails it back to Paris to cover his ass. That leaves us with the question of where Paul fits in...and what does he know?"

"I think this started out as a normal operation," Suzanne replied. "For Paul, at first, it was just another assignment. That's why the Agency and Craigwell and Kronovich did not suspect anything. Someplace in the process, while Paul is digging into the situation in Paris, he learns about the money being siphoned from the operation and gets his hands on half of the key Goestler's half. Maybe the gun was double-dealing. He sold his bits and pieces to Paul and Paul put the rest of it together himself. He figures this is his chance to cash in. No one knows about the money except Zimmerman and Goestler. Even if the Iranians know about it they are hardly in a position to file a complaint if Paul steals it. But he needs the other half of the key Zimmerman's half. When he finds out that Goestler is gunning for Zimmerman, he figures that's his chance. He offers to go halves with Zimmerman, cut Goestler out and split the stash. That was the real reason for the meeting in Chicago. He was there to make a deal with Zimmerman for the other half

The Nova Affair

of the key, the half we found in the address book. Paul must have been delighted when Craigwell shot the gun. That tied up a loose end for him."

"But before they could make the deal, the gun shows up again and spoils the meeting with the canister of gas. That explains why Zimmerman let Paul into the room."

"Once the alarm goes off, Paul can't stick around and talk to Zimmerman while we're with him every minute and Craigwell and Kronovich are in the background."

"So Zimmerman gets us back to Bermuda with Mutt and Jeff, while he takes off for Paris to make contact with Paul and to go after Goestler. He instructs Mutt and Jeff to get rid of us at the first opportunity, probably because Paul let him know that we were plants. Once Paul decided to go after the money we were just in the way and we gave Craigwell and Kronovich a chance to get too close to what was really happening."

"That's a beautiful theory," Roger said. "But it doesn't help us any. We need the other half of the key before we can get to the money. Zimmerman and Paul could be meeting any minute. If Goestler gets to Zimmerman first then he has the whole key and he may beat us all to the punch. If they shoot each other first, then the two halves may never get together."

"And if they shoot us first, we may never stop them," Suzanne commented. "What we have going for us is that Paul, Goestler and Zimmerman can't trust each other. They're like three scorpions in bottle. They are probably trying to figure out some way to open the casket together without each trying to eliminate the other the second after they have their hands on the money."

"Time is the problem for all of us," Roger agreed. "All three of them are looking for us. Sooner or later one of them will find us. Paul knows the cat's out of the bag. He can't keep Craigwell from blowing the whistle on him much longer. Now that the press is on to this thing, the French authorities will be forced to do something. Zimmerman and Goestler have only a few days to solve this before they're going to have to get out of the country."

"Look," Suzanne said. "There are two players with one half of the puzzle, Zimmerman and us. There are two with the other half, Paul and Goestler. Our goal now is not the money, that's just the bait. We want Goestler and Zimmerman behind bars if possible, at least shut down if not. We want Paul exposed to the Agency so they can deal with him in their own way. Most of all we want everyone to forget about us and for you to be able to clear your name in the states. If we can recover the money, that's all the better. How do we do all that in the next couple of days?"

Roger paced up and down the room for a considerable time while Suzanne stared out the window, lost in thought.

"Okay," Roger finally announced. "I think I have it. We contact Paul and offer to make a deal. Our half of the key for his. Tell him we just want the money and want to get out. We were both forced into the operation and could care less about the Agency or getting Goestler and Zimmerman. He won't feel threatened by us. If he takes the bait, Craigwell has the proof he needs to deep-six him with the Agency. In the meantime, we let Goestler and Zimmerman find out that we're making a deal with Paul. That will force their hand and flush them out. Either way, they have to come to the stash. If they make their own deal, they come together. If not, they're sure to be close so they can watch for us trying to get it."

"And how do we make the exchange?" Suzanne asked. "You know Paul won't hesitate to kill us if he gets the chance."

"We don't exchange anything," Roger answered. "Neither one of us could trust the other to give the right information. There's only one way to do it. We go into the crypt together and set the switches together. If either one of us fails to play straight, we all go up in smoke."

"And what happens when we leave the scene with the money. Paul will still eliminate us if he gets the chance. Zimmerman and Goestler will be waiting for all of us. We'll be sitting ducks for everyone."

"We don't just leave. That's when Craigwell calls in the authorities. They pick up Paul with the evidence in his hands.

The Nova Affair

Then let them go after our German friends. You and I do a fast fade in the confusion, leaving the money behind. No one needs us after that and if we don't have any of the money no one wants us. I'll try and square up with the Agency after the dust settles."

"There's plenty of room for something to go wrong," Suzanne said. "I don't like it. Why do we always have to be the ones up front in this deal. The guys who get paid to do this are always one step behind us."

"Maybe that's how they got to be old pros," Roger answered. "They use up other people first."

Later that night, they sold the proposition to Craigwell and Kronovich. The two agents weren't sure that Paul would take the bait, nor were they sure that the French authorities would react on cue. On the other hand, neither of them could think of a better plan.

Suzanne would call Paul at the safe house in the south of Paris to initiate the offer. Craigwell would arrange for one of their contract operatives tailing Goestler to sell the information that a deal was going down with Paul. Kronovich would make contact with the French authorities and also arrange for them to leak enough information to a known Iranian operative so that it would reach Zimmerman.

As was their habit now, before retiring, they checked all doors and windows and then set up an all night watch, so that one of them was always awake with a gun in hand. It was not, Roger decided, the way he wanted to spend the rest of his life.

13

Early the next morning Suzanne made the call to Paul from a public booth in a nearby hotel. It rang several times before it was answered by a voice she recognized as Abdul's.

"Oui?" Abdul spoke. This phone number was known to only the CIA and a few operatives. Suzanne was one of the few.

"This is Suzanne. I want to talk to Paul."

"He is not here. Where are you calling from."

"This is an emergency. Please get him."

"I tell you, he is not here. I will give him the message. Where are you?"

Suzanne ignored the question. "Tell him we know everything. We know where the money is and we have Zimmerman's half of the code. We also know how to program the device that guards the money. Roger and I will make a deal. If Paul will share the other half of the code, we will split the money with him and disappear. Paul can do whatever he pleases. We just want out and we want to be left alone. I will call back in six hours for his answer." She hung up before Abdul could reply.

Zimmerman also made a call that morning. Again, he used the public phones next to the Gare St. Lazare and called a public phone in Bonn, one of several that he used on a rotating basis. The person to whom he was to report, a functionary in the Iranian Embassy in Bonn, was his control. Zimmerman was in serious trouble. The whole plot was in the papers. Soon there would be names and specifics. Goestler had disappeared. There was no answer at the cottage in Bermuda and the staff at Mayberry had reported that Roger had not been in the office for several days, nor had they heard from him. Nor had he heard anything from his two operatives on the island. They should

The Nova Affair

have carried out their assignment and returned to Paris by now. The cottage was empty. Zimmerman suspected the worst.

He had lost control of the situation and risked exposing his sponsor. At the best, he would finish his career shuffling files in Tehran. At the worst, if they were to discover his plot with Goestler to divert part of the funds from the operation, it would mean his life. He knew that he would be ordered to return to Iran at once. His superiors would not risk having him taken into custody when the full story finally broke. He knew that the men he reported to suspected something. He and Goestler had been too greedy. A little money would never have been missed. But they had taken too much and now it was too late to cover it up.

As was the procedure, he let the phone ring three times, then hung up and moved to another booth to replace the call. This time the phone was answered on the first ring. The conversation was in German. It was brief and direct. He was ordered to destroy all his records and to take the next train to Bonn. He was to give Goestler the same orders but they were not to travel together or be seen together. In Bonn he would be provided with new papers and a ticket to Iran. Zimmerman acknowledged the orders and hung up. He left the phone booth knowing that he would not return and that he would never see Iran again. He had only a few hours to salvage anything. He must make contact again with the American agent and arrange to split the money. He must also avoid Goestler who was sure to be looking for him. He was at a disadvantage. The only two operatives who would take his direct orders had disappeared in Bermuda. If he tried to use any of the other Iranian agents in Paris he would arouse instant suspicion. He was very frightened. He had never before operated without an apparatus behind him.

Zimmerman had no idea how to contact Paul. He could have called the embassy, but any message he left might be seen by anyone. He did the only thing he could. He returned to his flat and began destroying his papers and packing a bag. He knew that he and Goestler had been under surveillance and that

Paul knew of the flat's location. But Goestler also knew of it and either of them could arrive first. He kept a pistol in his pocket as he moved about the flat. He tore what few papers he had into small shreds and flushed the scraps down the toilet. It took several hours. When he was done he walked to the nearest public phone booth to make one call to the Paris police. He informed them that the man they were looking for in connection with the articles recently in the press could be found at one of two locations. He gave them Goestler's home address and the location of the warehouse they had used for a number of operations, including the abduction of Roger two weeks before. He was sure that they would not find Goestler. But they would identify him and began searching for him. If Zimmerman could keep Goestler busy dodging the police, he might have time to complete his plans before his old partner caught up with him. Zimmerman was down to only three assets, his pistol, a few thousand francs in cash and his half of the key to the money. He returned to his flat and began cramming some clothes into a suitcase. He was not even sure where he was going but he knew the longer he stayed where he was the more likely it was that someone would come for him.

Paul had several advantages. He still had the full staff of the Agency at his disposal in Paris. He had expert operatives tailing both Zimmerman and Goestler. But he, also, knew that he had only a little time. Craigwell and Kronovich had not checked in and could not be located in Bermuda. He had learned that Craigwell had contacted the Agency directly to have the translation of Zimmerman's document done. There could be only one reason for this breach of protocol. The two agents were on to him. Roger and Suzanne had also dropped from sight in Bermuda, as had Zimmerman's two men. Paul put it all together and assumed that all of them were back in Paris. If he used all his resources, he could locate them soon enough. But he was at a disadvantage in that respect as he could not assign regular agents to hunt down other agents,

The Nova Affair

particularly agents that were supposedly reporting to him, without some kind of explanation.

Paul had deduced from Goestler's papers that the stash existed and that it was someplace in the Jardin Du Luxembourg. He knew that he held half the access code but did not know how it was to be used. His only real option was to contact Zimmerman and make a pact with the Iranian agent to share the money. That presented several problems. Any direct contact with Zimmerman in Paris would expose him to both the Iranians and to detection by the Agency. He had to be circumspect and quick. He knew that Goestler's only hope was to get to Zimmerman before he did, force Zimmerman to give up his half of the code and run with the money. If Goestler beat him to Zimmerman, his only chance was to follow Goestler to the money. Goestler, presumably, knew less than anyone. He had no idea that Paul had obtained his half of the code, he did not know that the three Americans and Suzanne were back in Paris. He had burned his bridges with Zimmerman and had thereby cut himself off from all Iranian support. Goestler was isolated and should be easy to pick off.

Paul had just about decided that his best bet was to eliminate Goestler, make direct contact with Zimmerman and play it out from there, when he received two telephone calls within a few minutes of each other. The first was from one of his sources within the Paris police department, advising him of the tip they had received identifying Goestler as being involved with the plot described in the papers. The second was from Abdul, who relayed the contents of Suzanne's message.

For the first time, Paul thought he might lose. He debated just dropping the whole plan and gutting it out with the Agency. So far he had done nothing that could convict him of a crime. His handling of the case would certainly appear unusual, even negligent, but they could not put him in jail for that. He wanted the money too much to quit, however. He had been waiting for such an opportunity for a long time. He found the prospect of retiring on an Agency pension repulsive.

He did not trust Suzanne. She had obviously fallen in love with the American. Was the American devious enough and greedy enough to double-cross everyone and make off with the money? Paul did not think so. His best bet was Zimmerman.

Goestler knew quite a bit more than anyone was giving him credit for. He had known that he was being followed for several days by at least two separate tails. After one of the tails, Suzanne's French operative, had contacted him with the offer to sell information, he had tortured the full story from the man, cut his throat and left him at the warehouse. He then slipped the other tail and left to find Zimmerman.

Goestler knew that Paul's man was watching Zimmerman and that someone else was watching them both. Goestler was in an apartment that he had broken into that morning, across the street from Zimmerman's flat. He had no idea to whom it belonged, and it did not matter to him. If anyone walked in while he was there he would kill them instantly. Roger had been right in his assessment of Goestler's personality. The man could kill with no compunction or hesitation. He did not do it for enjoyment, he obtained no particular pleasure from it, but neither did he feel any guilt at the act or empathy for his victim. He killed the way a normal man would brush aside some casual obstruction in his path.

He had seen Zimmerman enter his flat and immediately pull the blinds. Goestler began by locating the two tails he knew were following his quarry. One was surely the Agency's but he was not sure of the other. It could be someone working for Suzanne and the Americans, like the person who had approached him, or perhaps the Iranians were now watching Zimmerman themselves. In any case, he had to find a way to isolate Zimmerman, obtain the other half of the code and get to the money before the roof caved in on everyone. The first tail, the close one, was in the lobby of the building where he had arrived only a few minutes after Zimmerman. As Goestler had entered the building across the street, he had seen the man

The Nova Affair

sitting in a corner, his face buried in a paper. The second tail was probably in the car that had pulled up and parked half a block away from the entrance to Zimmerman's building a few minutes after the first tail had arrived.

Goestler decided to start with the car. He exited the apartment by the rear entrance, walked quickly around the block and then slowed as he approached the car from the rear. It contained one man, who was smoking a cigarette. He had rolled down the driver's side window to let the smoke escape from the interior. As Goestler approached the car, he reached into the inside pocket of his trenchcoat and grasped the handle of a silenced Walther. Reaching a position opposite the car, Goestler slowed and turned. He leaned over, smiled and began to ask the man directions to a local landmark. As the man pivoted his head toward the open window, Goestler shot him between the eyes, never taking the gun from his coat. The man slumped forward and Goestler quickly pushed the body sideways before the pressure of the body could activate the car's horn. He then rose and walked calmly on toward Zimmerman's building.

This time he reversed the process. He walked past the entrance, verified that the first tail was still in the corner, and then turned right and went to the back of the building. He used a service elevator to go to Zimmerman's floor and wedged the door open when he left the elevator. He pressed his ear to the door of Zimmerman's flat long enough to hear that someone was still moving about inside. Then he stepped into an unlocked linen closet between Zimmerman's flat and the door to the service elevator, leaving the door open a crack.

Within a half-hour it was over. Zimmerman left the flat with one large bag in hand. As Goestler had expected, Zimmerman did not attempt to use the public elevator but turned toward the service elevator in the rear, planning to elude the tail in the lobby. As he passed the linen closet, Goestler quietly stepped out behind him and shot him in the back of the head. He dragged Zimmerman's body and the suitcase into the linen closet and after a few minute's search found the address book. He stuffed the body and bag into the back of the closet and covered it with a pile of linen. It could be a full day before it was discovered. He exited the building as he had come in, passing the front of the hotel on the opposite side of the street. The man was still in the corner, but he was talking to someone else. Someone who looked very much like Paul Sullivan, the CIA Agency chief in Paris.

A free-lancer in Paris, known to both Goestler and Zimmerman, had made the locking mechanism that guarded the money. It had been constructed so that there were two separate steps required to calculate the code necessary to open the box without triggering the explosives contained within the casket. The first step was as Roger and Suzanne had already deciphered. The second part of the key was knowing with which switch, of the thirteen, one begins using the numbers generated by Zimmerman's half of the code. The second part of the key was Goestler's half and it was simpler and random. Between the layers of his belt he had secreted a small slip of paper with twenty-five entries in two parts. The first part was made of the numbers one through twenty-five, in order. The second part was made up of any number between one and thirteen, chosen in a random order by Goestler. The man who had made the device had explained to them how to activate it so that each man would know only his half of the key. Once Goestler had entered his twenty-five numbers, in order, into the machine and turned on the switch that armed the mechanism, it could not be safely opened again without the right code being entered first. Their only obligation was to replace the batteries once a year a task that was still several months ahead of them and which would now, presumably, be unnecessary.

Given the number on the counter and its color, Zimmerman's half of the code would always produce a sequence of thirteen numbers which would always run up to thirteen, back to one and then up to the number below the starting point. But it was Goestler's half of the code that indicated with which of the thirteen switches the sequence was

The Nova Affair

to start. Either man could have gone for the money at any time but he would have had only one chance in thirteen of making it. They had picked thirteen because of its unlucky connotations and because each agreed that it was enough to preclude the other from taking a chance, given the consequences of failure.

Minutes after Paul arrived at Zimmerman's hotel and checked with his agent he was in Zimmerman's room. Paul had told the agent to wait in the lobby, explaining that he had received a tip that Zimmerman wanted to defect and that he was going to make contact. A quick examination of the interior of Zimmerman's premises convinced him that Zimmerman had left for good. He had followed Zimmerman's path back to the service elevator, smelled the cordite in the air from Goestler's pistol and had quickly found Zimmerman's body in the linen closet. After thoroughly searching Zimmerman's clothes and bag, and not finding what he was looking for, he left the body where it was. He returned to the lobby and told his agent that Zimmerman had fled. He instructed the agent to institute a search of Paris for Zimmerman, concentrating on the airports and train stations. It would not hurt to have the Agency busy elsewhere while he tried to finish his business.

Goestler had made one mistake. There were three tails on Zimmerman, not two. The man he had killed in the street was working for the Iranians, who had wanted to be sure that Zimmerman reported back to Bonn as instructed. The third tail, Suzanne's operative who was working for Craigwell and Kronovich, had escaped detection. He had a contact who was employed as an assistant manager in the hotel. He had simply helped himself to a porter's uniform and had loitered about the lobby during the entire episode. When Paul and the CIA agent left, he had used a master key to let himself into Zimmerman's room. He, also, quickly deduced that Zimmerman had fled. Not being as clever or as observant as Paul, he did not find the body in the linen closet. Nor did he have any way of knowing about the body in the car a half block down the street. Within a few minutes he reported what he did know to Craigwell.

Paul knew that the noose had tightened further. Goestler now had the whole key and the German knew where the money was. Paul was certain that the man would waste no time in retrieving the stash and fleeing Paris. Suzanne's offer might now be his only hope. But first he had to stop Goestler. He called Abdul and gave the man a lengthy set of instructions.

Kronovich had spent the morning with the French police. He offered to release all that the Americans knew of the plot and the location of the money in return for the cooperation of the authorities in apprehending both Paul and the two Iranian agents. The catch was that it had to be done on the American's timetable. At first, he thought he might be arrested himself. The French were not at all anxious to either create an international incident or to be forced to admit that they had suspected the plot themselves but had not been able to stop it. Nor were they excited about admitting that the whole scheme had been blown open by two amateurs and two rogue foreign agents. They would have been more than happy to see Zimmerman and Goestler exit the scene and to recover the money, leaving the public and the press none the wiser as to the real story.

But Kronovich held the high cards. If the authorities did not cooperate his partner would see to it that the details were released to the press. The authorities had the choice of accepting Kronovich's terms and sharing the credit or of seeing themselves look even worse in the eyes of the public. In the end, they agreed to play the American's game.

When Suzanne called Abdul back later that day she was given terse instructions that Paul had accepted their offer. He would meet Roger and Suzanne at 4:00 PM that afternoon in the Hall of the Egyptians at the Louvre.

The Nova Affair

After leaving Zimmerman's hotel Goestler spent several hours in a rented room. He dyed his hair a non-descript brown, inserted two contact lenses that changed the color of his eyes from blue to hazel and donned a set of working man's clothes, including a worn, linen cap that he wore half covering his face. He then bought several papers and spent the next few hours watching the crypt from a convenient park bench in the Jardin du Luxembourg.

Roger, Suzanne and the two CIA agents spent the rest of the morning in a "council of war."

"Okay kids, we got problems," Craigwell began. The man ticked off the points on his fingers, one by one. "First, our man who was to contact Goestler has not reported back. We have to assume that he's history and whatever he knew, which thankfully wasn't much, Goestler knows. Second, Zimmerman has disappeared. He may have decided to report back to Iran, but I doubt that. He doesn't have the money and he's in such deep shit with his superiors he'd be stupid to go back. So, either he's just laying low, or maybe either Goestler or Paul got to him first. If Paul got there first, he wouldn't need us, so let's assume the worst, which is that Goestler now has both halves of the key. On the other hand, if I'm wrong and Paul did get to Zimmerman first, then his offer to meet us is a trap. We can't let him get all of us in his sights at the same time. Our insurance is that any one of us can blow the whistle on him, although it would be a lot better if it's either Hal or me, we have a little more credibility with the Agency. Finally, we have to move fast. If anyone of the three has all of the code, they'll go after the money as soon as possible."

"Here's what I worked out with the French," Kronovich said. "They'll stake out the stash as soon as we tell them where it is. They'll let anyone get to the money but no one leaves the scene once they touch the goods. As soon as the weapon is disarmed and the money is accessed, it's theirs. They take custody of Zimmerman or Goestler, or both, depending on who shows up. If Paul gets caught in the net they'll hold him for twenty-four hours, which gives us time to alert the Agency so they can take custody. If either Goestler or Zimmerman gets there first, alone, then the game's up and we're on our own with Paul. In return for their help, the French authorities get to break the story to the press. The only acknowledgment that we exist will be a general reference to assistance by American authorities. Roger and Suzanne don't get mentioned at all."

"It could get very crowded in the park tonight," Roger said. "What do we do if everyone shows up at once, draw straws?"

"If Goestler does have both halves, he's probably sitting in the park right now, waiting for dark and making sure that no one beats him to the stash," Craigwell said.

"Look," Roger said. "We want to catch Goestler, but it's important that we actually pull Paul into the scheme, so that he commits himself and gives us the evidence you guys need to turn him over. Why don't we intercept Goestler or Zimmerman, or both, whoever turns up, and just let the French arrest them? Then we have a clear field to come in with Paul later."

"Two reasons. First, because Goestler and Zimmerman are unlikely to cooperate," Craigwell answered. "They're both trained agents and they can spot a stake out. If we put that tight a ring around the park we won't see them. We have to stand off, watch the crypt from a distance and pick them up when they come out. Second reason, we need to be sure that someone opens that damn thing. We don't know yet that we'll work anything out with Paul. If we miss there, we're stuck with a booby-trap that no one wants to touch."

"How about a bomb disposal unit?" Suzanne asked. "Surely the French have them. Then no one has to worry about opening it."

"The French want no part of that," Kronovich said. "This is a one-of-a-kind, made by an expert with two very smart and very resourceful fellows looking over his shoulder. All the guts are inside the coffin. It's certainly got some kind of fail-safe mechanism in it. Otherwise, either of our two friends could have opened it at any time by disconnecting the device. Besides

The Nova Affair

not wanting to risk one of their men, this is a national monument. They don't want to scatter it all over Paris."

"We have to go through with the meeting with Paul first," Craigwell interjected. "We need to know if he's going to bite or not. If we get his commitment to help us open the coffin, then half the problem is solved. We get the money and we get him. He may know something about either Goestler or Zimmerman. I doubt that he'll tell us, but you never know. Let's concentrate on that part of the problem for the moment.

"Now put yourself in his position," Craigwell continued. "He doesn't trust you guys. He has to suspect that we're all in this together. He's a very smart man. If he thinks that Hal and I have made him, then he's going to know that we may have the police on our side. How does he get into the crypt, get the money, take care of us, slip the French and get out of the country?"

The question was followed by silence. None of them could think of a way they would do it.

"He's got one asset we haven't factored in," Kronovich commented. "That man Friday of his, Abdul, we know he's absolutely loyal to Paul. He's sure to be in this scene someplace."

"Well he's got to tip his hand somewhat," Roger said. "If he agrees to make a deal, we have to concur on a time and a method. He wouldn't be dealing with us if he had the whole code, so we have to go in together him and at least one of us."

"Maybe that's it," Suzanne said. "Suppose he sends Abdul and stays in the background himself. He knows it's him we want. If he sends Abdul then we'll be tempted not to spring the trap until we follow the money back to him. He probably figures he can beat us at that game and he's probably right."

"But what about the French?" Roger asked. "They're not going to let that money out of the park in any case. I think we just insist that it's Paul or no deal. Now, what worries me is what happens two seconds after we open the coffin. What's to stop him from eliminating whoever's in there with him, just out of spite and to improve the odds somewhat?"

173

Thomas Bloom

"We cover that on the front end," Craigwell said. "We just have an understanding that if the same number of bodies that go in don't come out that the odd man is fair game. Besides, it would be more his style to circle back later and take us when we aren't ready. I think right now he just wants to take the money and to be gone."

"I just don't see how he thinks he can do it," Suzanne said. "He knows that he has to deal with Roger and me. He must suspect that you two are involved, in which case the French may be also. Plus, he has to worry about either Zimmerman or Goestler showing up. If Zimmerman did decide to come in from the cold then the Iranians could show up too. And Paul has to handle all that without causing anyone else in the Agency in Paris to get suspicious."

"Well, that's his problem. Here's the way we play it," Craigwell said, exerting his authority for the first time in the conversation. "We get the French to put a lookout on the park right now, so that if anyone shows up we know about it. We keep the meeting with Paul and see if we can get a clue as to how he's going to arrange this. The whole thing is relatively safe until dark. There're too many people in the park until then."

Things were moving much faster than Suzanne, Roger or the Americans suspected. Paul had the advantage of knowing that Goestler had the code and he was sure that the German would not waste a minute. He had rented a room in a small hotel about a block away from the Jardin Du Luxembourg but with a clear view of the park. He now sat a few feet back from the window, in the shadow of the unlit room, examining the park through a high powered telescope. He had narrowed his suspects down to a man reading a newspaper on a park bench and another figure leaning against a tree and looking out over the pond toward the crypt.

The man with the paper rose and walked back toward the far entrance of the park. Paul turned his attention to the man leaning against the tree.

The Nova Affair

Goestler had seen his opportunity. He left the park bench and began walking toward a uniformed park attendant who was picking up litter with a broom and a long handled dustpan. He walked directly in front of the man and opened his coat, long enough for the attendant to see the gun in his inside pocket. Holding the gun inside his coat and pointed it at the man, he told the attendant, quietly but very firmly, to carry his equipment into the nearest restroom.

A few minutes later Goestler exited the restroom in the attendant's uniform, carrying the broom and dustpan. His victim now sat in one of the booths inside, with Goestler's pants around his ankles and a bullet in his head. Using the man's tie and his own handkerchief, Goestler had bound the body to the tank of the commode so that it would remain upright. Pausing occasionally to pick up a piece of litter, Goestler slowly made his way toward the crypt.

Paul almost missed it. Goestler was slipping through the door into the crypt when he spotted him. With a curse, he ran from the room and toward the stairs to the street.

Having done the computations earlier, it took Goestler only a few seconds, using a miniature flashlight, to set the counters on the mechanism in the proper sequence. He then flicked the switch next to the counters and breathed a sigh of relief when nothing happened. Surprisingly, he next stepped back from the coffin and leaned against the wall, glancing once at his watch. Only he, Zimmerman and the man who had made the device knew that the timer would wait two minutes before disarming the bomb inside the coffin. This was the last of the traps. They had decided that in case someone might successfully steal the codes that they would so arrange the sequence so that an interloper could still set off the device even after successfully programming the counters.

Paul had to make a fast decision. There were several couples on blankets within twenty or thirty feet of the crypt. They were only interested in each other but they were close enough to see and hear anything going on outside the crypt. Paul was sure that Goestler would come out fast, armed and ready for trouble. He would only have one chance to get off the first shot. Even if he felled his quarry on his first attempt, the commotion was bound to attract attention. Assuming that Goestler would be distracted in gathering up the money, he decided to risk going in after him. The back of the crypt was half covered by shrubbery. He slipped behind a bush and waited a few moments to see if anyone had noticed. The couples on the blankets continued their cooing, oblivious to him.

He went through the door fast and low and then dove to the right, his gun extended in the firing position. To his surprise the crypt was unlit. The partially open door let in just enough light to reveal the shape of the coffin lying on its pedestal in the center of the room. Nothing else was visible. He had just decided that Goestler must have already left when a bullet hit the granite floor in front of him, throwing splinters of rock into his left cheek. He felt a sudden pain in his left shoulder. The bullet had ricocheted up and caught him in the fleshy part of his upper arm. The muzzle flash had come from his right of the coffin. Their had been no sound. Goestler was using a silencer.

Goestler had not counted on Paul's reflexes. Paul had seen more than a little action in his career and his training took over without having to think through a plan of action. He rolled once to the left, cutting off Goestler's line of sight, and then rose and ran for the coffin. He dove directly for the top of the coffin and slid down its length on his stomach. Goestler was a fraction late. He rose and fired but did not have time to aim. The bullet missed Paul's ear by an inch. Paul's shot, a .357 soft-nosed shell, blew the top of Goestler's head off. Paul's pistol had not been silenced and the sound of the shot reverberated within the crypt. It seemed that all of Paris must have heard it. Paul waited a full five minutes. Nothing happened. No one entered and he could hear no noise coming from the outside. He stripped and searched Goestler but found nothing on the man

The Nova Affair

but the pistol, the flashlight, a small key and two large, plastic garbage bags stuffed into his pockets.

Paul spent several more minutes staring at the counters. Even with Goestler's half of the code he could not decipher how the system worked. He saw small levers pointing to thirteen numbers, beginning with the number seven on the first counter, continuing in sequence to number thirteen and then running from one to six. The counters, in turn, could be set on any number between one and thirteen. There was a dial on the machine with the number six showing. The number was in red but that had no significance to him. The half of the code he had stolen from Goestler was a random series of twenty-five numbers, all between one and thirteen. He could not see how that set of numbers had anything to do with the sequence before him. He stared at the top of the coffin for a long time then decided he could not risk it. Goestler had not opened the coffin, either because he had not reset the counters or because he had been aware of some other problem. He made his decision. He would have to make a pact with Suzanne and the Americans after all. He fashioned a crude bandage from strips torn from Goestler's clothing and wrapped his upper arm. The wound was not bleeding badly and the bullet had entered and exited within the space of not more than two inches. It was almost a graze. Nonetheless, he knew that the wound must be attended to or he risked infection. Worse, it would start to stiffen up in a few hours. By the end of the day he would not be able to use the arm at all. He stripped the uniform from Goestler and put it on over his own clothes. Then he pocketed both the key and the German's gun and left carrying the broom and dustpan, shutting the door firmly behind him and replacing the lock that hung loose on the chain.

Paul had serious problems but he had one advantage, he knew what the problems were and he had time to prepare his response. He was operating on the assumption that Roger, Suzanne and his two operatives were working together. That almost certainly meant that the authorities were involved. The French would want two things to recover the money and to eliminate Goestler and Zimmerman, a task that had already been performed for them although they were not yet aware of it. Roger and Suzanne wanted only to finish the assignment and to clear Roger's name so that they could be free to start a new life. Craigwell and Kronovich needed to catch him crossing the line, actually converting the money to his own use, in order to take him in. He had three things in his favor, Abdul, his wits and the fact that he could control the timing.

They agreed that Roger would go alone to the Louvre. They could not admit that Craigwell and Kronovich were involved with the plot to uncover Paul. If Roger and Suzanne were truly working alone, they would not be so stupid as to allow Paul the chance to take them both together. As Craigwell had pointed out earlier, their only weapon against Paul was the threat of disclosure. One of them had to be always free to carry out the threat.

The afternoon was warm and sunny. The Louvre was full of art lovers and tourists. Roger entered off the Rue De Rivoli. Signs by every entrance pointed out the way to the Mona Lisa, or La Giocondaù, in several languages. The employees of the Louvre had become so tired of directing tourists to the famous work of art that the museum was now posted with the information. It was amazing how many people came into the museum, found their way to this one painting, and then left without taking a moment to view the hundreds of other magnificent pieces in the building. They could then go back to Iowa and tell their friends that "they had been to Paris and seen the Mona Lisa."

Roger walked directly to the Hall of the Egyptians, remembering its location from his previous visits. He arrived a few minutes before four. He was sure that Paul was already there, watching, and he made no effort to be surreptitious. He was viewing a display of hieroglyphics when Paul came up behind him.

"I told you both to come," Paul opened.

The Nova Affair

"That would be stupid of us, wouldn't it. As long as one of us is free to blow the whistle you can't risk taking out the other one."

"You have no whistle to blow. I'm only carrying out my orders, recovering the money and putting Goestler and Zimmerman out of business."

"That's between you and the Agency," Roger replied. "I could give a shit. Suzanne and I just want out. We're tired of being played with. For a change, we know something that you don't. Like Zimmerman's half of the code and how to get to the money. We figure that you have Goestler's half. The deal's very simple. We combine our information to get the stash, split it down the middle and go our separate ways."

"You are referring, of course, to the cache in the crypt at the Jardin Du Luxembourg?"

Roger could not hide his surprise. Paul laughed.

"Perhaps," Paul said, "I know more than you give me credit for."

"If you have all the information, what do you need us for?" Roger asked. He was starting to worry that Paul did in fact have all the information, in which case his only reason for being here would have been to eliminate him and Suzanne.

"Everything but Zimmerman's half, I admit," Paul replied, "and how to use it. I will warn you, just having the code is not enough. There is something more to it. I have done some research on my own."

"We think we have it all," Roger replied. "We've been busy ourselves."

"Prove it," Paul said. "If you understand the entire procedure you should be able to tell me about my half of the code Goestler's half."

"You should have a series of twenty-five numbers, all between one and thirteen. Our half of the code tells us what sequence of numbers we need to set the switches on, in a specific order, your half tells us which switch to start with."

It was Paul's turn to be startled. "And how do I use my half to deduce that information?" he asked.

"I think that's best our secret until the time comes," Roger replied. "We don't want you getting too far ahead of us."

"And how did you manage all this? You've had some help from two of my friends perhaps?"

Roger smiled. He saw no reason to lift the charade. Let the bastard wonder, he thought. "We're working alone. We slipped your two boys in Bermuda and haven't seen them since."

Roger decided to add a little credence to his position. "I got Zimmerman's half of the code while he was passed out in his room in Chicago. We got the location from a map that was in the shoe of the guy that Craigwell drilled in the hotel. Craigwell told us in Bermuda that the stash existed but he didn't know where. We put two and two together. Suzanne and I came to Paris planning to make a deal with Goestler. It appeared that he and Zimmerman were falling out and we figured he'd be ripe for an offer to split the loot and run. By the way, how much money are we after?"

Paul looked at him skeptically. The story made sense but Roger could not tell if he was buying it.

"I don't know for sure. Assuming our two friends kept only twenty percent of what they had their hands on, it should be well over one hundred million dollars. The Iranians got the rest, of course."

Roger whistled. "Plenty for both of us. No sense either of us getting greedy."

"Enough talk," Paul said. "I'll meet you at the west end of the pool in the park at nine tonight. I'll have backup but you won't see them. If anything happens to me, or if anyone attempts to interfere, you go first."

"And what's my insurance?" Roger asked. "How do I know that you won't put a bullet in my head the second after we open the casket?"

"What're the odds?" Paul answered. "You've got Suzanne safely tucked away. If you don't come out in one piece, and with your half of the money, she starts calling everyone from

The Nova Affair

Paris to Washington. Why do I need that kind of trouble when I can just take the money home and bury it in the backyard?"

Roger was cleverly caught in his own net. If he and Suzanne were working alone, Paul's scenario made sense. Paul would only run if he knew that his two agents were on to him and Roger could not propose that possibility.

"One more thing," Paul said. "I've reason to believe that there's a second trigger to the mechanism, something more that has to be done besides just setting the proper code. If you have any idea what it is, now would be an excellent time to share it."

"No idea," Roger answered. "The mechanism only allows for the one setting. We saw no other trigger device. How can you be sure?"

"Yours to know in the fullness of time. It might be just a timing delay. But if so, what time? Do you wait a certain minimum or do you have to open the casket within a certain window?"

"I don't know," Roger responded. "But we've thought of one other possible problem. Suppose we open the casket lid and find another device inside?"

"Easy," Paul answered. "We run like hell. One way or the other, we'll know soon enough. At the pool nine o'clock. Be alone and no games. Remember, if I have any trouble, I go after you first."

Paul turned and left the hall without a further word. Roger resented the implication that Paul could take him out at will, not even allowing for the possibility that Roger could protect himself. On the other hand, given the difference in their training, Paul was probably right. Their timing was going to have to be awfully good or he would have a problem.

When Roger returned, they reconvened the council of war. They had finally given the French authorities the location of the stash. The French were establishing a ring around the park, well out of sight but with enough men and equipment so that they could close off the entire area on a moment's notice. Craigwell, Kronovich and the French supervisor would be hidden in a van parked at the edge of the park and situated so that the crypt was visible from a window cut high in the van's body. Craigwell had insisted on having the authority to sound the alert. No one would move until he gave the signal. They anticipated that Paul would keep Roger hostage until they exited the park, where they assumed Abdul would be waiting with some kind of vehicle. If Paul kept Roger hostage after he left the area, the French had cars and surveillance teams in place in every direction and they would follow the escape vehicle until Roger was finally released.

They all knew that it might not be enough. Paul was clever and he suspected a trap. They might have to improvise. They also believed that either Goestler or Zimmerman could show up first. If so, when either man exited the crypt, with or without the money, he would be apprehended immediately. If anyone got to the money before Paul arrived then the rest of the plan was off. The Americans would have to deal with Paul on their own. The French only wanted Goestler and Zimmerman eliminated and the money recovered. The Americans could wash their own dirty laundry.

They spent the hours before it was time to leave considering alternatives. They could not improve much on the basic plan. Roger was given two weapons, a .38 special to carry in his coat pocket and a small, snub nosed pistol which held five shots in its clip. Craigwell insisted he secret the pistol in his jockey shorts. It was cold, uncomfortable and made walking difficult.

"He's sure to search you," Craigwell said. "Let him find the first gun. If he's a little careless he might miss the second one. He's not liable to grab you in the crotch."

In addition, Roger still carried the equipment Paul had issued him at their first meeting, the 22 caliber lighter, reloaded courtesy of Craigwell.

Once again, Paul came up behind him before Roger heard him. He had been waiting by the pool for over ten minutes. It was a few minutes past nine. The park was almost deserted as

The Nova Affair

darkness fell. A few last strollers wandered toward the exits in the distance.

"Arms out and spread your legs," Paul said. "I'm armed and I will not hesitate to use it if you provoke me."

"That's the trouble with you government guys," Roger quipped. "None of you have any sense of humor." He complied with Paul's orders.

Paul quickly found the thirty-eight. He threw it into the middle of the pool with a snort of disgust. "Now empty all your pockets. I want to see the knife and the lighter I gave you. I assume you're still following orders."

Roger threw the contents of his pants pockets on the ground and turned the side pockets of his sports jacket inside out. In addition to a money clip, and some change he disgorged the lighter and knife. Paul threw them into the pool after the revolver.

"Now open your shirt and pull up your pant legs, I want to be sure you aren't wired." Roger complied.

"Where is your half of the code?" Paul asked, his voice revealing a teneseness, despite himself.

"Up here," Roger answered, pointing to his temple. "It's simple enough to remember, once you do the decoding. Where's yours?"

"When we need it," Paul replied. "Walk ahead of me to the crypt."

When they arrived at the chained door, Paul handed Roger the key and instructed him to open the lock. Paul held his left hand inside the pocket of a light trenchcoat. Roger assumed it held a gun. As they entered the crypt Paul produced a flashlight from his right hand coat pocket.

"Stop here," he said to Roger, just inside the door. "Just so you don't do anything stupid, Goestler's body is behind the coffin. He has a very large hole in his head as will you if you fuck this up."

"So that's it," Roger said. "You two weren't trading the same half of the code with each other, so he must have gotten Zimmerman's half somehow and you followed him here. What went wrong? Did you interrupt him before he had time to set the counters?"

"I'm not sure," Paul answered. "He had plenty of time to disarm the mechanism before I came in but he was just standing here in the dark, like he was waiting for something. That's why I think there's another step to this thing. In that your ass will be scattered all over Paris with mine if we don't do this right, do you have any ideas?"

"No. But your theory of a time delay makes sense. It would be their last protection. If anyone else had stolen both halves of the code, they would have eliminated themselves if they just walked in, set the counters and opened the coffin. Let's see how it's set. It's time to let me see yours."

Paul laid the flashlight on top of the coffin and produced a small sheet of paper. "Don't fuck with me," Paul said. "I want to know exactly what you're doing and why."

"Easy enough," Roger said. "The part you didn't figure out was this counter. It tells us which one of twenty-six different possible sequences to pick. As I told you, your half tells us which counter to start with. What number is opposite number six on your list?"

Paul switched the flashlight to the sheet of paper. Opposite the sixth digit on the left hand side of the page was the number five.

"Okay, the sequence for today starts with eleven, runs up to thirteen and then from one to ten. Your number means we start the sequence with the fifth counter. If the counters are already set in that pattern then it means that Goestler either knew he had made a mistake or he was waiting for something."

Paul focused the flashlight on the counters. Roger said "bingo." The counters had already been set to the correct sequence and the disarming switch was turned off.

"We've got two choices," Paul said. "If Goestler was waiting for a simple delay, then it's okay to go ahead now. The bomb must be disarmed. But if there is only a time window of a minute or so and then the thing rearms, we should reset it now. But if we reset it, we have no way to know how long to wait, either way."

"How far ahead of you was Goestler?" Roger asked. The macabre aspect of the scene struck him. They were ignoring Goestler's mutilated body like it was some litter in the corner. He knew that Paul would not hesitate to kill him at the slightest provocation. Yet they stood over the booby-trapped coffin of a long dead hero, which could blow them to pieces at any minute, chatting like two neighbors over the backyard fence.

"Two minutes, two and a half at the most," Paul replied.

"I'd gamble on the simple delay. They would only need to build in a minute or two to serve their purpose. You said he was standing in the dark, but if he were waiting for the right window to open up, I think he'd have had his flashlight glued to his watch. Besides, the window option would have only complicated things for them. My guess is it is a delay of a minute of so. He probably decided to wait a little longer, just to be sure."

"If you're wrong, we're hamburger," Paul said.

"Big prize, big risk," Roger countered. He hoped Paul could not see his knees shaking or the tremor in his hands. He wanted to get it over, one way or the other. He was confident of his logic. If he were wrong he would never know it.

"Okay, you take that side," Paul said. He lowered the lid that covered the arming mechanism and laid the flashlight on top of it, pointing the beam down the length of the casket. Then he moved to the center of the casket.

Roger moved opposite him and they slowly lifted the lid off the coffin. Nothing happened. They walked the lid toward the door and leaned it against the wall of the crypt.

"Good guess," Paul said. His relief was evident. He raised the flashlight and pointed the beam into the interior of the casket. There was another box attached to the inside of the casket, opposite the arming mechanism. It presumably held the rest of the controls and the timing device. From the box ran several sets of wires attached to two large pieces of Plastique that lay along the sides of the casket. Neither man was looking at the explosive. They were both mesmerized by the sight before them.

The casket contained no body. But it was nearly full of neatly bundled stacks of bills in large denominations. Most were French but there were also some dollars, marks and Swiss francs. It was impossible to even estimate the amount of money they were looking at.

After a few moments during which both men remained frozen before the tableau before them, Paul finally spoke. "The end of the rainbow, plenty for everyone. Our friend here was good enough to bring along a couple of large trash bags. You fill them both up. I'll watch. When your done, I'll pick the one I want, then we leave together. You will stay with me until I'm sure there's no one waiting outside. Same rules, if anyone comes after me, you go first. Understood?"

"Sure thing boss, no problem." Roger began to stuff the bundles into one of the bags. He was careful to put all the dollars, marks, and Swiss francs in one bag and finished filling it with French francs. He then put as much of the remaining money in the second bag as it would hold. There was still a considerable amount of money left in the coffin.

"I'll take the first bag," Paul said, when he was finished. Now you walk out in front of me, go about ten feet out the door, then stop. I'll be right behind you."

Roger understood the implicit threat of a gun at his back. He did as he was told. He turned just enough to watch Paul out of the corner of his eye. Paul stood in the open doorway, still shielded from sight in three directions, and turned the flashlight on and off several times in succession. After a few seconds, two huge explosions broke the quiet of the night, one coming a few moments after the other. They seemed to come from the periphery of the park. Roger could feel the shock of the concussions where he stood. He took the opportunity to reach down the front of his pants and retrieve the small pistol. Then, after a few more seconds, a whole string of smaller explosions went off in the park. It seemed as if they were under an artillery bombardment. Each of the smaller explosions produced huge

The Nova Affair

clouds of white smoke. In a few moments the park was filled with smoke and the stench of cordite. In the distance, the sounds of sirens could be heard. Roger looked back in time to see Paul raising his right arm, which now held a gun. The barrel was leveling at his head. Paul evidently wanted all the money after all.

Roger half spun, fired two quick shots from his waist, and dove for the cover of a small group of trees about ten feet to his side. The shots missed but had the desired effect, Paul ducked, hesitated a minute, and then turned and fled into the obscuring mist that now filled the park, carrying both the pistol and the bag of money in his right hand.

Craigwell was with him in a minute, a drawn gun in one hand and a portable radio in the other. "Is he gone?" the agent asked.

Roger pointed in the general direction that Paul had fled. "What the hell happened? It sounded like Omaha beach here for a minute."

"This guy means business. It even looks like Omaha beach out there. He set off two car bombs in the street next to the park. There's debris and injured people all over the place. The stuff in the park was meant to cover him. The worst thing is, when the French heard the explosions, they assumed you guys had set off the bomb in the crypt and they all broke cover and came to the park. Our cordon is blown. He must have had Abdul set up the bombs and then detonate them by radio when he gave him a signal. At least we got him to break his cover. His ass is meat with the Agency, not to mention the French. It's too bad we didn't get him here. Now we'll have to hunt him down the hard way."

"Do you still have that direction finder you used to track me?" Roger asked.

"In the van, yeah, so what?"

"The pen, he didn't take it from me. I turned it on and slipped it in the bag of money he's carrying."

Craigwell looked at him with surprise and admiration. "You may make it yet kid." He turned and began to jog back toward the street.

As they ran, Roger told him the rest of the story.

"Incidentally, Goestler's in the crypt, with the top of his head blown off. Apparently Goestler got to Zimmerman and then Paul followed Goestler here. I assume Zimmerman's dead. At least they did part of the dirty work for us."

"That explains the body in the car," Craigwell commented cryptically.

"One more thing," Roger said. "He seems to be favoring his left arm. I think maybe he's wounded or hurt it somehow."

As soon as they reached the van, Craigwell turned on the direction finder. Its needle flickered a moment and then swung west.

"Going west and almost out of range. Looks like he may be headed for the coast. Hey, Hal," he shouted at Kronovich, who was in the driver's seat of the van. "Let's go. Due west. We'll see if we can keep him in range. In the meantime, I'm going to get on the horn and see if someone can get us a chopper. My French liaison left me when the car bombs went off. As soon as we're sure what direction he's headed we'll have the French start setting up road blocks, although I don't think we'll be lucky enough to catch those two that way."

"By the way," Craigwell looked at Roger. "Where's the money, didn't you get half?"

"Oh shit," Roger said. "I left it lying in the weeds." He had been holding more money than he ever dreamed of having and had completely forgotten about it.

"Never mind," Craigwell said. "The place is crawling with gendarmes, I'm sure they'll recover it quick enough."

Paul had planned his escape well. They were using a dilapidated panel truck. Abdul was driving and Paul sat concealed in the back of the vehicle. Anyone looking for two men speeding from the scene would not have looked twice at the truck. It was actually CIA property, one of a number of

The Nova Affair

vehicles kept stored around the town for various purposes. It would eventually be missed, of course, but by that time Paul expected to be far away from it. Although the body of the truck was rusted and full of scars, the engine had been expertly tuned and was quite up to any reasonable demand.

Paul knew it would be stupid to attempt to flee the country immediately. The French would have every exit route blocked and heavily manned within a few hours. If they had any hint as to his whereabouts roadblocks would go up immediately. It would be even more difficult to run the gauntlet carrying the huge amount of money he now had with him.

Paul also knew that such a degree of alertness was unsustainable. As time went on, other emergencies would demand attention. Routine work would back up beyond tolerance. The cost of overtime and special equipment would attract the attention of the bureaucrats. Every day that went by without his discovery would increase the possibility that he had already eluded the authorities, made his escape and that the cost and trouble of the search for him had become purposeless.

In anticipation of this need, Paul had long since acquired several houses in the countryside surrounding Paris. Abdul had leased them as "summer hideaways" for his employer, supposedly a rich industrialist in Paris who was very protective of his privacy. The amounts offered had been generous and it had been made clear by Abdul that his master might arrive and depart on any schedule or might choose to never use the property at all. All the landlords lived well away from the properties in question and were quite pleased with the arrangement. All the transactions had been conducted under aliases provided by Paul through his access to forged documents within the Agency. It was to one of these homes that they were now headed. Abdul had stocked each with ample supplies. They could stay under cover at least a month before having to show themselves anywhere.

Paul emptied the bag of money onto the floor of the truck, planning to transfer it to several small suitcases. The pen that Roger had secreted in the bag skidded across the pile of bills and fell to the floor of the vehicle. Paul stared at it in shock and disgust. He realized the implications immediately. It had never occurred to him that Roger could react that quickly or think that far ahead. His first inclination was to simply turn it off. Then he had a better idea. He shouted some instructions to Abdul.

Within a few miles they pulled up behind a stake truck filled with crates of produce. A canvas held in place with semi-circular ribs running over the top surrounded the bed of the truck. The rear of the truck had a two-foot high tailgate. Paul lowered the passenger window and, as Abdul pulled alongside, threw the pen over the tailgate and into the back of the stake truck. They pulled off the highway and on to a side road at the next opportunity. They then drove about five miles north and pulled into a car park next to the local train station. They quickly transferred everything in the van to a Citroen that Abdul had left at the station earlier in the day. The van would not be noticed for some time. Abdul donned a chauffeur's hat and jacket and Paul sat in the back seat. They left the station, continuing north, driving well within the speed limit.

14

The chase ended in a dramatic and fruitless anti-climax. The unsuspecting grocer, headed home from a local market with a supply of produce, suddenly found himself surrounded by a half-dozen police vehicles. By the time they sorted it all out, the trail was cold. The grocer had seen nothing. Their quarry had certainly gone to ground. The French would conduct the usual surveillance on all ports, trains and airfields, but Roger and the two CIA agents knew it was hopeless. They would not

The Nova Affair

find Paul using standard procedures. If he were already out of the country, they would have to wait for him to surface. If he were still in France, they would have to find him their own way.

They feared that the French would not really want to find Paul. That would mean a messy trial with all the details of the case coming out in the press, including the authorities' own relative ineptness. Also, the amount of damage done by the two Iranian agents, presently not suspected by the public, would become known. It would not look at all good for the administration. It would also involve them in a custody fight with the Americans, who would want to prosecute Paul for reasons of their own. It was better that Paul left the country. The Americans could track him down and wash their own dirty laundry in private.

Roger was sure that the authorities would soon lose all appetite for the chase and would go on to other things. He was also sure that Paul had known that it would develop this way.

The French were satisfied. They had recovered a considerable sum of money, Zimmerman's body finally had been discovered by a maid and the two foreign agents were dead and posed no further threat. They released a short and self-serving explanation to the press. As agreed, the Americans got only small credit.

The press release was just sufficient to answer the questions previously raised in the information that Craigwell had leaked. It was reported that the two Iranian operatives had been subverting certain Common Market business enterprises and had committed a number of murders to cover their tracks. The bombs in the park had been a last desperate ruse to throw the police off their trail. The operatives had been killed in the process of apprehending them and much of the money recovered. There was no mention of Paul, Roger or Suzanne. The Iranians denied everything. The French did not challenge the denial and in a few days the whole affair began to work its way to the back pages.

Roger, Craigwell and Kronovich had returned to Paris and their flat late that night to tell Suzanne what had happened. They had to decide what to do next. Craigwell had a lot of explaining to do to Washington, including two bodies in a freezer in Bermuda. Against that he could claim credit for having stopped Paul's plan, in the process avoiding a potential international incident and, in a roundabout fashion, having completed the assignment of taking both Goestler and Zimmerman out of action.

It had struck Roger on the way back to Paris that he was done, he had completed what he had contracted for, the plot was uncovered and the guilty had been punished. Paul had never been part of the deal. He was the Agency's problem. Craigwell and Kronovich would now be able to work within the system to pursue him. They didn't need his help any more. He and Suzanne were free. He would only have to return to Bermuda to wind down the U.S. activities of the Mayberry a few days work. Why did he not feel finished?

"I see your point," Craigwell acknowledged, when Roger proposed that he now be released from the project and cleared of the charges still pending against him. "On the other hand, you're still an officer in the Marine Corps, in case you've forgotten, and still attached to the Embassy, which is to say, to Paul. As I was Paul's second-in-command on this project, until somebody does the paperwork, you still answer to me. Besides, maybe Paul wasn't part of the deal but the money was, and a good bit of it is still missing. Actually, Courtney, I've gotten used to your smile. Let me talk it over with Washington, keeping in mind that there are a few aspects of this matter that will take up more of their attention initially than processing your discharge."

"Shit," Roger said. But he was not as disappointed as he should have been.

As expected, the French were of no help. They agreed to keep their surveillance teams in place for a week but everyone knew they were only going through the motions. The French

The Nova Affair

had recovered almost seventy million dollars in the park, about half in Roger's bag and the other half still in the coffin. That indicated that Paul had at least thirty-five million with him.

"What about the General's body?" Roger asked. "Does anyone have any idea what happened to it?"

"They found it buried in a corner of Goestler's warehouse," Kronovich answered. "It's already back where it belongs. Neither the public nor the good General's descendants are any the wiser."

The four of them sat around a kitchen table in their rented flat, sipping red wine and eating cheese and sausage.

"Washington's not being a lot of help here," Craigwell announced. "They're not too happy with the way this whole thing has developed. We've left bodies scattered from Chicago to Bermuda, not to mention the four people that were killed when the bombs went off here. We made an unauthorized entry into the United States, where we're not supposed to be operating. I went out of channels several times and then didn't tell them what we were up to when we came back here. They can't do much to us because we were right in the long run but they're pissed all the same. They don't want any publicity about Paul's absconding with the money, let alone that he ordered the bombs planted. He was a senior agent and they don't need the bad press. They think Paul's long gone, so I don't get any help on this side unless I can come up with some evidence that he's still in France. They've given me one week. If nothing turns up by then, we're all to report back to Washington. That's good news for you, Roger. That means debriefing for us and decommissioning for you. You're almost out of this after all."

Suzanne surprised them all by leaping to her feet. "Are we going to leave it here? Someone must look for Paul. He has betrayed us, betrayed his country and France, killed four innocent people and he would have killed Roger if he could have." She spoke with vehemence, spitting out the words.

"It's not that simple," Craigwell answered. "A search like that takes time and resources. We have neither. Remember, this guy's a pro. He won't be easy to find. We don't even know if he's still in the country."

"I know that he's still in France," she answered. "I can feel it. He would not risk leaving the country while anyone is still looking for him. I am sure that he is in some out-of-the-way place, under an assumed name, waiting for the right time to move."

"Good theory," Kronovich said. "But where in the hell do we start looking?" No one had an answer.

Kronovich got two pieces of information from his contacts with the French police the next day. A careful analysis of the evidence in the crypt indicated that someone beside Goestler had been wounded there. The blood type matched Paul's. Also, the two CIA agents had checked out all the vehicles in the Agency's inventory in Paris. There was one van missing and the French had found it in a suburban commuter station northwest of Paris. It was empty and had been wiped clean.

"Okay, the pattern is clear," Craigwell said. "They ditched the van, picked up another vehicle that had been left at the station previously and went on their way. This also explains why he was favoring his left arm. He must have gotten clipped in the fight with Goestler."

"Look here," Roger said, laying one of the many area maps that they had acquired on the table. "If you connect the center of Paris to a spot a few miles in back of where the produce truck was picked up, then on to the train station, you get an almost straight line. They were not wasting any time. It seems to me that they must have been headed in this direction." He drew the line on out into the countryside.

"Great," Craigwell said. "That narrows it down to only one fourth of the country. If we check every house we might be done before the last of us dies."

"We've got one thing going for us," Kronovich said. "We're pretty sure that he was wounded. Roger said he was hardly using his left arm. It's possible that he might have to

The Nova Affair

have someone look at it. At least it's something we can check out."

Two days later it paid off. They had gone to the local telephone office and copied the names and phone numbers of every doctor within a fifty-mile radius of the northwest environs of Paris. Then they divided the list and started calling. In Chantilly, home of the famous lace, they found that a country general practitioner had disappeared the previous day. He had not returned from a house call he had made on an elderly widower a few miles outside of town. His worried wife had instituted a search and his abandoned car had been found on a side road off his route. There was no sign of a struggle and no sign of the doctor. He had disappeared.

"It sure isn't much but we may as well check it out," Craigwell announced. "We still can't investigate every house, even in one town. But let's visit every realtor and see if we can locate anything recently listed to someone that might fit our guys' descriptions."

It took two more days to make the next connection. The two agents had a bottomless pit of phony identification. They had conjured up some ID cards from an obscure French bureau, just official enough to get someone to talk to them. They were supposedly looking for some artwork, loaned by the Smithsonian Institute, which had been stolen from the national galleries in Paris. The suspects were thought to be secreting the pieces in a safehouse in the area. To allow for Craigwell and Kronovich's terrible accents, they identified themselves as U.S. Treasury agents assigned to the case.

"See, I told you," Craigwell laughingly explained. "We occasionally do liaison with the Treasury Department."

It was Suzanne who finally hit paydirt. She found a realtor who had recently rented out a local property and whose description of the customer fit Abdul fit perfectly. The cover was exactly right for the circumstances.

"We will have to check it out first. I don't have enough to go to either Washington or the French yet. If they're in the house, we back off and call for reinforcements. We don't want to lose them again and we don't want anyone getting hurt, at least not anyone on our side. They probably have a small armory with them and they won't hesitate to use it. They're facing a death sentence in France and life with no parole in the States."

They revisited the realtor to get a full description of the house and the grounds. It was an old chateau, which had been renovated a number of times over the years, sitting on about five acres of ground several miles to the south of the city. It was situated well back from the road and was surrounded by trees. This time of year it was barely visible from the road. In the summer, once the foliage was out, it would disappear altogether. There was a large barn to the rear of the house and several small utility sheds scattered about the property.

The ground floor of the home contained a great room, with fireplace, a library, a large kitchen and several smaller rooms, once reserved for servants, in the rear. The second floor was divided into several suites of bedrooms. There was a large cellar, which once held wine and a storage area for fruit and vegetables. The home had electric service and a telephone which, according to the realtor, had not been connected for some time.

After scouting the area for several hours, they found a spot from which the house could be observed. By taking the next road to the east of the house they could enter a small woods which brought them to within several hundred yards of the suspect premises. From there, with binoculars, they could see enough to identify anyone if they showed themselves. It would have to do.

They divided into two teams. Craigwell and Roger in one and Kronovich and Suzanne the other. Craigwell had intentionally split up Roger and Suzanne. He wanted one pro on each team. They would take turns standing twenty-four hour watches until something happened. They set the time to switch

The Nova Affair

watches at 2:00 AM. This would be the easiest time to evade discovery. They had taken rooms in a small hotel in the city and rented a second car, so that each team had its own transportation available.

The surveillance was grueling. This was a part of the agent's lives that neither Roger nor Suzanne had fully appreciated. Each team took turns at the binoculars. While one person watched the other could nap in a sleeping bag or eat a cold snack. Once on the binoculars, one could not waver for an instant. If anyone did show themselves, it might be for only a moment.

They established early that the house was occupied. Lights could be seen to go on and off and smoke rose from the chimney. However, for the first two days, no one came in or left and the blinds remained drawn.

Things broke on the morning of the third day. Roger and Craigwell were on duty, with Craigwell on watch. A figure came out of the house and walked to the barn in the rear, carrying two suitcases.

"Shit," Craigwell said. "That's Abdul. We've got a winner here. But it looks like they're getting ready to leave. They must have the car back there."

Abdul made two more trips, carrying several bags and parcels. After the last trip, he exited the barn in a green Citroen. He drove to the side of the house and got out, leaving the motor running.

"Fucking rotten luck," Craigwell exclaimed. "They're going now. If we go back to our car we could lose them again. No choice, sweetheart, we take them now or maybe lose them forever."

Craigwell had had the foresight to arm their little expedition. Each man had a .38 special and an army issue M-16. Roger had never fired the revolver and had not used an M-16 since basic, many years before. He wasn't sure he remembered how to take the weapon off safety and arm it. Craigwell checked out both his weapons for him, talking at the same time.

"We split up. You go as far as that small grove of trees by the barn. I'll get behind the house and try to take them both when they come out. Your job is to cover me and to warn me if anyone tries to blindside me. No heroics, this is what I get paid for and I'm better at it than you are."

"No argument," Roger said.

"Okay," Craigwell said. "Both your weapons are ready. Here's the safety on the pistol, keep that in your pocket. The M-16's ready to fire. It's on semi-automatic. To move it to full automatic, push this lever. For Christ's sake don't trip over anything. You let me get fifty yards ahead and then follow."

Craigwell moved off at a rapid trot, his rifle carried at ready arms. Roger had to admire him. He was decisive and brave. Whatever they paid him, he earned it.

A few moments later Roger moved out, at a slower pace. By the time he made it to the far edge of the small grove of trees, Craigwell was already at the back of the house. The agent held his weapon upright in his right hand and moved around the house just enough to peer around the corner to Roger's left, where Abdul had parked the car. The Citroen still sat in the driveway, spitting exhaust fumes. Roger lay the rifle in the crook of a small tree and aimed at the back of the car. That was almost a deadly mistake. As he focused along the sights, Abdul had come around the far side of the house and was moving toward the corner to Roger's right. Once he rounded the second corner, he would have a clear shot at Craigwell's back.

When Roger saw him, Abdul was almost at the near corner. He held what appeared to by an Uzi sub-machine gun. There was no alternative. Roger swung his weapon to the right and fired. The gun kicked but he could see no result. Abdul dropped to the ground and sent a spray of fire in Roger's direction. Roger could hear the bullets cutting a swath through the branches above him. Realizing that his position was exposed, Roger dropped to the ground and rolled to a tree to his right. At the same time he tried to remember what lever to push to put the weapon on full automatic. He had two extra clips in his coat pocket.

The Nova Affair

Craigwell was exposed. He had obviously been spotted from the house. He couldn't see who Roger was firing at or tell where they were. If he stayed put he would be an easy target for anyone coming around the corner to his right. If he went around the corner he would have the same problem to his left. There was no other cover near the house. He ran for the rear of the car and dove to put it between him and the house. He had almost made it when a spray of shots chewed up the gravel drive in back of him. As he hit the ground behind the left rear wheel of the car he could feel a burning in his right calf. He'd been hit. He tried to draw his right leg under his body so that he could crouch on both feet. The pain was instantaneous and severe. The bullet must have hit a bone. He was momentarily safe, but immobile.

Roger saw Craigwell's dive for cover and heard the second set of shots coming from the house. In the meantime, Abdul put another spray of bullets into the branches above him. Twigs and dead leaves rained down on him. When he raised his head again Abdul was gone. He could just see Craigwell lying behind the car, flat on the ground. The man did not move and Roger feared that perhaps he was dead. There was no way that he could leave the agent alone and exposed. He backed up through the trees and then started to run to his left. He planned to get the barn between himself and the house, go in the back and come out the front. He ran faster than he knew he could. He kept waiting for another spray of bullets but nothing happened.

He reached the back of the barn, only to find that there was no door on that side. He wasted several moments breaking out a window with the butt of his rifle and then crawling through. He had to put the weapon inside first and then use both hands to pull himself through the small frame. If anyone had been in the barn he would have been hamburger. The structure was empty except for some rusting equipment lying along the outside walls. The barn smelled old and musty.

Roger ran to the two large doors at the opposite end of the barn. He started to peer through the crack between the doors when some sixth sense stopped him. He had been too lucky, getting through the woods without a shot being fired at him. He picked up an old tarpaulin lying in the corner and, using a rake handle, held it out so that it hung in front of the crack between the two doors. He was rewarded with a solid spray of bullets that cut the two doors to pieces and shredded the tarpaulin. The crossbar holding the doors shut was cut apart and they swung halfway open. Roger dove to the side and at the same time screamed at the top of his lungs. He retreated to a corner and after a few moments risked a peek through the very dirty window that faced the house. Nothing moved.

Roger had no idea what to do next. The two men in the house knew where both he and Craigwell were. They were well armed and ready to fire to kill. He didn't know what condition Craigwell was in or what the agent intended to do next.

Craigwell heard Roger scream and decided that it was a little too dramatic to be real. He had seen men cut down by automatic fire. There was normally no sound from the victim at all. If the man wasn't dead before he hit the ground, the body was paralyzed by the trauma. He was in a bit of a spot. He couldn't run and he couldn't hide. He knew he didn't have much time. The two men in the house weren't about to sit around and wait him out.

Craigwell reached up and opened the driver's side door, throwing his rifle across the front seats. He pulled himself half onto the floor of the car, leaving his legs dragging out the open door. He reached up and pulled the shift lever down, putting the car in gear. As the car started to creep forward, he pushed the gas pedal down with his hand. The car picked up speed and began to bounce down the drive, away from the house. He reached up to grab the wheel, steering as best he could. He almost passed out from the agony of his injured leg dragging over the rough ground.

The car was suddenly swept by automatic fire. Abdul appeared on the open porch, firing his Uzi from his waist. Metal parts and glass flew everywhere. The car started to spit

The Nova Affair

smoke. Craigwell guided it off the drive in a slow turn to the right, so that the vehicle stayed between him and the house. About a hundred yards from the house the car went nose first into a small drainage ditch that paralleled the road. Abdul stopped firing and reached to replace the clip in his weapon. That was his mistake. Three quick shots came from under the left rear of the car. Craigwell was right. He was good at this.

Abdul fell backwards, the Uzi clattering to the floor of the porch. The man lay still.

Roger, watching from the barn, was quite sure that Abdul was dead. He debated going for help. Paul was now trapped in the house, without any transportation and without support. Craigwell could obviously take care of himself. On the other hand, Craigwell might be injured. In any case, if Roger left for help he would allow Paul a free route out of the rear of the house. The man might be injured but he was dangerous and resourceful. He wouldn't need much of a crack to slip through. Roger wondered where the money was. If it was already in the car, then Paul was sure to attempt to recover it. If he had it with him in the house, which Roger decided was more likely, then he would surely take it with him. The house was not so isolated that the gunfire would not have attracted attention. Whatever Paul did, he did not have much time.

The front door opened and a man Roger did not recognize stood in the doorway. At first he had a terrible thought that they had made some kind of mistake. Then Paul appeared behind the man. He had the man's collar gripped in his right hand, which also held a pistol. The pistol was jammed firmly against the back of the man's neck. Paul held a suitcase in his left hand. Undoubtedly the money!

Of course, thought Roger, this must be the missing doctor that had brought them to the area in the first place. They had been holding the man in the house. Paul guided his hostage directly toward the car, which shielded Craigwell.

Oh shit, thought Roger, if Craigwell were hurt Paul could take him in an instant. He had to let him know that he didn't have a free hand. Roger stepped to the half open door and fired a shot about ten feet to the left of Paul, kicking up a spray of gravel from the driveway. To the man's credit, he hardly flinched. He glanced over his shoulder at Roger and resumed pushing the frightened doctor toward the car. At that moment, Craigwell rose from behind the rear of the car. He leaned against the left rear fender, supporting himself on his left leg. His lower right leg was covered with blood. His rifle was still at ready arms. Not knowing what else to do, Roger came out of the barn and followed Paul down the drive. He kept the rifle aimed at Paul's back.

"Bag it Paul," Craigwell cried. "We're in front and in back of you, this car isn't going to take you far, if it moves at all. Someone must have heard World War III down here. The place will be crawling with gendarmes in a few minutes. Nice try, boss, but you lose."

"Sorry," Paul said. "No giveaways today. Throw down the weapon and move away from the car."

"Not a chance boss. You've got two choices. Shoot the hostage and I take you. Shoot me and my friend in back gets you. Either way, you die."

"Your friend in back isn't a good enough shot to try for me without risking the doctor here and he knows it."

Roger listened to the exchange and knew that Paul was right. From this angle, he couldn't risk a shot. He began sidling to his left, trying to get an angle from where he could risk a shot without having a miss hit the doctor. He was about thirty feet away and closing slightly. Then things happened very fast. Paul twisted his wrist and fired the pistol past the doctor's neck. Craigwell fell backward along the side of the car. Roger couldn't tell if the man was hit again or only shielding himself. Paul then swung the doctor to his left and pushed the man directly at Roger. At the same time he let go several more shots. Roger felt pain exploding in his left thigh. For the first time in his life, he was hit. The doctor stumbled, or had the sense to hit the ground. Roger dove left, easy to do as his leg was no longer supporting him, and fired a steady succession of non-aimed shots in Paul's direction. He was glad

The Nova Affair

that he had never put the weapon on full automatic, he would have used up the full clip. He tried to burrow into the tall grass at the edge of the yard.

When he raised his head, Paul was gone. The doctor was running down the drive as fast as his old pair of legs would carry him. A shot came from the general direction of the house and the running man sprawled face first in the drive and lay still.

"Goddamn," Roger cursed under his breath. He burrowed deeper into the weeds. Then he saw Craigwell half hobbling and half hopping toward the house. He was using the rifle as a crutch, thrusting the barrel into the ground at each step. The man's right chest was covered with blood and he had the .38 in his left hand. He had managed to circle around the house, using the ditch for cover, and was coming in from the side opposite the porch. Once again, Roger had no idea what to do next. He lost sight of Craigwell as he reached the far side of the house. There was several moments of quiet, followed by the sound of breaking glass and several shots.

Thinking back on it later, Roger had no recollection of making any conscious decision to rise. He just suddenly found himself moving toward the house. Once moving, he had little choice but to keep going. It was the same reaction many men have in combat. Some subconscious part of their mind just took over their actions, directing them to do things they would never have the resolve to do normally. He found he could hobble like Chester in the old *Gunsmoke* series, keeping his wounded leg stiff at the knee. His pant leg was soaked with blood but he felt no pain. He made it to the porch as several more shots came from the back of the house. He went through the still open front door and stopped. He was in the great room. Two doors were on the opposite side of the room, both closed. One presumably led to the kitchen and the other to the library. He decided that the library was probably a dead end and that the kitchen must lead to the rear of the house. But which was which? Then he remembered that the chimney from which they had seen smoke each morning was on the far side of the house from the woods. That would place the kitchen as the door to his left.

He approached the door slowly, not sure how to enter. He surely couldn't kick it open. He finally just reached out with his left hand, slowly turned the doorknob, and swung the door away from him. Paul stood in the center of the kitchen, behind a wooden pillar. His gun was leveled at one of the two windows at the rear of the room. Craigwell must have been playing guess which window with him, first one and then the other.

Roger didn't hesitate. He raised the rifle, aimed it directly at Paul's back and pulled the trigger. The first shot slammed the man into the pillar. Roger couldn't see any blood. He pulled the trigger again nothing happened! He had two full clips in his pocket and had never thought to reload. He started to reach into his coat pocket for the .38.

Paul turned toward him, a look of surprise and contempt on his face. He raised his pistol, holding it surprisingly steady.

"Once an amateur, always an amateur," Paul said. Roger was frozen, watching the tableau as though he weren't part of it.

For the second time in his life he heard a shot that he was sure was directed at his brain. And again for the second time he watched the other man die. Paul let out a long breath and fell forward. Craigwell stood at one of the open windows, his pistol pointing through the broken glass.

"Once again, sweetheart, I pull your fucking chestnuts from the fire. Are you sure you want to stay in this line of work? Us warriors load our weapons before we go into battle."

Roger managed a wan smile. At that moment both men broke out laughing. His leg suddenly hurt again.

They hobbled down the drive, each with his arm around the other's shoulders, past the still body of the doctor and toward the road. Each man used his good leg. They looked like two men in a sack race, without the sack.

"I'm really getting too old for this shit," Craigwell said. "I think I'll put in for a desk tour."

"I just think I'll resign," Roger replied. "The hours stink."

The Nova Affair

They tried to flag down three cars before one finally stopped.

15

It took two more weeks to wrap it up. Roger and Craigwell, both hospitalized, left the messy details to Kronovich. Between the local authorities and the Agency's staff in Paris, they covered up the whole thing. The abduction of the doctor was described as a foiled kidnap attempt. Unfortunately for the doctor, he had been shot during the process of rescuing him. The kidnappers, also dead, had been obscure members of the Paris underworld. Except for the doctor's widow, and his patients, no one paid much attention.

Roger and Kronovich were due to return to Washington immediately upon Roger's discharge from the hospital. Suzanne would go with them. She and Roger planned to be married as soon as he was discharged and cleared. They all visited Craigwell on the last day. His leg was healing nicely, but the chest wound would require more time. His lung had collapsed and he had lost a considerable amount of blood. Only Roger's testimony convinced the Agency that Craigwell had led the charge after receiving the second bullet.

After a few minutes of small talk, Kronovich stood and indicated that he had an announcement.

"I've got good news and bad news."

They all groaned.

"The good news is that, under French law, there is a reward due any civilian that assists the authorities in recovering money under the circumstances surrounding this case. Specifically, one percent of the take. That's about one million dollars and change, in this particular case. The bad news is that it is not payable to any employee or agent of any government, foreign or domestic. That means that Jay and I are both out and, sorry Roger, but you too. You're an officer in the Corps, remember?"

They all groaned again.

"I've got more good news and bad news and good news," Kronovich announced.

This time Suzanne threw a pillow at him.

"Technically, Suzanne is entitled to the whole thing. The bad news is that the French didn't want to give her a thing. They claimed that she was an agent of the CIA and that, in any case, her contribution was not documented. I offered to document the whole thing in the Paris press and they suddenly saw the light. The long and the short of it is that, in return for signing this release and pledge that you'll never discuss this with anyone, they will cut you a check today. By the way, the law also says that any such reward is tax-free." With a huge smile on his face, Kronovich thrust an official looking document at Suzanne.

The rest of them stared at Kronovich, dumbfounded.

Three days later, Roger and Suzanne strolled down Pennsylvania Avenue in Washington. He was no longer an officer in the Marine Corps. He did have a civilian commendation in his pocket, signed by the President, as reward for his work. The Marine Corps had never given him anything, not even a paycheck. He did not intend to make an issue of it.

Using the reward that Suzanne had received, he had wired a money order to the Cook County Prosecutor's office for about $460,000, everything that he was short, plus interest. That had made it much easier for Grover to issue a press release announcing that full restitution had been made and that all charges had been dropped. He had also sent a check for $100,000 to his attorney, with instructions that it be distributed to his former employees as severance.

The Nova Affair

They also sent a check for $100,000 each to both Craigwell and Kronovich. It seemed like the right thing to do.

"Well," he said to Suzanne, "where do you want to get married?"

"I don't care where, as long as it's soon."

"I still have a few days work to do in Bermuda, I understand that they have churches there."

She answered him by stepping to the curb to hail a taxi.

As their plane lifted from Washington National, she turned and kissed him on the cheek.

"How do you feel," she asked.

"Good news and bad news," he said. She frowned.

"The good news is I've cleared my name, paid my debts, we still have close to three hundred thousand in the bank account and I've made a new friend."

"And the bad news?"

"I don't have a job. We'll have to work on that, after the honeymoon."